The Summer Escape

LILY GRAHAM

The Summer Escape

LILY GRAHAM

bookouture

Published by Bookouture

An imprint of StoryFire Ltd.
23 Sussex Road, Ickenham, UB10 8PN
United Kingdom

www.bookouture.com

Previously published as *An Invincible Summer*.
This is a new extended version.

ISBN: 978-1-910751-86-2
eBook ISBN: 978-1-910751-85-5

For Catherine, the best friend a girl could ask for.

PROLOGUE

Her hands were like old parchment: brown, mottled and thin; yet to my five-year-old eyes they were capable of anything, magic not least among them. Today, they were a domestic symphony rolling out the dough; the flour, like fairy dust, sprinkled on the long, flat marble. Her arms were strong and wiry, and as she kneaded she beguiled me with stories from far away. Stories that conjured wisps of sun-drenched olive groves, plum-coloured wine sipped out of short glasses on cobbled sea-front tavernas, honey drizzled over thick, creamy-white Greek yoghurt, and wild, pink-tinged peaches warm from the sun.

'Yew kno' the story of how yew got your name?' asked Yaya in her heavy Cretan accent. Flour smudged on her soft, brown cheek as she peered down at me, a smile edging the corner of her mouth.

I grinned my gap-toothed grin, perched on the counter, legs swinging, and clutching my latest and most cherished possession, a collection of fairy tales.

'You named me, Yaya,' I said. My name was collateral damage from my Greek heritage: I was doomed to walk through life with the rather foreign-sounding name of Ariadne.

'Yes-a, but do yew kno' who I named yew after?' asked Yaya, holding up the index finger on her left hand, which curved ever so slightly at the tip, as if she would lift each vowel along with it in her lyrical burr.

I shook my head, espresso-eyes wide.

'I named yew after one of the most famous princesses of all-a time, eh… the one who suffered the most-e,' she said, with a sense of pride about the latter. 'Unlike these silly princesses from your fairy book.'

My mouth formed an 'o' of surprise, my feet paused mid-swing.

'Why I do this, eh?' she asked.

I shrugged. She was a bit mad. This wasn't exactly news. I loved her anyway and maybe a little because of it.

'Well *meli mou*, the goddess Ariadne suffered most terribly, and it was her bravery and courage, not her beauty, that made her a hero, which I think-e is what really makes a hero, a hero, no?'

I supposed so. I liked the idea of the girl being the hero, though.

Yaya continued. 'She was the daughter of a king; a mad Cretan king 'ho ordered a young man named Theseus to enter a maze and kill a wild, monstrous beast that had killed many people before. Knowing that this young man was facing certain death, Ariadne helped 'im escape and they fell in love. Together they fled the kingdom, Ariadne believing that she 'ad found a love that would last-e forever. Only, it wasn't to be.'

'Why? What happened?'

'He left her. He left her sleeping in a cave one-a night, so they say, and he run away.'

I gasped. That was not how the story was supposed to go. 'What happened to her?'

Yaya looked at me with her beetle-black eyes. 'Well, there are many different stories, and everyone tells different ones. But for me, the story my own yaya told me is still the best-e. After Theseus left her, Ariadne sank-e into despair, barely able to keep going. Feeling sorry for the woman who had sacrificed everything for this man, Dionysus, a god 'ho knew all about suffering, rescued her, though there are many who would say that in the end, she rescued him too. You see, *meli mou*, life is never what we think it will be; it's not always like these stories,' she said, tapping the green cover, leaving behind a faint film of flour. 'It can be filled with joy or misfortune, but mostly it's a mixture like this dough. A real hero is like the bread – rising after it has been beaten.'

ONE

It's not that I hate my job.

Hate is a strong word. I don't *hate* it.

I mean there are parts of it that I don't like, but that's common with all jobs, isn't it? No one loves every minute of their job. Except maybe Jeremy Clarkson on *Top Gear*. And, well, look how that turned out.

But the rest of us? Not so much *love*. Sometimes when I think about my job on a Sunday evening, I get this odd feeling where I lose all sensation along the left side of my body.

But that's normal.

Completely normal... I'm sure. It's the Sunday blues, right? And, anyway, it doesn't last that long. By around midday on Monday, I'm fine. Mostly.

I'm an obituary writer for the somewhat insalubrious London paper *The Mail & Ledger*, which comes out on Monday morning, and part of my job involves dealing with irate phone calls, tear-soaked letters and the occasional little old lady queuing outside my cubicle.

Like yesterday morning when Rosa Greenberg called after *The Mail & Ledger* hit the stands. Rosa was phoning about her late husband George's obituary. My hands shook as I took the call. I slouched down in my seat as low as I could, trying to avoid Kimberley's gimlet gaze – Kimberley is my colleague, who sits in the cubicle next to mine. She was busy writing her 'action list' for the day with different coloured Biros to underline things like 'priority item #1' and 'red flag – follow up before 12'.

I despise Kimberley Mondsworth-Greene.

Meanwhile, Rosa Greenberg sobbed into the receiver, 'I just wasn't ready. I mean it's not like Pauline, you know, Pauline from next door. I told you about her when we spoke after, after... it happened,' she sniffed.

I closed my eyes, hoping that just this once my tear ducts would behave. Today I vowed, as I do every Monday, I would be strong.

Rosa continued, 'Pauline had time; Roger had had two heart attacks already, and even then she says she had been preparing for it. But George was... just gone. I know he was seventy-eight, but he was fine. He wasn't young, but he wasn't old, not really. It was too soon.'

A loud foghorn sound announced that Rosa was blowing her nose. I took the time to surreptitiously reach for my ever-ready box of Kleenex and mop up my own eyes.

I'd have to be strong some other time.

Alerted to the sound like a vulture circling from above, Kimberley turned to raise an eyebrow at me. I ignored her, swivelling my chair as far away as I could to the wall opposite, while Rosa prepared to send my leaky tear ducts into overflow.

'So beautiful, what you wrote... that's why I'm calling, it's like you *knew* him. I was worried about it... you know, worried that it wouldn't be George, but it was. I know this probably sounds silly, but George would have loved to have read it. He would have been so pleased that you wrote about his time in India, dear,' she said before ringing off.

Afterwards, I put the phone back in its cradle and stared at the horrid blue speckled carpet until I had regained control of my wobbling chin.

Kimberley would never cry at her desk.

'Journalists', she told me haughtily a few weeks ago, 'are meant to be objective, to report the facts without emotion. Try to be more of a journalist, Ria,' she rebuked, while I considered that the first action on my own 'action list' would be to staple her stupid list to her forehead. I suppose that wouldn't be an objective act, though, would it?

The thing is, being objective is fine for Kimberley, who gets to report about current affairs and breaking news. In the entertainment world anyway. Like when Kim Kardashian insured her bum.

Oh yes.

They ran a whole piece asking if it was worth insuring body parts and what the point of it all really was.

People wrote in.

There were debates.

There were polls.

There were people with a bit too much free time on their hands, if you ask me.

But I digress. My point is that it's hard to be impartial when you write about death every day.

I've been doing that now for close to three years. Three very long years. I never planned on being an obituary writer – it's not something you study for at university. No one says, 'I'd like to do a course on financial journalism and obituary writing.' And, anyway, when I joined the paper the job wasn't advertised as 'obituary writer'.

The advert had read: *writer required for popular London broadsheet* (yes, they actually called themselves a broadsheet, not a tabloid – I remember that clearly), *graduate level acceptable.*

And when I started I wrote about other things too, like films, events, and just once, for a single glorious moment in my career, about travel. It was a little B&B just outside Sheffield, but still it was nice, er… ish. Or it would have been if there hadn't been a dead body in the dining room. But that's another story altogether.

Although in retrospect it may have been a sign, too. You know, of things to come?

Because two days following the death of ninety-seven-year-old Mr Wimple from Sheffield, John Marshland, who wrote the obituaries, retired, and I was asked to fill in for him until we could find a replacement. That was almost three years ago – I'm still waiting for that replacement. But it's just a glitch. Even Janice says so. Or at least she used to.

My boss. Janice Farland. She hasn't said much about it being a glitch lately, to be honest. Not that I haven't broached the subject, I have – quite regularly, to tell you the truth. The last time, well, let's just say it didn't go so well.

There were words.

There were tears. (Mine.)

And threats. (Janice's.)

Then there was wine. (Me again.)

And anyway, it's fine, really. Most of the time I enjoy what I do; okay, not *enjoy* really, quite the opposite actually, if I'm honest. But I do feel a sense of purpose, of value in a way. Especially after what happened to Christopher. Maybe I was meant to do this. Like some really horrible calling? Which I realise is probably just a bit morbid. But I figured, for a long time anyway, maybe you don't get to choose your calling? I mean we can't all be called to be singers or doctors. Perhaps this was my calling, being a professional mourner?

Or, you know. Not.

The thing is, and what gets me through, is that somebody has to do it. And it may as well be someone like me who gets it. Though in hindsight maybe it would be nice if I didn't get it quite so much. And the crying will stop eventually. Everyone said it would get easier. And it will. Someday. Still, you'd think after three years that I wouldn't cry every time someone called to thank me, or, worse, to shout at me for getting it wrong. Or just crying because it's a Monday and I have nothing else planned that day. Crying has become my thing. You know, like how some people are good at darts. I've become abnormally brilliant at crying.

I'm not saying that my job is always hard. It isn't *always*. Some days are actually sort of all right. It's just that a lot of the time it's a bit, well, brutal.

I mean, you're dealing with the very worst day of a family's life, and you're taking notes about the person they've lost, which is kind of horrible when you think of it that way, which I try not to. And if you get it wrong, well, let's just say you know you haven't actually ruined anyone's life, but it sure does feel that way. Which is why sometimes, on a Sunday, when I think about work I get a bit panicky because that's when the obituaries race through my head, and I know if I've made a mistake it's too late. It will be there in print for the entire world to see, or London, or the people that read *The Mail & Ledger* anyway, or the obituaries at least, and they're a tough crowd, let's be honest: retired school teachers, grammarians, my mum.

She doesn't read it to be gloomy or anything, she just likes to read what I write and put it in a big scrapbook; it's nice in its own macabre way. I mean imagine bringing that out to guests.

Although since Christopher, Mum doesn't read them any more. I can't blame her. If I didn't have to, if I didn't feel that I was needed, that perhaps what happened to me made me understand the pain of people who had also lost someone close to them, neither would I.

Later in the day my mind was in a comfortably numb state after having spent the morning worrying over everything that could possibly go wrong yet hadn't, when quite suddenly my body developed a will of its own and gave in, having decided that it had had its fill of anxiety for the day, thank you very much. Or maybe the meds had kicked in. The ones Mum insists on force-feeding me every morning, despite Dr Rushma telling her that perhaps it's time for me to just go off them and see what happens. I can never really tell. It's a comfortable sort of hum, like white noise for the nerves. I had just sat down to a cup of tea when Kimberley appeared: short and rather square in shape, with square glasses framing her square, sharp-eyed face.

Her breathy little girl voice, so out of place with all her boxy, square angles, caused the hairs on the back of my neck to stand on end before I could process what she was saying. I was good at tuning her out. At some point, though, she raised her square-shaped hand in front of my face and asked, 'So, what do you think? We need about four people for the feature.'

I frowned. 'Sorry, what feature?'

She gave me a look. It actually looked a little like sympathy. She even seemed a little nervous, or what constituted nervousness for Kimberley. It looked like she needed to pee, actually.

'We're doing a feature about surviving unimaginable tragedies – you heard about the guy who won the lottery, only to have his money stolen out of his bank account, and now he's completely destitute, and his wife left him, right?'

I shrugged. She cleared her throat, not meeting my eye. 'Janice is thinking of calling the feature "When the best day of your life becomes your worst", and she wants to know if you'd share your story?'

My throat went suddenly dry.

Share my story.

I stared at her in horror. Janice's awful, pithy title tearing through my brain: 'When the best day of your life becomes your worst'.

Who were these people?

Then she said it. As if I could have had any doubt as to what she'd been referring to. She cleared her throat, and said, 'About what happened to Christopher.'

As if she knew him. As if she had any right to say his name.

The room started to whirl. I pushed back my chair, not bothering to look at her as I rushed to the bathroom, my heel breaking on the tiled floor as I fled to the nearest stall and vomited my shattered heart into the cold porcelain bowl.

TWO

But I'm getting ahead of myself, you see. Or behind myself, as it were, because my life changed on the Tuesday, really. As usual I was on the M4 on my way to work in my wheezy, gobbled-up-and-spat-out Renault, a relic that had been lovingly passed down to me from my grandmother. I reached down for a slug of the filter coffee that I had prepared bleary-eyed at six in the morning, my hand groping while I kept my eye on the road in front. Instead, my finger brushed the radio knob and tuned into Sam Cooke's 'Twistin' the Night Away'. I blinked in the grey light, my throat constricting and thought, simply: Yaya. The word itself was a balm. Unbidden, the memory swam in front of my eyes and I saw us: my feet in their new sparkly red ballet flats. The ones that Mum said I couldn't have. The ones Yaya went and bought me anyway. And us, together in the kitchen with the radio turned to her favourite station, the soundtrack of my childhood: Aretha, The Temptations, The Supremes.

I remember watching the cake rise through the glass door of the oven, her smile as I tried to help, while we both twisted the day away, our hips in time, on a sunny afternoon.

I bit my lip and couldn't help the watery smile on my face as my hands tapped along on the steering wheel. I barely noticed as the tears slid down my cheeks.

I swallowed and tried to push the image from my mind. Please, just not yet. Not today.

A car passed and honked its hooter as I'd been holding up traffic without realising it. With a fright I changed lanes and found myself taking the airport lane by mistake.

The driver who passed shot me an odd look, mouthing the word 'lunatic' at me.

I shrugged. Despite popular belief, lunacy isn't exactly a choice. But I'm not sure if he got my mental message. He just continued to gawk. It's not like I could exactly blame him.

It was then that I gave a thought to my hair.

I'm not someone who usually concerns herself with hair. Well, beyond it being clean and neat, anyway. There was a time when I did, sort of. There were hairdresser appointments, and highlights, and the obligatory consultations with Christopher before I lopped any of it off – he was such a typical bloke that way. He'd actually frowned for most of a day when I came home with a bob once, but that had been a long time ago. From the look I received from the driver, I had to wonder… had I brushed it?

I glanced in the rear-view mirror at myself and looked away just as quickly. They were still there, the dead things in my face where my eyes should have been, and above them, the nest that was my hair shoved into an all-purpose, ratty topknot.

I really must brush it properly, instead of just giving it a quick wash and combing my fingers through it before I shove it up and out of sight. But then I've been promising myself that for a long time now.

Okay. *Focus.*

At the closest exit I'll turn around, and with any luck I won't need to explain my latest insanity to my boss. But the thought of Janice – or The-Devil-Who-Wears-Birkenstocks, as I sometimes like to call her – and our weekly 'catch-up' meeting makes me put my foot down flat on the accelerator. My breathing turns sharp, and my hands tighten on the steering wheel. Basically, what happens in these meetings is that Janice goes through my copy, line by line, and she lets me know what she likes. And what she doesn't. To the point where I begin doubting my own name. Like last week.

'Why do you mention this?' she snapped, tapping the obituary of Sarah Gilbert, and the bit about her tennis career; she was one of the first pro women tennis players after World War II. 'Honestly, Ariadne,' she said, using my full name, which she pronounced wrong. Granted, no one can pronounce it. But still, her gall for even using my stupid bloody name made me want to stab her in the eye with my pen. 'That was so long ago, who would care?' she said, eyes narrowing at me as if I were an imbecile. I didn't take the look seriously: she looked at everyone that way. I clamped my teeth in frustration, and stared at her in disbelief – was she serious?

Sarah Gilbert would bloody care, which is precisely what I told Janice, which only made her hawk-like nostrils flare. Sarah Gilbert had been a housewife for most of her life, but before that she was a nurse in France who had seen the horrors of World War II and had done what she could to help. She'd raised three children and had been a doting grandmother. And once, a long time ago, she'd won at Wimbledon. It was an important part of her, a part of her legacy. I'd fought to keep it in, and almost won, but when the copy ran over, Janice cut it anyway. I was beside myself with anger. And rage. And, when I got home, with wine. I was beside myself with lots of wine. This was when, for an unreasonable half a day, I considered taking up drinking professionally. God knows I need a hobby.

I'd taken two hours to open the email that came from the Gilberts the next day, dreading what it said. When I had finally opened it, I found that they had thanked me. It was polite, kind even.

Which just made it worse.

The signs for Heathrow get closer.

I try to signal to get into the far-right lane, but a car is flying past me and cuts me off. My heart starts to race.

Three exits.

Crap! How do I get out of here?

Two.

No one wants to let me out! Why are people so rude?

One.

Oh God… *I'm stuck!* Okay, keep calm, Ria, I tell myself as I take the entry lane for Heathrow International, hoping to do some kind of drive-through while I press for a ticket, only to join a mad throng of cars in bumper-to-bumper traffic. Seriously? It's barely 7 a.m.! What a mess. We're inching forwards. What is going on? I lower my car window and stick my head out, trying to see where the drop-off lane is so I can drive through; instead, I see that one of the cars in front has broken down.

Are you kidding me? It's taking forever and only one car seems able to get through at a time. I'm miles behind. How long is it going to take me to just drive through the drop-off area? I quickly wind the window back up again. It's freezing. What the hell am I going to tell Janice? Finally, after twenty minutes of slow inching forwards, my temper inching upwards accordingly till I'm in a slow, steady burn of rage, there's a little gap in the traffic in front of me, only it's to take me in the opposite direction of where I want to be, to the parking bay. Several airport security guards have come to see what the problem is and to help some of the frantic drivers who look as impressed as I am. It looks like it will take at least another half-hour to get out. I head towards the nearest open parking bay, pull my car in, turn the ignition off and head inside, deciding I'd rather pass the time with a cappuccino than wait for that mess to clear. I'm also in desperate need for something to steady my nerves.

My phone starts ringing and I check inside my bag, the one I had to change this morning when the handle on the old one snapped just as I was about to leave. I'd made a mad rush to my closet, grabbed the first one I saw, which I haven't used for years, and shoved in my wallet, phone and keys. I reach for my phone, only to see Janice's number flashing on the screen. Seriously? She can't give me five minutes grace? It's not like I'm even late… yet. I swallow and decide not to answer it.

Entering the airport through the automated doors, I breathe a sigh of relief as I feel the warmth of the interior envelop me. I'm walking blindly, blinking at the sudden racket. All around me, the airport is teeming with people. Men and women dressed in business attire, wearing serious expressions, tap away at their laptops and iPads, pausing only to take a sip of coffee, ready to depart for some or other business engagement. Young adventurers wearing excited grins huddle in groups with their large backpacks in place and maps open while they chat animatedly with one another.

There are the holidaymakers, the visitors, and the people coming home with exhaustion etched in the creases of their clothes and in the dark shadows under their eyes. Every wall, pillar and balustrade is densely populated, the larger groups creating a cacophony along the perimeter of the building. Some people are just milling about. Others have luxury luggage on hand while they hug their friends, lovers or families one last time. The air is thick with excitement and infinite possibility, a tangible feeling that anything could happen.

It's infectious.

You could go anywhere. Be anyone. Do anything.

I've always loved the airport, even as a child. I remember feeling this familiar sense of longing whenever I had to fetch or drop off a friend or relative, someone visiting from abroad, leaving for some far-off – and to my child's eye – exotic destination (everything is exotic when the farthest you've ever been is Wales), and I'd experience an overwhelming desire to go somewhere too.

I still feel that way sometimes.

A woman draped in a scarlet coat bumps into me and shoots me a nasty look as she wheels her luggage past. She comments to the man alongside her in a snarky tone, imbued with self-importance, 'Who just stands stock still like that in the middle of a corridor?'

My face colours and I give myself a mental shake; the rational side of my brain finally shows up. I decide to find the nearest coffee shop. A message comes through on my phone. Janice again.

'WHERE ARE YOU?'

Like that, all in caps. God, that woman! I could have been run over, for all she knows. She'd never buy what happened to me, she'd just look over her steel-rimmed glasses with that hawk-like gaze and say to me, her voice how I imagine a hawk would sound if it were a middle-aged woman who was really fond of mannish German footwear – a sound rather screechy, like a pair of fingernails scraping a blackboard – like she did the last time I was late for work because the car broke down – 'I don't like excuses! Why do you always insist on making them? It's your grandmother's funeral all over again… honestly, who needs a whole day off for that?'

Yes. She said that.

Yes, I managed somehow not to commit an act of violence. Unless you count what happened with the vodka bottle later, which was rather violent indeed.

Incredibly, Janice sends another text. One that sends me over the edge, despite the fact that it's now in sensible lower case. The words seem written in indelible ink, leaving an impregnable scar.

'Kim will interview you at 10 for the feature, make sure you're here'.

I blink. Feature? Suddenly my blood runs cold, as I realise what she is referring to... that awful article they were talking about the day before: 'When the best day of your life becomes your worst'. Had they honestly thought I was going to take part? Did they think I would meekly sit there and have them pick apart my life like carrion birds? My hands start to shake. I see red and all I can think of at that moment is that I need a drink, past caring that it's barely 8 a.m. I look around rather manically and spy a little airport bar where I go in and order a vodka neat, not concerned if it's appropriate or not. Thankfully the barman doesn't raise a brow, but returns quickly with my order, which I down in one gulp, only to ask for another. He has kind, hazel eyes and thin shoulders, which he shrugs while he does as instructed. After the second one I'm starting to feel better. Still angry, but calmer. He holds the bottle up to offer me a third, I shrug *why not*, and down that one too. 'Better?' he asks. I nod, noticing that he has a bit of an accent, Russian I think. I watch everyone going to and fro outside the bar and there's a part of me that can't help wishing that just this once I could be like the people surrounding me: going somewhere; doing something, anything else.

God knows that I need an escape from everything. It's a feeling so profound, so consumed by its precipice of grief, that it eclipses everything else. I see Yaya's face for just a second, her tired, worried face, and in that moment I make a choice. One of those snap decisions that changes the course of your life forever.

Only, of course, I don't realise it at the time. I pay for my vodka, thanking the barman for 'All the betters', who gives me a half smile and says, 'Is no trouble, call on Sven whenever you need.' As I stand I feel the blood rush to my head, and salute him. It's good to have a Sven in your life, I think as I grab my bag. There should be more Svens like this. 'Well, you've got a Sven in me,' I say seriously. Then blink. That wasn't right, was it?

He doesn't seem to mind. His eyes have lit up with interest. I blush furiously, giggling as I back away, hands in the surrender position. I'm feeling a bit more sloshed than I realised. To my right are the doors that lead out to my car and the drunken sleep I'm likely to have before I'm anywhere near okay to drive and face Janice; on my left is a row of counters manned by travel consultants. Their cubicles are lined with man-sized posters selling exotic destinations, each claiming a diverse and unique adventure: the magic of Europe, fun in Disneyland, tango in South America. Beneath these is the strapline: *Travelstar: Your Dream, Our Promise.*

I stand transfixed.

Minutes pass.

I turn left.

THREE

WHAT HAVE I DONE?

Why am I on a plane? *To Crete?*

There has to be some mistake.

Surely someone should have said something? Tried somehow to stop me? It shouldn't have been that easy, should it? Even when I was about to pay, there was a tiny part of me that didn't believe I would actually do it and something would go wrong, and when the agent asked for my passport to book my ticket, reality finally checked in to my drink-addled brain.

Of course. I need a passport.

Which was, I was quite sure, in the dark recesses of a drawer somewhere at home. Dejected, I tried to ignore the sudden stinging in my eyes. How could I go back now? I stood biting my lip, my throat tight with unshed tears. At the agent's kind but expectant look, I'd opened my bag to mime looking for it and felt my mouth fall open in shock because there it was in the side pocket. As if that was where it had always been.

I'd taken it out with shaky hands and stared at it in astonishment. Then realised, '*Of course*! I must have left it in this bag! The last time I used it was when we went on holiday…' I babbled, happily. 'I switched bags today,' I said with a bit of a drunken wink, as if that explained anything.

'That's, er, nice, love,' said the travel agent, an older lady with short, bristly blonde hair and a fondness for electric blue eye shadow, who was looking at me as if I'd gone mad while holding out a manicured hand for my passport.

'It *is* nice, isn't it?' I'd replied, nodding happily at the solar-powered toy plant on her desk that was bobbing its head and telling me to 'Have a good day'. I touched it on its little petal head to the agent's surprise.

'I will do that', I told it in a loud carrying whisper, like the fake plant and I were sharing a secret as I handed my passport over.

And here I am.

The travel agent had said that I'd get a special rate if I took the flight that was boarding in an hour.

It made sense, at least, financially. Except it doesn't really make sense at all. Maybe I actually dozed off in a drunken stupor and I didn't realise it? And this is just a bizarre dream. Only I feel wide awake, and worse, horribly sober, like I've been hit with a course of electric shock therapy; which at this point, I could probably do with.

My chest is tight and I'm finding it hard to breathe. I've been ushered to a seat by the window. I'm clutching my bag like a misshapen leather teddy bear, my eyes darting frantically around.

I must calm down. I must.

My mobile begins to ring and I can feel eyes from all around staring at me. I scramble in my bag to switch it off, feeling like claws have attached themselves to my throat. I glance at the screen.

Oh God.

Janice.

Why did I look? Why?

I cut the call.

My vision lightens, and I sway in my seat. I think I'm going to be sick.

I try desperately to calm my breathing. A second later my phone starts to ring again and I stare at it in abject horror.

A flight attendant comes over to ask if I'm all right. She has wide, gentle brown eyes and seems genuinely regretful as she asks to switch my phone to flight mode. 'I'm so sorry. You can make a call from the plane if you need to once we're in the air,' she says with a kind smile.

I must have nodded because she's leaving.

I want to shout out, to tell her I've made a mistake, that I shouldn't be on this plane… that they shouldn't sell plane tickets to drunk people and that actually no, we don't need more Svens in our lives, but she's already halfway down the aisle.

I stare dumbly ahead. I jump as the phone starts to ring again.

I switch it off and put it in my bag; I take a deep breath, then another.

Soon the flight attendant is coming round to check that we've all fastened our seatbelts.

I'm looking around somewhat feverishly when I feel a pair of eyes boring into me. I look up – a young girl with very large amber eyes and wild curly red hair is peering at me over the top of her seat. 'Are you all right?' she asks in a loud probing voice.

I swallow my fear, will my hands to stop shaking, give her my 'I'm not mad, really' smile (it's well-practiced) and say, 'Ah yes, quite so, I was just about to read… this,' reaching for the in-flight magazine in front of me. Inquisitive eyes watch, as I search for my perpetually lost inner calm. A woman's head pops up next to hers and she mouths 'Sorry' at me, turns to the child and says, 'Leave the lady alone, Olivia. Turn around and sit properly, we need to put our seatbelts on.' I close my eyes when I hear her say 'poor thing', wondering when my grief will no longer be etched on my face. I check my lap to see what I had pulled from the flap. It's a folded newspaper titled *Eudaimonia: The Guide to*

Good Cretan Living. Absently, I flick through the pages. It's an English–Cretan newspaper featuring profiles, reviews, travel tips and island news. An article about a vineyard that burnt down catches my eye. There's a picture of a young man with his arms folded, wearing a white shirt with the sleeves rolled up, looking intently at the camera. He's tall, with vivid blue eyes and dark brown hair. There's something about his eyes, though, that makes me look harder, something dark and familiar. As I turn to read the article, the captain announces that we'll be starting our ascent. I take a breath and look up.

I've never been very good at this part. Across the aisle an elderly man gives me an encouraging sort of look and I take heart.

As the plane levels out I breathe easier again. The flight attendant is handing out drinks, and I choose orange juice, wishing I could also ask for a family-size pack of aspirin for the headache I'm developing, and turn my attention back to the article.

Resurrecting Elysium

When a fire destroyed Elysium, the thousand-year-old family-run winery in the mountainous region of western Chania, Crete, ten years ago, everyone believed that the vineyard would exist only in our memories.

That is, until thirty-three-year-old Tom Bacchus returned just eighteen months ago determined to resurrect his family's legacy. Bacchus is the half-brother of Tony Bacchus, whose wife, Iliana Kirosa, is the daughter of the ex-mayor of Chania, George Kirosa.

The cause of the fire has long been shrouded in mystery; Bacchus himself was at one point suspected of starting the fire. However, nothing was ever proven. Continuing strife in the family led to mounting debt and the eventual liquidation of the vineyard despite Bacchus' attempt to hold onto the farm.

Despite these setbacks, Bacchus returned, and managed to buy back several hectares of the old farmstead. 'I'm hoping that in time I'll be able to buy back as much of the original farm as I can,' says Bacchus, who will have his first public harvest later this year.

The first-ever Greek Pinotage?

In a bold move for Bacchus' first harvest, the intrepid young wine grower has planted Pinotage (amongst the traditional Protected Designation of Origin [PDO] varieties including Cabernet Sauvignon, Carignan, Grenache rouge and Syrah), the red wine grape hailing from South Africa. The variety has an almost equal share of acclaim and disdain, with many wine critics referring to it contemptuously as a 'new world' wine. In fact, the irascible French wine critic Arnold Prisane once claimed that it had all the charm and taste of 'old paint', while the New Yorker's food and wine connoisseur Mathew Sprint famously declared it as the only wine that tempted him to extend his holiday when he visited the beautiful city of Cape Town. Whatever the feeling about this long-contested wine (its origins lie in the winelands of Stellenbosch, where it was bred in 1925), the grape is a cross between the Pinot Noir and Cinsaut, producing a deep, smoky, earthy flavour which has become a signature variety for the country, known for its bold distinctive taste, which has proven quite popular across the globe, with some countries attempting to grow their own. However this will be the first for Greece.

The feeling with Pinotage has long been that you either love it, or you hate it. Let's just hope in Bacchus' case, the Cretans love it.

I study the series of photographs printed alongside the article; one shows the old vineyard before and after the fire, with the before picture depicting a lush valley in the Cretan countryside. The men of the Bacchus family are outside: an old man with dancing blue eyes has his arms around his two sons. The eldest, presumably Tony, is medium height and stocky; the angle of his body and his stiff posture make it clear he doesn't want to be there. Tom, the younger brother, who couldn't have been more than sixteen in the photo, appears young and carefree. He's tall and lean, already showing signs of the striking man he'd one day become: his eyes amused, lips wide, clearly mid-laugh while his father beams down at him.

The next photo was taken after the fire, showing remnants of the large country home, most of which was swallowed by the flames. The last photograph is of the farm as it stands to-day, the newly planted vines in neat rows shrouded by the early morning mist. Tom Bacchus, his face thoughtful, stands in his newly planted vineyard, so altered from the carefree youth of the photograph before. I touch the photo, almost in benediction; it looks like he needs it.

I close the newspaper and return it to the flap in front of my seat, only to retrieve it, fold it up and place it in my bag. There's something... something intriguing about Elysium, and Tom Bacchus. An unanswered question, something that I can't quite put my finger on. Perhaps it's his haunted eyes, but I can't help but feel that there's more to his story.

FOUR

I'm in Crete.

Technically I'm in an airport in Crete. But right beyond those doors lies Crete. I have nothing to declare, no baggage to claim, and the word Crete is running through my head at warp speed *Crete Crete Crete Crete Crete Crete*, creating a peculiar, almost mechanical tattoo in my head.

All I have to do is go outside. *Oh God.*

I must not panic. I. Must. Not. Panic.

I. MUST. NOT. PANIC.

Did I just think of what my mother would say? Seriously?

Oh God, I'm panicking.

I'm trying to remember what to do in a panic situation – something about brown paper bags. Where the hell would I find a brown paper bag? Suddenly my body jolts; someone walked smack bang into me. I look around and see a familiar scarlet coat. I blink, stunned. The woman shakes her head in disbelief and says in a loud voice to her male companion, 'The same woman. The VERY same one from Heathrow. Standing stock still. Again. What a lunatic.'

I blush furiously and bolt outside.

I'm so tired of that word. I mean, it's not funny when it's sort of true, right? A large group of taxi drivers are standing by alongside their cabs, their noisy chatter interspersed with laughter. As soon as they spot me, they all stand to attention and begin shouting destinations.

Or at least that's what I hope they are shouting.

One breaks away and starts jogging along backwards beside me, his swarthy face lit with a smile. He starts rapid firing words at me. I blink. The words are all in bloody Greek.

And the thing is, I should be able to understand at least some of it, as I am part Greek.

'Chrissoskalitissa! Samaria? Georgioupolis! Elafonisi? Xeno-docheío?'

I'm walking fast, trying to get away, when he says it.

'Chania old town?'

I pause mid-step. For just a moment, I smell the faint aroma of wild lavender, taste the sweet tang of honey on my tongue and feel the fine texture of flour between my fingers. I stare at him. He stops too and his smile broadens. 'Chania old town?' he asks, again.

I feel a lump form in my throat, close my eyes and nod. During the drive, I get lost in thought. Back to another time. A time of plastic bubble-gum shoes, only child hopscotch, imaginary friends, and how it all changed when an old woman with eyes like warm coffee came to stay.

Yaya.

She sold her house in the Cretan countryside and moved into the garden cottage at the back of our house, which she filled with treasures that spoke of all the wonders of the island. Filling the window boxes with wild Cretan herbs, she planted a garden that seemed to be in perpetual bloom, bringing with her the sun, scent and stories from far away.

Chania.

I can still remember her teaching me how to say the word, which made a pleasing rasping sound at the back of my throat, like an enchantment. A word that matched the tales of the strange, beautiful and ancient city; coloured by the people who made it their home throughout the centuries from the ancient Minoans to the Venetians and Ottomans, till finally freedom hard won.

I can't quite believe that I'm here.

I'd spent the taxi ride lost in memory, the countryside rushing past me, each sight a reminder, a promise. The scents were indescribable, a heady mix of wild herbs strong in the air. Yaya had said that Crete had its own distinctive scent, but I'd never imagined this. Having only English money with me, I'd left the taxi driver with ten pounds, which he said he was certain he could exchange. He directed me to the new quarter, where he said I'd be able to get euros with my credit card. He'd been kind. Not once mentioning my lack of luggage, and, sensing that I didn't really want to talk, he'd left me to soak it all in.

My legs carry me, almost with a will of their own, to the old harbour; the water, a shining reflection of the biscuit-coloured buildings perched along the coastline, with the stone sea wall winding around the harbour. Up ahead the old Venetian lighthouse stands sentry, as it has for centuries. As I stand in awe, a small white dog, of unknown breed, jumps onto a nearby bench to doze in the sunshine. With the sun on my face, I feel suddenly free. It's hard to be sad or anxious now that I'm here. I walk over and take a seat next to the dog; he opens one languid eye, which closes instantly as I scratch behind his ear.

There's an easy warmth that heralds the start of spring. It's hard to believe that just a few hours ago my breath was forming a mist in front of my face in icy London. I unwind my scarf and put it in my bag, seeing my passport again as I do.

I pick it up and look at it once more, in wonder. How was it that on the day that I ended up with a bag I hadn't used since my last holiday with Christopher, a bag that had held my passport for three years, I took the airport lane by mistake?

I know what Yaya would have said. That there are no coincidences. I'd never bought into that way of thinking, not really. But this? How did I explain it? A small part of me can't help but wonder if she'd had a hand in bringing me here. It would be like her, too.

The photograph on the inside of my passport makes me catch my breath. Taken three years ago, my hair is long and loose, my eyes alight, trying hard not to laugh at Christopher as he made model poses at me from behind the photographer. I swallow hard.

I'd forgotten about that day. Or, at least, I'd been trying to forget. Not just that day but all the days since. No one prepares you, though, for the sudden jolt of memory, transporting you back, against your will. I shut the passport quickly.

I wipe a tear away, almost hearing her voice, 'Ria, why yew sad? My *meli mou* is no reason to be sad, not now that you're finally here. *F-i-n-a-l-l-y.*' The word stretched out, with a roll of her big brown eyes. I can't help the small smile it causes.

I put the passport back in my bag and stand up; the little dog gives me a look, holds my gaze, then seems to make up his mind as he jumps down to follow. I grin, grateful for the company.

We amble past the waterfront, with its lively atmosphere; the noisy hum from people selling their wares, the air spiced with the rich aroma of delicious Greek food, and head up a narrow cobbled street, where the sounds of the bustling harbour fade away.

We walk beside buildings shaded in varying hues of russet and ochre, windows overflowing with begonias in countless colours. I buy a coffee to go from a taverna spilling onto the pavement with wicker-paned chairs and blue-checked tablecloths:

an intersection of business lunches and groups of relaxed holidaymakers. My faithful companion stays silent at my feet.

An old woman in a black dress smiles at me from outside a flower shop, as she places fresh, pale pink peonies in one bucket and yellow roses in another. '*Kalimera*,' she says. I return her greeting. She looks at the dog with an expression of amused bafflement. 'Yamas,' she says.

I frown in confusion, then raise my takeaway coffee cup at her. She gives a deep throaty chuckle and shakes her head. 'No, I meant your friend. You haven't been formally introduced? This is Yamas,' she says, patting the small white dog staring up at her adoringly.

Her voice is melodic and low, with a strong Greek brogue, achingly similar to Yaya's. I smile at her and thank her for the introduction. She returns the smile and gives me a wink. 'Yew must have found his favourite place – right here,' she says, scratching behind his left ear.

I laugh, seeing the expression of delight cross Yamas' face. 'I did,' I admit. 'Is he your dog?' I ask, curious.

The woman shrugs. 'Yes and no – he's all of ours, we all look after him. If he belongs to anyone, though, it's the people at *Eudaimonia*, that's where Yamas sleeps most nights.'

I look at her in astonishment. *Eudaimonia* was the newspaper that I'd read on the plane, the one still folded up inside my bag. I couldn't help thinking about the burnt-down vineyard, and the young man with his daunting task.

'They're based here?' I ask.

'Just up the road, next to the Spinalonga café. Yew arrive today?' she asks, noting my long trousers, boots and jacket with a curious expression. It wasn't quite holiday wear.

'Just a little while ago.'

'Have yew been to Chania before?'

'No. Although it feels a bit like I have.'

She looks at me curiously and I explain. 'My grandmother was born near here, and she told me about it.' I pause. 'She had a way of describing things that captured so much.'

'Seeing is something else, though?'

I have to agree, it definitely is. 'I'm Ria,' I say, holding out my hand, which she shakes.

'Sofia. How long yew in Crete?'

I feel the familiar panic settle around my throat at the question, but manage to squash it somehow. 'I'm not sure yet,' I say.

She gives me an understanding sort of look, but doesn't say anything. Just then a customer comes, pointing and giving her an order. I turn to leave, calling goodbye. She turns back to me with a grin, beckoning me to come back. 'Here,' she says, handing me a peony, 'something to brighten your stay.'

'Thank you,' I say, touched. As I walk away I can't help but laugh, as Yamas comes tearing after me. I bend down and pat his salty fur, looking into his big brown eyes, which are regarding me rather seriously. 'I'm not sure what I did to deserve you, but I'm grateful for your company.'

Together we walk the old town, silent companions along narrow cobbled lanes. I stop at a money exchange and, with a combination of pointing and broken Greek, manage to get some euros. We reach a patisserie decorated in green and gold with tables and chairs haphazardly arranged on the pavement. The enticing scents of sweet honey-scented pastries flavour the air, and Yamas comes to a halt, his tail wagging hopefully. Loud, indecipherable Greek follows and a grouchy-looking man, with large pop-out eyes, flings a scrap of bread Yamas' way, which he vacuums up.

I get a croissant – not exactly traditional fare, but I haven't eaten all day. It's soft and delicious, still warm from the oven. I pause to eat, Yamas staring at me, so I throw him a piece. After I finish eating, I take my jacket off and fling it over my bag, rolling my sleeves up too. Sweat forms at the back of my shirt and my clothes are starting to stick to my skin, my feet are hot and pinched in my boots – clearly these boots weren't made for walking. Looking at them properly, I blink.

They're purple.

Not black, as I had assumed since wearing them every winter *for two years.*

I had been wearing purple boots for two years, and no one told me? A mad chuckle bubbles out. My feet look like two oversized bruises. Had I just never seen them in the sun?

Out of the corner of my eye, I spot a small, beach-shack-style shop brimming with sandals on display, which seem like a good idea. I finish my croissant and cross the uneven cobblestones to pick out a pair. Inside the shop a stack of blue and white beach bags catches my eye and I choose one too. Five minutes later I've swapped my boots for orange sandals, and am feeling decidedly more comfortable in my own skin. Even though with my – thankfully not purple in this light – corporate slacks, blouse and beach bag I probably look... well, a bit like I feel, which admittedly is like a raving lunatic.

I suppress a manic giggle when Yamas lets out an enthusiastic bark and runs up the street. I hurry after him and find him greeting two casually dressed men sitting at a café surrounded by the usual paper debris involved in a business meet, albeit with a large carafe of red wine. *Vive la Crete!*

'Yamas, you silly devil, where've you been?' greets the older man, who must have been in his late sixties, with dark auburn hair and tawny, heavily freckled skin. He speaks with a clipped, rather posh British accent.

The younger man barely looks up and simply continues with their previous discussion, heroically ignoring the intrusion of the dog. 'I think if we move the Iraklion piece to page six that should solve the problem, but then should we put the Easter festival on page two?'

The older man agrees while scratching behind Yamas' ears. He catches me staring and calls, '*Yasou*.'

I blush, and return the greeting. Yamas comes trotting back to me, and I explain, 'We made friends earlier, and he's been keeping me company ever since. I wondered where he had bolted off to.'

'Just me, I'm afraid,' says the older man. 'Hope he hasn't been a bother?'

I shake my head. 'Not at all. He's been giving me the tour.'

His smile widens. 'Ah, you couldn't ask for a better guide. Nico and I only wish we knew what this old boy has forgotten – we'd offer our readers the real taste of Crete.'

I grin back. 'You run the paper... *Eudaimonia*?' I ask, remembering the name from earlier, unconsciously tapping my bag in the process.

'Yes. Well me, and Nico here, actually,' he says, patting Nico on the back. He is quite young, probably just out of university, with dark hair and skin, and a pair of square-cut black glasses that give him an intellectual air.

'How did you hear about *Eudaimonia*?' he asks.

'Oh – I got it on the plane,' I say, taking the paper out from my bag. 'And then when Yamas started following me, I met Sofia from down the street – and she told me that as far as everyone is concerned Yamas is everyone's dog, but if he belonged to anyone it would be the owner of the English paper, *Eudaimonia*.'

Loud barking laughter follows from the older man. 'Quite right, too! I can't claim ownership to Yamas either – I inherited him when we opened this office,' he says, gesturing to the narrow building on his left, where a small faded sign on the wall proclaimed the name of the paper. 'He came with the deal.'

'Not a bad deal,' I say, giving Yamas a pat.

He chortles. 'That's what I always say. You in town for work?' he asks, eyeing my suit and orange sandal combination with a wry expression.

I blush but grin anyway. 'No, I came from work, but didn't count on this heat.'

His eyes crease in amusement. Yamas leaves my side and settles by his feet, closing his eyes.

'Would you like to join us for a glass of wine, Ms—?' he asks.

'Ria… Ria Laburinthos,' I supply.

'Laburinthos – Greek, hey?' he says. 'Nigel Crane… and this is Nico Stephako.'

'Thanks for the kind offer…' I find myself declining. Even as I have nowhere to go, I'm not sure about human company right now: I know I need to spend some time alone just to think. So I lie. 'I have to get back, but it was very nice to meet you both,' I say.

'Next time, then,' says Nigel. 'You can always find Nico and me here if you change your mind.'

I smile. 'I'd like that.' Turning to go and seeing that Yamas is happily ensconced at Nigel's feet, I feel a sense of loss that I try to ignore; I bend down and give him a farewell pat.

As I make my way up the street, I feel lost without my furry guide. I walk the streets, watching families eating and speaking loudly in Greek. The city is a heady mix of old and new, where large chain stores vie with traditional Greek tavernas. Even the people are a delicious melange. I spy an old man leaning against the wall, dressed in traditional Cretan garb, while a group of teenagers saunter past, iPods in place, talking loudly, their neon-coloured T-shirts ripped and torn in the latest eighties revival fashion.

Up ahead I spy a large, beautiful church in a baroque style, and I hurry over to take a closer look. According to the plaque on the wall it had been built during the Venetian empire. I try the door, but it's locked. Turning to go, I walk up the side, stopping when I see a large noticeboard along the wall. A sign catches my eye, for accommodation nearby; it isn't far, just near the harbour, and the picture looks inviting. There are a few more advertisements like that, and I scan them as well, deciding against them as they are far away and I don't have a car. I take down the address of the place and make a mental note to buy a map as soon as possible, doubting I will find it otherwise. As I turn to leave, a note pinned to the board grabs my attention.

Writer's assistant required for well-known English author/ mad cow

Ability to keep herbs alive (a plus), coffee-making skills (non-negotiable)

Tea drinker (tolerated, depends on the tea, really)

Biscuit baker (an added benefit)

Use of chocolate and/or wine in a crisis situation (fundamental)

Sense of humour (vital)

Contact: Caroline 28215-73930

I laugh aloud. She sounds great. Anyone who considers chocolate fundamental usually is.

I drag myself away, thinking: map. And I head down the street, only to stop, go back and take down Caroline's number.

FIVE

An hour later, map in hand, I'm standing in the heart of the bustling waterfront, outside a large, ornate sky-blue door, the faded paint a perfect patina, enhanced only by the vivid red begonias flanking it on either side. A sign on the amber-hued walls reads Water's Edge Lodge.

I push open the doors and head inside to a small cobbled courtyard, overflowing with flowers in pots, from roses to night jasmine, begonias and lavender. I enter the building ahead, where a small signs reads in Greek and English: Reception.

Behind a heavily polished oak counter sits an old woman with fluffy white hair, a curved back and a face browned like the flesh of an apple exposed to air. She greets me in heavily accented English. The sound of her voice tugs at my heart; everywhere here reminds me of Yaya.

'Yew are with luck,' she says after I ask her if she has any vacancies for the night. She points to the long flight of stairs behind her. 'I haf one,' she smiles conspiratorially. A finger taps near her nose. 'The best-e one.' She winks.

This is a small miracle, I'm made to understand, as accommodation can get quite scarce in the old city this close to Easter. After I pay for the night, thanking the heavens that my credit card works here, she leads me up the six flights of stairs. She is surprisingly spry, despite her age.

'Is the last-e room, most people don't-a always want it because the climb,' she says, in her sing-song voice that lifts up the last letter of every word like a question. She opens a bottle-green door with an elaborate copper handle and declares, 'But it has the best-e view...'

I gasp. A row of windows that lead out to a small balcony offers a sweeping view of the harbour, stretching as far as the eye can see, taking in the elegant column of the Venetian lighthouse in the distance.

She smiles at my expression. I would climb twenty more flights of stairs just to see this view, I think.

'So okay they bring luggage later?' she asks.

I shake my head. 'No luggage – just this,' I say, indicating my handbag and the recently purchased beach bag.

She shrugs. 'O-kay. I am called Nessa,' she says, tapping her chest with a gnarled brown finger.

'Ria,' I say.

'Okay,' she repeats, and runs me through the facilities in the apartment, which include a double bed, a tiny kitchen, a TV, and thankfully an en-suite shower and toilet.

'Yew call me if yew need anything? I cook yew a nice breakfast tomorrow,' she says, eyeing me in the way only Greek grandmothers do, with a look which implies that she's going to start poking your ribs and feeling your collarbone and lamenting at how skinny you are in about a minute.

She narrows her eyes and peers intently at me. 'Yew hungry now? I make you something?' she asks.

'No, no, I'm fine, thank you.'

She narrows her eyes further, taking in my frame, and shakes her head. 'Okay... I make you a sandwich.'

Resistance is futile.

'Thank you, Nessa,' I say with a grin.

She smiles. 'My grandson, Nicky, will-a come bring,' then she gives me a long searing look. 'Yew stay as long as yew need, is my last-e room but… no one else booked zis one since yesterday… Mebbe is meant for you?' she says with a shrug, before closing the door behind her.

I swallow hard. Could it be? I put my bags on the white bedspread and sit down, taking out my phone and switching it on. I take a deep breath and wait.

There are fourteen missed calls.

And one text message. It's from Janice and says only one word. But it's one word too far.

'Unacceptable.'

It's like I've been plunged into ice. My breath comes in gasps. Soon another emotion surfaces, obliterating the ever-present sorrow. Anger – full dark and white hot.

I was unacceptable?

How dare she?

When she hadn't even asked me – not once – how I was after everything that happened. Even in the beginning when I asked – begged – to be moved to do something, anything else besides writing obituaries, when she'd pretended to understand and said she'd see what she could do, and never did. While watching me hang on by a thread, pushing myself every day to write about the one thing I found impossible to accept. She, who now wanted to create some morbid horror show from it all: a mishmash of a bunch of people's lives that had all ended on the day they all thought they were beginning. This person, who could never have been accused of showing some semblance of humanity, found me unacceptable?

I knew then with sudden irrevocable clarity that I would never be going back.

'I quit.' I hit 'send' and felt immediately free.

A second later, she replied again. *'Unacceptable.'*

I had to laugh. Thinking that I may as well rip off the plaster completely, I did the next impossible task: I called my mother.

SIX

'Crete?' came my mother's oddly calm voice. 'Do I understand you correctly? Instead of going to work today, you decided to fly off to Crete, is that correct?' she says, as if I were on trial.

My mother is a retired barrister.

Although there is little retiring about her.

You can just imagine the bliss that were my teenage years.

Or you know, *not*.

'It wasn't planned... I was at the airport and it just happened.' I didn't mention the alcohol – that wouldn't exactly help my case.

Silence greets my answer. I can picture her trying to make sense of my words while she sits beside the phone in the hallway in the blue Queen Anne chair that Christopher's mum, Trish, picked out for her.

'Right...'

I wait for it, but she doesn't ask why.

'I just couldn't do it any more.'

She sucks in air, a small sound that makes me close my eyes. Then, so unexpectedly it makes my eyes brim with tears, she says, 'Oh.'

I hear a faint sniff, then, 'I love you.'

'Oh Mum,' I choke. 'I love you too.'

'No tears,' she says, her voice breaking.

I use my palms to dash them away, nodding, even though she can't see me.

'I quit my job,' I say.

I'm gobsmacked when she starts to laugh. '*F-i-n-a-l-l-y*,' she says, in perfect imitation of Yaya, and I can't help but chuckle too.

Then she says, 'So, you had to wait-a until I kick the bucket to do this – eh? Just so I couldn't say I told you so? Eh?'

Her accent is terrible, but in a delicious way. It's so morbid, I can't help myself – I'm crying I'm laughing so hard. That's exactly what Yaya would have said.

It takes about a full minute for either of us to settle down.

Rather unexpectedly, she says, 'She'd be proud of you, my darling.'

'I don't know about that… it wasn't the smartest move.'

'Life isn't always about doing the smart thing, my love, sometimes it's about doing what's in your heart too, and after everything you've been through… the idea of you doing that every day, well it's been breaking my heart.'

My throat constricts. I'm a little bemused by her response. My mother has always been the practical one, the one who played by the rules, the one who told me that she had installed cameras at my school so that's how she saw me smoking behind the maintenance shed. I had the last laugh, of course – we all smoked behind the old school bus instead. But she was the last person who would have thought that abandoning your job would ever be a good idea.

'Mum?' I ask.

Her breath catches; the sad sound twists in my heart. 'I miss her so much. She knew what to say after what happened to Chris. How to just be there.' She gulps. 'And now…'

My eyes start to spill over again. I don't say it aloud, there's no need, we're both thinking the same thing: now she's gone too.

A million different feelings in one day, but it always comes back to heartache.

I wonder if I will ever be the same again. After losing them both, so soon after the other.

I realise even more that I'm not the only one it has changed. 'Mum,' I say, my palms brushing my eyes, trying to still the inevitable, 'no one knows what to do or say – you've been wonderful, there's no guide for this, you've done so much, really.'

I hear her intake of air and wish I could hold her tight; instead I try to break the mood. 'No tears,' I admonish. She laughs in response. 'Dad will want to hear too, hang on, let me get him.'

I feel a sudden flicker of apprehension, as Dad is liable to lecture. I hear her calling him from his home office – Dad refuses to retire, he's an applied mathematician and professor at the University of Reading. When I was little he started doing classified work for the government, which naturally turned him into James Bond in my young eyes. Of course, Dad never discouraged this: he used to walk into the house and say, 'Laburinthos, Michael Laburinthos,' every time he came back from a meeting with them.

I hear them talking in the background, hear my dad's voice go up in surprise, then suddenly he's on the line. 'You're in Crete?' he asks in surprise, needing me to confirm. His voice is still mildly Cretan. It's funny, I'd stopped noticing it but now that I'm here I can hear it. 'I am.'

'Where?'

'Chania.'

I hear him take in a breath, then, 'Ah, *meli mou,* she would have wanted you to see it.'

I swallow. 'Thanks, Dad.'

'So I hear... you quit?'

'Bad news travels fast…'

'The fastest,' he agrees. 'Look, *meli*…' says Dad in his firm but kind voice. 'You should have come to us first. You should have resigned, worked out your notice, so you could have got a good reference. I understand you've been unhappy but to just quit…'

I close my eyes. Should. There's lots of things that 'should' have happened. Christopher should still be here. So should Yaya. Why *should* I do what's right when nothing else goes the way it should?

I hear my mother speaking in the background but don't hear what she says, though I can imagine it's something along the lines of 'Not now, Michael'. There have been a lot of 'Not now, Michaels' over the past two years, I think. I feel a sudden curling of shame. No one likes to be a burden. A grown-up daughter, nearing thirty, living in her childhood bedroom for the past two years, definitely qualifies.

Next thing Dad is back on the line, trying to put a positive spin on what he clearly thinks is my stuff-up. 'Look, *meli*, have a holiday, you've earned it. Take some time, see the old country, have a break. Then when you get back we can help you look for a new job, put that degree to real use, mmm? Maybe you could retrain, get out of journalism, find something that uses your skills but pays better, maybe communications, or marketing?'

I sigh. This is an old argument. My father never really wanted me to be a journalist. It wasn't that he didn't believe in me, just rather that he felt that if I was sensible I'd find a job where I could use my skills and get paid properly. Journalists aren't the best paid people in the world. Considering how unhappy I've been lately in a job I hate, getting paid peanuts just didn't add up. Not to Dad, and well, perhaps not to me either. I'd made peace with the salary. But although a small salary was fine if you had job satisfaction, it was adding insult to injury when you didn't. But still… marketing? A career change? Honestly, I didn't have the strength to consider that right now.

Next thing Dad asks. 'You got money?'

'I'm all right. I've got my savings.' Some things never change, and my parents worrying about me is one of those things. It's a nice thing to be sure of. After I gave up Christopher and my flat in London – I just couldn't be there, emotionally, or financially – I moved back home to Reading to figure things out. My parents insisted that I save what I would pay on rent for the future. It was meant to be a temporary measure, six months tops, but time moved differently, slower somehow, and I found myself stuck in a kind of limbo for two years. Until Yaya passed two months ago, taking with her the small bit of solid ground beneath my feet. I wasn't in limbo any more, that's for sure.

Mum comes back on the line. 'You've got somewhere to stay?'

I look around the small apartment, like a little treehouse perched over the harbour. 'I do. You'd love it here.'

'Maybe I'll come one day too,' she says, surprising me further. My mother, like me, has never been one for spontaneity.

'Promise me.'

'I promise.'

As we say goodbye, I hope that she will. I try not to think of what Dad said. I can't help feeling, for perhaps the first time in a very long while, that while I don't have anything figured out, it just feels right to be here, to be doing something else.

Looking out of the window at the harbour, I can picture Yaya, the way she used to look at me, especially after Christopher. When I used to get the jitters on a Sunday, she'd shake her head and make me promise that I would live my life; that I would see that I didn't have to live the same one over and over if

I didn't want to; that I would see that there's more to living than that. I used to sigh and say, 'Yes, Yaya, I will, I promise.'

'When?' she'd ask, her beetle-black eyes boring into mine, wanting an answer: a date, a guarantee.

'One day,' I'd assure her. 'Not just yet, things are very busy at the paper.'

'Pah! The paper?' she'd exclaim, throwing up her hands. 'Writing about death every day, Ariadne, is no way to live. Don't keep putting off your "one day" until there are no days left, trust me on this, *meli mou.*'

Watching the light hit the water, the reflections from the buildings above making paint-like rivulets in its depths, I speak aloud and say, to my own surprise, 'Seems it's today, Yaya.'

A tap on the door gives me a start. I get up to open it and find a young boy, barely a teenager, holding up a plate with a large sandwich filled with lamb and tzatziki. 'From Yaya,' he says.

I blink. For just a second I think my dead grandmother has brought me a sandwich from beyond the grave. And then I realise. 'From Nessa?'

'*Nai* – yes,' he answers and dashes off like a racehorse down the steps, while I call after him, '*Efharisto* – thank you.'

I take my sandwich outside and eat it ravenously while watching the boats in the distance. It even tastes like something she would have made.

Being here makes her death both harder and easier to bear, somehow. I want to ask her about so many things. It's a feeling that I suspect won't go away. I understood when I chose Crete, even before I bought the ticket, that this was the only place that I wanted to go, despite knowing that at every point I'd be reminded of her. And of Christopher too, the two events, like the two halves of a coin – heads I break, tails I start again.

I suppose in a way that's what has made it easier too.

Here, I don't need to move past it, to try not missing her or Chris, both of which are impossible.

Here, I feel that I can just accept that I will always miss them. I only hope that in time it won't always hurt as much. Perhaps here I can just let it be. There's a certain freedom in that.

SEVEN

I've never been a fan of lists.

Perhaps it has something to do with Kimberley and her co-lour-coded 'action plans'. Perhaps it's the way she seemed hell bent on mapping out every second of her day. A task, no doubt designed to suck out any marrow of fun that she or anyone in her vicinity might ever experience, that caused me to treat them with disdain.

Even when lists are meant to be fun, they're really there just to tell you what to do.

Like those '100 best books of all time' lists. Translation: all the other books you've read don't count. Or the 'Top 20 places in the world to visit' lists that make every other place you've visited, likewise, irrelevant.

Been to Allhelgonagatan? Really? Doesn't bloody well count, does it? Not unless it's on *the list*.

And don't even get me started on the '100 things to do before you kick the bucket' list because, well let's face it, all that really happens is that right before you kick the bucket, you're trying desperately to plank in the underground. Or take up cross-fit, and learn Taiwanese and, yes, read all those bloody books that you should have been reading while all you really wanted to do was get on with the latest Nora Roberts.

Yet there comes a time in everyone's life when a list isn't just a list any more; it's a lifeline.

Sitting on my bed, I sort through what constitutes my 'luggage', which is:

1. A beach bag (empty)
2. A small handbag containing a notebook, my passport, some make-up and a packet of hard mints (Best before 2013, er *gross*)
3. A pair of worn, and as it turns out purple, 'bruiser' boots (hellishly hot in this heat)
4. An English–Cretan newspaper
5. A jacket and scarf (ditto point 3)
6. A pair of orange sandals (the answer to point 3)
7. One loose-stemmed peony (wilting)
8. The very uncomfortable clothes I am wearing

And considering that I have:

1. Quit my job
2. Hightailed it to a foreign country

With no plan of return, no job, a dwindling cash supply... and more importantly no clean underwear to speak of, I am forced to concede that I am in desperate need of things, things in want of a list...

A while later this is my list:

1. Toothbrush
2. Toothpaste
3. Underwear
4. Summer clothes

That's a bit short, I muse. Where is bloody Kimberley when you need her? Oh yes… at work. Ha-ha, cue evil laughter.

Okay, focus Ria.

I do a quick run-through of my room, mentally visualising what I might need, and add:

5. Clothes – tops, shorts
6. A towel (why are there none here???)
7. A swimming costume
8. Body wash and sponge
9. Some anti-crazy meds (just kidding). Or not…

Lists are pretty good, it turns out, useful really, except two hours later I have returned with:

1. Four slabs of chocolate (essential – rookie mistake for not putting them on the list in the first place)
2. Wine (ditto point 1)
3. A Bodum and a bag of hazelnut filter coffee (ditto point 1)
4. Underwear
5. Three pairs of shorts
6. Five assorted spring tops
7. A duck-egg blue shawl (love at first sight)
8. A grey and yellow sundress (ditto)
9. Two pairs of sandals
10. Body wash
11. Face wash
12. Toothpaste
13. Sponge
14. A beach towel and a bath towel

15. Aching limbs from lugging this lot up six flights of stairs and nine blocks of cobble-paved roads in scorching heat (we are so not in London any more)

I unpack my things into the tiny kitchen, bedroom and bathroom. I open the wine to 'breathe' – five seconds should be fine, right? I take a shower, combing my hair out under the spray, tackling each and every snarl until the water turns cold.

I finally feel comfortable in my own skin. Dressed in a pair of cool linen shorts and a loose T-shirt, my hair wrapped up in a towel, I take a seat on my little balcony with my wine in hand to watch the sunset. A sweeping mix of pink and violet bathes the harbour in a rose-tinged glow.

I phone Tamsin, my best friend since our secondary school days, to tell her what I've done.

'You did what? You? The person who ordered the exact same pair of boots as the ones you wore for three years before that, which you wore almost every single day of winter and autumn these past two years, even though they were purple... *you* got on a plane to Crete?'

Hang on... now really, hang on just a minute. 'You knew they were purple?' I gasp.

'You didn't?'

I start to laugh and she joins in. 'No,' I admit.

'I can't believe it, Ria,' she says in wonder between giggles.

'About the boots, or Crete?'

'All of it! And you quit via text? God, I would have *loved* to have seen Janice's face! What did you say, please say you texted the word "unsubscribe"?'

I laughed, 'I should have! But that was the gist.'

As a well-known beauty blogger, with a strong eco focus, Tams knew many of London's media editors, surprisingly including Janice, who she despised for never telling the truth when a beauty product was less than kosher.

'I haven't got a plan, not yet… but for now it's enough to just be here, I feel so close to Yaya here.'

'Ah my lovely, I can imagine. Look, the blog is expanding, I've been looking for an assistant, maybe you could come work with me… when you're back? I know beauty isn't your thing but there's some travel and the events are a lot of fun… plus you'd get as much free product as you could wish.'

She's being sweet. I mean, me, a beauty blogger? Ten minutes ago I was feeling proud of myself for giving my hair a proper brush. It's not that I don't like beauty products and things, I do in a casual sort of way, but I'm not sure I could ever be really passionate about them like Tams. Or that I'd cut it. Obituary writer turned beauty blogger? That was insane even by my standards. Her readers would spot that I was a fraud, I'm sure. Or my ghastly boots would give me away…

I know she's just trying to help, but when had I become this person… the one everyone needed to fix? I used to be a lot tougher than this. Didn't I? I didn't like that my father and my best friend saw me as some problem that needed to be solved, even if they meant well. I didn't care for it, not at all.

I thank her for the kind offer and say, 'Right now I just need time to think, really… see what my next step is.'

'Yeah, I know… was worth a shot. I know it's not your thing. I mean the last time I told you about wing tips you thought I was talking about shoes,' says Tams.

I laugh. 'Good point.' We say goodbye, and I promise to get in touch soon to let her know how I'm getting on.

It's only later when I'm getting ready for bed that I realise: I forgot to buy a bloody toothbrush.

Bloody lists.

EIGHT

It's 1 a.m.

I know this without having a clock nearby to confirm, or the plaintive wails of Travis, the bulldog next door back home, who'd got stuck in the flap of the door again (poor pudgy soul).

I know it's 1 a.m. because even a thousand miles away (where I can't help Travis by pumping his fat little legs and propelling him head first through the door, to his immense slobbering gratitude) my body is, as usual, getting on with its job of grudgingly providing light, mostly broken sleep, then switching gears and giving me a healthy wallop of full-blown panic instead.

Self-love: it's such a crock sometimes.

I sigh loudly and try the deep breathing exercises I had practised with Dr Rushma. I try to think calming thoughts as she had suggested, picturing Travis' wrinkly fur and the demented yet funny-as-hell way he ran at me whenever he saw me and often (due to his failing eyesight) missed his mark and went barrelling into the wall instead. I love that stupid dog.

I sigh again, get out my phone and text Mum: *Is Travis stuck?*

And Mum, in typically retired barrister-Mum style, responds straightaway: *Travis needs to go on a diet. Go back to sleep.*

Come on, Mum, he's probably wondering where I am.

She replies: *Get a grip. I'm not breaking in next door to squeeze a 100-pound dog through the cat flap.*

'Okay… Maybe Mrs Smythe will get him… when she remembers.'
She says goodbye with: *'Fine, I'm going. Go back to sleep.'*

I lie back against the cushions with a grin. Mrs Smythe is rather deaf and ninety-seven years old.

If she hadn't been mostly deaf and ninety-seven years old, I would most likely have stolen Travis and built him a bigger flap. Perhaps with her poor eyesight she'd assume he was still in her backyard when she looked out her window.

Chris would help, too. With a sudden mad laugh, I picture us: thieves in the night with Travis under my arm, his long, pink ribbon-like tongue lolling in the wind.

My grin dissolves and my throat turns dry. Two years and I still do that to myself. I can't believe I just forgot. The dreams don't help either.

Reality is hard, uncompromising and inescapable during the day. At night, during sleep, wishes rooted in the depths of the heart take over. The worst dreams are the ones where he tells me that it was all just a nightmare, and that this is the truth; that he's still here. Waking from that is unbearable.

I press my palms against my eyes – stemming the inevitable. I get out of bed and head to my little balcony.

The harbour is still and silent in the night, the air crisp. I turn back inside and brew myself some coffee and fetch the soft blue shawl I bought yesterday.

I take my coffee outside and sit at the little table with my arms wrapped around myself. There's this part of me that doesn't really know how to do this. How to just be okay with not knowing what to do.

Mentally I run through my finances.
Four weeks.

If I live very frugally, I could live here for four weeks, maybe six if I switched to peanut butter on toast. It wouldn't be luxurious living, but I'd have a real break… and just have enough for the plane ticket home.

Except I can't reconcile what I've done, the enormity of it all; from quitting my job to walking out on my 'life' (or whatever you call the last two years) for a short break.

I head back inside and fetch my bag. Inside I find the scribbled piece of paper with Caroline's telephone number on it – the writer looking for an assistant.

I thumb the paper over and over, thinking. Then take a sip of coffee and decide.

Several hours later I'm standing in an olive grove in the picturesque village of Ouranó. From somewhere deep inside, the meaning of the name reverberates in my head: heaven. It's not far off, with fat, juicy olives ripening on the branches, the impressive backdrop of the Lefka Ori mountain range, the sparkling blue ocean, and the beckoning lushness of the rolling vineyards in the distance. It's bliss.

The sun is warm on my bare shoulders as I make my way up a long sandy driveway towards a sprawling, honey-hued stone farmhouse complemented by pale blue shutters, the scent of wild thyme and lavender thick in the air. A friendly-looking woman sporting a navy wide-brimmed sunhat and a bag of chicken feed at her heels stands on her tiptoes and waves.

Caroline.

It's only as I am standing there that I realise… I know her. With the sudden drop of my jaw, I realise.

Caroline freaking *Murray*?

BBC's Caroline Murray, world renowned presenter of *Off the Beaten Trek*, author of *Falling for Crete*, responsible for at least sixty-five per cent of the British exodus to this beautiful island during the nineties, not to mention the subsequent holiday home price increase, apparently. Though, thankfully, few seem to have followed her here to this beautiful village; she fastidiously kept private the location of her home. It had been a delicious secret. Well, till now.

If I'd known it was Caroline Murray, I'm not sure I would have dared calling her. I would have stuttered and stumbled over my words and probably gushed something embarrassing, like that Yaya and I used to watch every single episode of *Off the Beaten Trek*, or that I developed a habit of calling my school chums 'darling' when I was nine, like Caroline did. Cringe.

Instead, she'd responded with, 'Ah! A fresh victim, what providence is this?' when I asked if she was still looking for an assistant. She'd then demanded I come over straightaway. I'd got the impression she wanted to get me there before I changed my mind.

Which is how, barely ten minutes after I'd rung, I found myself to my utter bemusement summoning a taxi from Nessa's little office and making my way to Ouranó.

'Just feeding the hens,' greets Caroline, scattering the rest of the chicken feed as she makes her way down the drive. She has the effortless grace of a woman who is comfortable in her skin, hair a loose tangle of blonde-brown curls, and a brilliant smile. It would be just as easy to picture her as comfortable in heels as she was now with bare feet. Up close, though, I can see she's older than I first imagined, perhaps in her late sixties. She welcomes me with a kiss. 'Hullo darling – wow… what gorgeous eyes,' she says. She peers at me intently, then winks. 'Creamy Italian espresso.'

At my raised eyebrow, she explains. 'Hazard of the trade, you know. Writhers,' she says with a roll of her eyes.

'Writhers?'

'Writhers.' She explains. 'Tormented souls, forever doomed to writhe in agony at the sight of a misplaced Oxford comma, an unused adjective, or a dearth of apostrophes... commonly referred to as writers by those not afflicted with the problem.'

I laugh aloud. Was she for real?

'Come in, come in, it's a bit of a mess – I'm knee deep in THE BOOK, as you'll see, but I have a roast in the oven and we can have some wine in the garden in a bit and you can tell me all about yourself.'

'Oh, that's so... that's such a lot of trouble,' I say, overwhelmed. I wasn't expecting this. A glass of water, maybe a taste of her olives (I'd planned a slightly illegal hand raid of an olive tree on the way out)... but a roast?

Caroline's eyes dance and she taps her nose conspiratorially. 'Darling, I'm not above bribery...'

'Bribery? Why would you need bribery?' I mean, she's Caroline Murray, for goodness sake – I'm sure people would work for her for free. Or okay, well, maybe for wine, and roasts, and raiding her olive groves at will.

'That is what I'm going to show you in a minute.'

I feel a flicker of trepidation as I follow Caroline's slim form into the house, where she takes off her sunhat and places it on the hall table. She leads me to a large sitting room with floor-to-ceiling views of the olive groves, and the iridescent blue ocean in the distance.

The room is awash with faded old-world elegance. A battered roll-top desk stands before the large picture window, and in pride of place is a vintage Remington typewriter. Opposite the desk are two inviting wing-backs, and a daybed piled with cushions sits alongside the enormous fireplace.

Here and there are eclectic pieces and ornaments; I spy a blue-grey glass swallow, a moss-covered stone, and even a small yellow minion character that gives the room a happy, lived-in feel.

A low coffee table holds a mass of photographs, a precarious stack of typewritten notes and an assortment of intricate botanical watercolours.

'My writing den,' says Caroline. 'It's rather a permanent mess, I'm afraid – much to my late husband George's despair.' She points to the collected jumble on the coffee table and grins. 'Pandora's box – or chest, in my case – and now it's been opened I can't very well put it all back. A pity really because I've been ignoring it for twenty years, so you would think that I could just carry on doing so for at least twenty more.'

It's then I notice the large open trunk next to the coffee table, a trunk that would look at home in the possession of someone rather rich and fabulous, from a bygone era.

Caroline's trunk looks thoroughly well travelled and is overflowing with a collection of memorabilia: what appears to be thousands of photographs, stacks of handwritten letters, postcards, botanical drawings and manuscript pages.

'Wow,' I say.

'Yes. That's one way to put it. I thought I'd show you this first – because this is what I'll need your help with, if I'm ever to finish.'

I look at it in awe; it's a lifetime's worth of memories from her unusual, remarkable life.

I can't think of a nicer way to spend my time. I'm longing to look through the chest already. I sit down next to it, picking up some of the photographs: Caroline in what must have been her early twenties with long hippie hair sleeping in the back of a VW bus; Caroline getting a piggyback ride in front of the Eiffel tower from a dishy guy sporting a fedora; Caroline and a friend in matching swimsuits lying on a beach, laughing uproariously. Each photograph held a story, a promise, an adventure.

'I'd love to help you with this, truly,' I assure her, trying to avoid saying what I really want to say, which was, 'Pick me! Pick me!'

She smiles, a wide relieved smile. 'You're sure?' she asks. 'It's roughly forty years of travelling and memorabilia – my life really. It drove my last assistant from here screaming.'

'Really?'

'Well, no,' admits Caroline. 'But almost – he had to get back to school, exams. Nasty things,' she says.

'Assistants or exams?' I ask with a quirk of my lips.

'Touché, darling. I'll need someone on a full-time basis, really – I don't know how long it will take, but I think a year at a minimum.'

I sit back, slightly alarmed.

A year.

Here?

A few hours ago I was wondering if I could stretch my quarter-life crisis to six weeks. Now I'm being asked if I want to make it a year. While I'm having a mild internal freak-out, Caroline continues in a rush, 'It won't be every day of course – er – maybe four to five days a week? We can chat about that. Regular sort of hours and pay, though with writing I do think naps should be included. Writing is nauseatingly, thrillingly exhausting, but you know that already. You said on the phone that you also suffer from the writing disease?'

I laugh, thinking that 'virus' seems more apt. Once you catch the bug, it's there for life.

'What else? Oh, I have a cottage at the back – it's nothing fancy, but you'd be welcome to stay there if you'd like. Of course you don't have to make up your mind straightaway – let's eat and then you can tell me what you think.'

NINE

'So you write obituaries for a living?'

I look up at Caroline's carefully impassive expression and give her a lopsided smile. 'Yes. Well, it's complicated.'

She raises a delicately arched brow and says, 'I'm sure.'

We're sitting outside under a large olive tree at a long wooden table with the kind of faded patina that some people spend hours trying to recreate. The table is expertly positioned to capture the best view of the sweeping olive grove and the neat lines of a vineyard in the distance. It is beautiful.

She passes me a salad and I pile my plate with juicy green olives (from her trees, of course), feta cheese and cucumber, and slather it all in olive oil.

'It's... interesting,' I say, 'the way people live and love, poignant really. But it's hard too, trying to sum up someone's life and knowing that they're gone. It became a bit of a problem – seeping into other areas of my life. Like where a friend would tell me something, a new plan for her life and I'd wonder – would this be one of the things that would define her life? Would it be one of the things that may be put in her obituary? It was all a bit morbid.'

'I can imagine,' says Caroline, pouring red wine into two glasses and handing me one. 'But in a way that's quite a gift... being able to see how your life would look on your eulogy instead of on your resume.'

'It is, though I've learnt that life isn't just about the big moments, it's all the little things in between that make a life worth living. They're often what makes that person remarkable – the husband who woke his wife up every day of their married life for sixty years with a cup of tea, or the little girl who wouldn't leave home without first hugging her dog. The little things that make a person who they are, yet often don't get included in the bigger picture – or the small print at least – when they should.'
I think back to how many of these little moments Janice had ruthlessly spliced with her ever-ready red pen, the marks hitting something deeper, leaving a small, irreversible rip inside of me.

'You're right, of course. The everyday joys. It's what made us decide to move here in the first place, me and my late husband George, wanting those moments – wanting to create a simple, yet richer life together – and we did, although it didn't start out that way,' says Caroline.

'Your move to Crete?'

She takes a sip of her wine. 'Yes, although not just Crete, but the travel, all of it. Crete was just a small part of the adventure. I mean, our whole way of living, really. George and I met at university, in Accountancy 102.'

I splutter my wine. 'You studied accountancy?'

Somehow I can't reconcile the idea of Caroline Murray – the woman who had encouraged a nation of reserved English people to rediscover their wanderlust – with accountancy.

I stare at her in wonder.

'I know, I know, but what can I say? There's a certain beauty to a well-balanced spreadsheet, darling.'

My mouth must be hanging open, because she laughs. 'I think accountants get a terrible reputation – they really aren't the boring bunch they're portrayed to be.'

Well, if Caroline was anything to go by, she had a point.

'But then—?' I start.

'Well, after graduation I joined a really big firm, so did George. We got married, all those usual things and in many ways life was good. Then my friend Jill, a free spirit if ever there was one, invited us to India. We couldn't find the time – there was this big thing happening at work, George was due a promotion – so we put it off, you know how it goes. We were trying for a baby anyway, then we got the news – I had ovarian cancer, stage one. I was only twenty-seven. It was devastating. And just like that it changed everything. The whole "plan" we had for our lives. For the next year I battled chemo and radiation and finally when I went into remission, we both took a very long, very serious look at our lives. We were only in our late twenties, but already we had fallen into that trap to which so many of us become prey: we put off what we want to do. The trouble is that life doesn't work that way, as much as we like to pretend that it does. It isn't a re-hearsal. It's a cliché, I suppose, but seeing how quickly our whole life could fall apart we realised that we wanted to make the most of it. So while I enjoyed my job, I realised that I didn't want to spend the rest of my life doing it. I just wanted more freedom, re-ally. George was the same. When I went into remission, we sold our house, packed up our bags and hit the road.'

'But wasn't it hard – just letting it all go?' I ask, wondering if I'm on the verge of doing something as scary, and as exciting – right then praying like hell that I am.

'The hardest, yet best decision I have ever made. There were people who just couldn't, or refused really, to understand. There were those who thought we were living a fantasy – one that would come crashing down around us, and there were some who believed that we were being utterly irresponsible.'

'Irresponsible – because you were walking away from a steady job?' I ask, feeling a matching shiver of guilt at the idea.

'That – yes – but more than that, there were some who thought that I was treating myself and George irresponsibly. Being away from home was a risk – and if the cancer returned or I died, I'd be putting George in jeopardy. I think, for some, it was seen as selfish – at least, I was seen that way.'

I shake my head in disbelief. 'But how—?' I exclaim.

'Well, I was asking George to let go of a particular life for a journey with me, one that there was no guarantee that I'd be around to finish. It was a lot to ask. The thing was I'd been thinking all of these things myself. George had his own demons too, and it's what kept him focused. I remember just before we were due to start our adventure, we'd decided on Paris as the start – all great journeys should start in Paris – I think you saw some of those photos in the trunk, we were such kids, really.'

I nod, eager to hear more.

'I was ready to call it all off. Feeling guilty at what everyone must be thinking of me and imagining the worst. But then he said, "Caro, it could come back whether we stayed or went, and if we carried on as if nothing changed, then I would have to live knowing that we could have tried but didn't." So we went,' she finishes simply. 'And it changed everything. Though you never know how life will turn out, do you? I never expected George to go first. Heart attack four years ago,' she explains.

'I'm so sorry,' I say.

She sighs, dipping her head in thanks, then gives me a smile edged with sadness 'I'm afraid you got me in a very contemplative mood today – finally bringing that trunk through this weekend has brought back a lot of memories.'

'It's fascinating,' I say sincerely, telling her not all but part of my own story. I can't quite bring myself to talk about Chris, though I'm sure she would understand. I still can't talk about it, not yet, and of course I leave out the part where I quit my job and ran away on a whim. There are just some things you shouldn't tell your future employer.

We finish lunch and I dare to ask, feeling quite nervous suddenly, 'Er... so you'll let me know if I have the job?'

Caroline's eyes widen and she laughs aloud. 'Of course you have it! You had it the minute you showed enthusiasm for sorting through forty years of photographs and history!'

I smile broadly, thanking her, perhaps a little too eagerly. We settle on a start date. 'The coming Monday, in four days' time,' she says. 'Gives you a chance to get yourself packed up or back out if you want.' She winks.

I assure her that won't happen.

'A toast!' she declares and rushes off to get a special bottle for 'just such occasions'.

She returns clutching an old bottle, the label faded, covered with a thin coating of dust. She pops the cork and sniffs the bottle, breathing deeply, before pouring us each a glass of red wine. I take a sip and close my eyes. It's dark, full-bodied and rich, like dark chocolate on a winter's evening.

'Heavenly,' I say.

She touches the label, almost reverentially. 'Close... Elysium.'

I pause mid-sip, with a frown. A faint tugging at the corner of my mind, then suddenly it dawns on me... a fire, a young man, his arms crossed ready to face an impossible task.

'From the vineyard that burnt down?' I ask.

It was Caroline's turn to look amazed.

'Yes, one of the few bottles left, I should imagine. Did you know it?' she asks.

I shake my head. 'No, I read about it, though... that one of the sons is trying to rebuild it.'

She smiles sadly. 'I'd also heard. It was such a tragedy – that fire.'

'Do you know what happened?'

She sighs. 'No, no one does – that's the problem.'

I take a sip. 'So it was just an accident?'

Caroline's brows shoot up. 'Oh no, that's the one thing we can all be sure of: that fire was no accident.'

'But how can anyone know that if they don't know the cause?' I splutter.

'There were examiners, enquiries, people from the bank's legal department – they examined it thoroughly, and the way the fire started and spread, it was found that only a deliberate act could have started it. There were many who suspected Tom, the youngest son, as the culprit.'

I look at her in astonishment. The young man who looked so altered and so serious about resurrecting his family's legacy? How could it be him? I ask as much and Caroline shakes her head. 'I don't know – it's all a dark, awful rumour. But it's one that has followed him for most of his life. I think many people were stunned that he came back and wanted to try again.'

I stare at the faded label on the old wine bottle, its corners turning upward, the elegant script proclaiming a near thousand-year-old legacy, now forever lost. I wonder what drove someone to destroy their own inheritance, and the will it must have taken to come back and try to restore it.

TEN

There are two typewriters.

Two prehistoric, non-electric typewriters.

And apparently one of them is for me.

I stare at the first and biggest Remington that I'd noticed as I came in. It was a black behemoth, which, if it landed on your foot, would take not just the appendage but a sizeable chunk of the floor along with it.

The other is sky blue – one of those vintage typewriters that I've dreamt of owning for years. We were leaving through the writing den when I noticed the second typewriter. I'd commented on how beautiful it was… how quaint… and Caroline had waxed on enthusiastically, telling me she'd bought it in the sixties, that it was just like the one that Jack Kerouac used. She was thrilled that I loved it. Then she said something that made my blood turn a little cold. 'And don't worry, it works beautifully – there's fresh ink and a new ribbon, it was serviced recently too.' She smiled and then continued with a frown, 'Was a bit hard to get it serviced out here but I made some phone calls and a lovely man came past, so you shouldn't have any trouble. I think between the two of us we'll be able to type out most of THE BOOK fairly easily.'

Hang on.

Now, hang on there just a minute. Does she really expect me to help her compile her memoirs – my eye fell onto the gigantic treasure chest filled with forty years of material – on a typewriter? Is she mental?

That's what computers were invented for.

There are times in your life, like now, just before I'm about to exit Caroline's house, where providence mercifully intervenes. I stare at Caroline, my smile freezing a little, and I take a breath. Okay, Ria. Gentle, but firm.

'Erm… look, it's a lovely typewriter, and while the idea of writing on one is sort of… romantic,' I start off awkwardly, 'you don't think it would be a lot more…' I search for a better word than sane, and try, 'efficient… with a computer?'

Caroline blinks. 'Ah, well, I suppose it probably would,' she agrees.

I sigh in relief. A relief that was not, however, built to last.

She looks at me earnestly. 'Unfortunately I'm really ignorant when it comes to computers. Haven't a clue how to use one.'

I smile in sympathy. 'That's no problem, I'll show you… or I'll type up your notes on your computer. That way we have a backup, and can change anything we like fairly easily, it's no problem.'

'Oh that sounds wonder—' she stops. 'Oh, did you say my computer? Sorry darling, we never bought one, wasn't really a need. Do you have one?'

The answer is yes – only it is a thousand miles away at home with everything else I left behind. I mutely shake my head.

Perhaps it's my dumbstruck expression. Or Caroline's fear that she may lose me forever. But next thing I know she's hurrying off. She reappears with a thick wad of bills, which she presses into my hands, her normally affable face showing deep concern. 'Why don't you get yourself one, darling, before you start? I think this should cover it.'

I stare at the pile of cash in my palm – it would probably cover a few computers. I look at her in amazement; surely she shouldn't just hand over all this money to someone she just met? What if I was some sort of criminal? She seems to read my mind, though, because she snorts at my expression.

'Darling, if I didn't think I could trust you, I wouldn't be inviting you to come live on my property, never mind work for me,' she assures me.

I leave speechless with a stuttering mix of disbelief and assurances that I will bring her back a receipt and her change, all of which she dismisses with a casual wave of her hand as she sees me out the door.

Which is how I find myself, bright and early the next morning, in a computer shop in Chania, a MacBook Pro under my arm – I'd always wanted one – with less change than I would have thought. Particularly as I had factored in a 3G internet provider, sold to me by the assistant, who was appalled that I would be stuck in the mountains without a connection.

It had taken me around a half second to see the wisdom of his words, and I'd asked for a package – one that I could top up when the need arose. I hoped that Caroline would see the sense in this, or that I could at least make her understand that there was a logic to it. I mean, email is a basic human right. Isn't it?

The sales attendant looks at me rather suspiciously when I hand over my wad of euros.

'Have you robbed a bank?' asks a clipped British voice behind me.

I spin around to see Nigel Crane, the red-haired editor of *Eudaimonia*, in the queue behind me, looking fit in a pair of khaki chinos. He is clutching a length of computer cable and his ruddy face is amused. A familiar wet nose presses itself into my palm. Yamas, his tail wagging so vigorously it appears his whole body is wagging.

I greet them both in delight. 'Something like that.'

'New hardware?' asks Nigel with a raised brow, eyeing the computer box.

'For the new job.'

'New job, eh? I wondered if it was business or pleasure when we met. The sandals said yes. The suit said otherwise,' he quips, referring to my odd 'needs must' outfit when we met.

I cringe, but can't stifle my grin while he pays for his computer cabling, and we exit the store together. I offer an explanation. 'Crete was just meant to be a visit, but I saw a job ad and well, let's just say it came at the perfect time.'

Nigel looks at me curiously. 'So you decided to stay. It must have been a very tempting offer. What's the job?'

I'm still beaming. I can't help myself – I still can't believe my luck. 'A writer's assistant to a well-known travel writer.'

'A travel writer?' says Nigel. He gives me a look. 'How well known?'

'Very.'

His eyes widen. 'It's not… Caroline Murray, is it?'

My mouth falls open. How did he guess? Nigel pauses mid stride, eyes agog. 'Really?' he says reverently. '*Caroline Murray?* Now, that's something. Amazing writer, astounding life… bit of a recluse, though, these days, so I hear.'

His hazel eyes glaze over, he looks far away. 'She did for Crete what Peter Mayle did for Provence. I'm sure I'm not the only one who fell for Crete because she did. Although like Mayle she also brought her fair share of tourists to the country – and many who took up idle olive growing because of her. What's she got you doing?' he asks, curious.

'I'm going to help her sort through all her memorabilia, type up her letters – help her put together her memoir,' I explain.

Nigel stops and gives me his full attention. 'You serious?' he asks.

I nod, surprised to see his ruddy face flush with excitement. 'Well, I never. She'd always said that after *Falling for Crete* she wouldn't do a follow-up. Wouldn't want to tempt the gods, as it were. It's not always possible to top something like that,' he says in awe.

'Well, perhaps she's ready to tempt fate. I didn't get to look at everything, but I'd say she has enough material for at least ten memoirs, judging by the size of the chest she has filled with photographs and bits of manuscript.'

'Brilliant,' he says, shaking his head in amazement. 'Do you think she'd be willing to do an interview with us about it? It would be such a great story – I could send Nico up if she agrees? Or I could do it myself,' he says, looking rather thrilled at the prospect.

Before I know what I'm doing, I blurt out, 'Or I could do it?'

He looks at me curiously.

'I'm a journalist,' I continue in a rush. 'Well, a writer really.' I omit the fact that up until two days ago my only claim to either was that I wrote obituaries for a living.

For a second, I think about how weird and wonderful it would be to use the present tense when writing.

Nigel, however, is looking at me with interest. 'A writer, hey? That makes sense then, you helping her. That would probably work out – you'd have plenty of time to get a good story – with her permission, of course. Can I see some of your work?' he asks.

Ah.

I cringe a little inside.

'Unfortunately, I don't really have a portfolio with me,' I begin.

Nigel, thankfully, seems unfazed. 'All right. Where did you work before?' he asks.

'*The Mail & Ledger*,' I say.

'Ah.' Thankfully he doesn't say much about the *Ledger*. Or its dissolute reputation.

'Look, we're right around the corner from *Eudaimonia*, why don't you come have a coffee and we'll chat about it some more?' he asks.

Shifting the computer's weight under my arm, I agree. The offices are up a steep flight of stairs, which seem to cause Nigel some trouble. 'Gout,' he explains. 'Nasty business – should cut back on the vino but life's too short, right?' He laughs a great booming laugh that reverberates off the narrow stone walls.

It's a very old building that overlooks the café where we'd met before. We enter *Eudaimonia*'s empty offices, which house just two tiny rooms. One is an office crammed with four desks, the other holds a sliver of a kitchen. He makes us some coffee, his broad frame filling much of the space, and leads me to his crowded desk, where he clears a green tweed-covered chair of papers, files and old newspaper so I can sit opposite him. 'We don't get much company – but this is where the magic happens,' he says, sweeping his arms wide and giving me an unruly grin.

I set my package down on the floor and grin in response.

I love this. It is the real deal. A place where writers write because they love it. Not a glass-fronted building held up by the broken spirits of its exploited staff.

I take a sip of coffee and he hands me a stack of newspapers. 'The best way to get our style is to have a read through of a few of our old papers. We cover it all, really – travel, food, profiles, entertainment, wine, expat living, restaurant openings, festivals…'

I look at the small stack and begin leafing through them. 'We use a range of freelancers dotted throughout the island, otherwise it would be too much for Nico and me.'

I look up. 'Is it just the two of you?' I ask, noting the other desks.

'For editorial, otherwise we have Maria, the secretary/office manager, Steph, who sells advertising, though she's based at home, and Milo, he does the accounts.'

'That's impressive,' I say, thinking of the vast teams we had at the *Ledger*.

I turn back to flick through the papers. There are some really great articles – travel pieces, features on the top farmers' markets in each prefecture. I turn to read further but am interrupted.

'Obituaries?' asks Nigel.

I freeze.

Oh God. I look up at him a little hesitantly from the top of my newspaper; he's staring at his computer. Dammit. Of course he googled.

'Er… yes,' I say, clearing my suddenly dry throat. 'And… erm, some features…' At his inscrutable expression, I come clean. 'But mostly obituaries, yes.'

Fortunately, he replies, 'That's brilliant – absolutely brilliant.'

Perhaps it's my puzzled frown, or maybe he deduces something from my expression, because he explains it anyway. 'I think this story would be told best by someone who knows how to capture a life.' He shakes his head. 'Someone with your kind of exceptional skills… and to just meet you off the street like that.' He snaps his fingers in wonder, looking pleased. 'That's extremely lucky for us,' he says enthusiastically.

I blink.

Well, that went far better than I ever would have expected.

I don't argue, mainly because I realise that maybe in an odd way writing obituaries does make me uniquely suited to writing profiles. Later I'd wonder why I always sell myself short.

But right now I beam rather like an idiot and we exchange email addresses and telephone numbers, me promising that I'd first clear it with Caroline and only write the story if she's okay with it. I pick up my package off the floor and balance the stack of papers under my arm. As I turn to leave I see a pinboard on the wall opposite. It showcases an impressive collection of clippings and news stories and, like a flashing beacon, my eyes find a familiar photograph. The one of Tom Bacchus and his solemn, haunted eyes, arms folded, standing in his newly planted vineyard. I take an involuntary step closer, reaching out, but stop myself as Nigel appears on my right.

'I read the story you ran about the vineyard that burnt down,' I begin, not meeting his curious hazel eyes.

'Ah,' he says, shaking his head as he regards the picture as well. 'Dreadfully sad business. He looks so...'

'Haunted,' I supply.

He nods. 'Poor mite, he really changed after that fire. Not surprising, though. Everyone suspected him... like he would have done that to his father,' he shakes his head, his expression grim. 'He and Tony were the only family he had.'

I look at Nigel curiously. 'Did you know him?'

'His father, really. Wonderful chap, the jovial sort, rather authentically Cretan. So friendly. What happened to him was awful.'

I look at him, perplexed. 'What happened?'

'During the fire he went missing, and when they did find him... it was too late.'

I gasp in horror. 'He got caught in the fire?'

'He was trapped in one of the barns and couldn't get out. Smoke inhalation. He died the next day. It was a terrible double tragedy – losing him and the vineyard on the same day, and from what I hear it just broke the family apart. The brothers never got on well to begin with, but afterwards... well.'

'What happened?' I ask.

'They just cut ties completely. Tony went to live in Elounda with his new wife, and from what little I heard Tom left the country. No one knew where he'd gone, you can imagine the surprise when he returned to buy back the land and start again.' Nigel looks out the window. 'Well, good luck to him, very determined lad, I wish him all the best.'

I look again at his photo and frown, wondering why he came back, even when, as Nigel had said, there was no one left.

To say everyone back home is a little surprised when I tell them that I've found a job and intend to stay here for a year is a bit of an understatement.

'That was fast, I thought it was just going to be a holiday?' my dad had said. I don't blame him. Two years in my old room with the same awful job and now not even a week later I've found myself a whole new country, job and place to live.

Mum is a bit awed when I tell her that I'll be working for Caroline Murray. She tells me that it's a once in lifetime opportunity, one I'd be crazy to pass up, exactly the kind of thing Yaya would have said. Which I'm a little surprised at. Like I said, Mum is very practical and not at all spontaneous, but I guess she understands more than anyone how stuck I've been.

Dad is the most reticent, which I suppose I expected, though he doesn't come up with half as many objections as I would have imagined. He says something half-hearted about a lack of long-term prospects, but in the end he wishes me well and tells me to make sure that I do a lot of exploring on my days off.

I think even he understands that I need this: the chance to stand on my own two feet again, make my own decisions.

At the very least, I'm happy that I have their blessing: it wouldn't have changed my mind, to be honest I feel like for the first time in ages I actually have prospects, but it does make it easier knowing that they are on my side, even if they have a few reservations.

I spend the next few days exploring the old town, falling deeper under her spell. In the mornings I find myself waking early to catch the sunrise over the harbour – a routine so different from London, where I used to resent waking up, never feeling rested. I used to begrudge the mornings that came too quickly or not fast enough, accompanied by panic and remembered pain.

Now the mornings bring light, and the first glimpse of the ocean and mountains. As the days pass, for the first time in years I find that my 1 a.m. internal alarm doesn't go off, and I sleep the whole night through. I don't dare hope that this means it will always be so, but it's a little shift that brings hope nonetheless.

I eat in little waterside tavernas, and trawl the large food market in the day, bringing home fresh fruit and vegetables; and once a particularly lovely green melon that perfumed the air of my tree-top apartment, causing my mouth to water as soon as I climbed the stairs. I shop the back streets, picking up a few more items for my wardrobe, trying to think long term. It's wonderful to not have to include anything that's remotely corporate in that plan. Yamas often finds me at the waterside, and settles by my feet while I gaze at the boats and nurse a cup of coffee, and more often a glass of wine.

In London I had rushed. Coffee was gulped, never sipped. I hurried instead of strolled, and food was shovelled, never savoured.

I'd been so caught up in the busy, I'd forgotten how to just sit and be, without needing to do something. Perhaps I had welcomed it too, after Chris, but since I'd lost Yaya too something had changed; I'd found that I didn't want to race any more. Here, I'm finding a different pace, one that suits me or the me I hope to become, and while I expect it to change somewhat when I start working with Caroline, for the first time in years I find I'm actually looking forward to something, rather than always looking behind.

ELEVEN

'It's small, I'm afraid. It was meant to be my writing cottage – back in the days when I believed I might become a novelist,' Caroline says with a self-deprecating smile, marshalling me into a little stone cottage with a blue-painted door, hidden within the olive grove.

There's a double bed with fresh white linen, a small cream French-style dining table with a chipped milk jug filled with purple wild flowers, and just next to it is a kitchen the size of a postage stamp with azure-blue cupboards. What it lacks in size, it makes up for in charm, especially when I notice, from my bedroom window, a hazy glimpse of the sea and the spread of vineyards beyond.

If my apartment at Nessa's was a treehouse, this is a story-book cottage in the country, equally magical.

'It's idyllic,' I say truthfully.

I'd just arrived, taking a taxi through the mountains to Ouranó, captivated by the wild, rugged beauty of the mountainous village. After the sophistication of Chania's old Venetian port, being here is like being in a golden-hued otherworld filled with sunshine, vines and olives.

On the drive I'd worried about what she'd say about the article I wanted to write featuring her. Would she mind? Would she take it the wrong way? What if she thought that I was using her somehow? I decided not to do it if she wasn't enthusiastic about it.

But I hoped she would be. I knew that it was a chance to prove something to myself. For far too long writing had become associated with death in my mind, with pain, and the acrid taste of tears in the back of my throat; yet something that Nigel said had stayed with me, and I'd spent the last few days pondering it. Perhaps writing obituaries had helped me, taught me how to be a better writer. Maybe writing about death had taught me to write about life. It's funny how it can take a stranger to help you see yourself in a new light.

Uncharacteristically, as soon as my bags were out of the trunk, I blurted out that I'd run into Nigel and how when I mentioned I would be working for a travel writer he'd guessed somehow it was her, and how interested he was in Caroline. To my relief she seemed rather amused. 'What is it about us writh-ers, that in a city as big this we all find each other... like happy flotsam, I suppose.'

'Shared pain? Trauma counselling over the Oxford comma?' I ventured.

She grinned. 'That must be it. I can picture it: across a crowded path, eyes meet, knowing instinctively like twins who feel each other on opposite sides of the continent, that there is someone who has sat up nights in horror lamenting the death of the apostrophe.'

'Or culpable commacide.'

Her eyes were grave as she patted my arm in mock sympathy. 'A life sentence, that. No wonder we find each other – it's group therapy.'

I nodded, face deadpan. 'No choice, really.'

When I told her that Nigel wanted a profile written about her, and that I'd offered to do it – with her permission of course

– she seemed really moved. 'Darling Nigel, as if anyone even remembers an old codger like me. Of course you can do it – I'd be honoured, Ria, really – thanks very much.'

I'd beamed as I followed her to the cottage.

I set my bag on my bed. Caroline went back to the main house and left me to get acquainted, as she put it. I look around at the stone walls, and the soft white bed pushed against the far wall. The word 'haven' seems about right.

TWELVE

The sun is warm on my shoulders and the scent of lavender in the air makes me smile as I walk to the sprawling farmhouse. I dodge a chicken migrating to Caroline's vegetable patch and let myself in. She's sitting crossed-legged in the writing den, wearing a loose cream caftan-style shirt over navy silk trousers. Next to her is the open trunk. Her reading glasses are perched on the edge of her nose, and a yellow legal pad is on her lap, where she's already written a few notes.

I place my new computer on the desk next to the old blue typewriter, suppressing a laugh as I give the old behemoth a fond pat. Caroline had seemed bemused when I'd handed her the receipts and change as I got out of the taxi.

I take a seat on the floor next to her, while she runs through her notes. She hands me a cup of mint tea and says, 'So, I've given it some thought and I think the best approach is to divide it by certain periods: childhood, young adulthood, marriage, and then chapters of my life. So working for the BBC, my show, moving to Crete, the book, etc.'

She tears off a piece of a paper with years, indicating each period. 'On the back of the photographs you'll find years, names and dates – a good habit my mother got me into, darling. Thank goodness, otherwise I'm not sure I'd remember everyone or where we were.'

I set about going through the photographs, unable to resist looking at each one. These were the days before digital photography, where every photograph felt like a work of art. Most of the ones I'm sorting through are from the sixties and seventies. Each photograph tells a story, captures a pulse – straight hair, doe eyes, miniskirt. It's so, well, *rock 'n' roll.*

Caroline, it seems, was in the heart of it. I can't help studying them. I'm used to looking at photographs of people's lives. But it's a completely new feeling, looking at someone's life and having the person on hand to tell you what happened. It's marvellous, and I ask about a million questions. 'London in the sixties,' I say reverently, with a touch of awe. 'I'm so jealous. Was it as good as I think?'

She winks. 'Better.'

I grin back.

Caroline gets a faraway look on her face. 'It was all about breaking the rules, letting go, being free. They called it a movement, and in many ways it was. It was a different way of life, really.'

I stare at a sepia photograph of Caroline in my hands. The sun is behind her, framing her form with an amber glow. She's in a miniskirt, her feet bare in the sand, hands outstretched as if she could touch the sky, face tilted in laughter. She's young and carefree. I wonder if I was ever like that. Perhaps, maybe just after I met Chris.

I stack the picture on top of my sixties pile, and gasp as I turn to the next. It's Caroline, sitting on a couch in a rather serious discussion, her beautiful hair long and straight, a glass of wine in her hand while next to her, his hand casually draped over the couch, is *Mick Jagger.*

A young Mick Jagger too, his shirt is slightly unbuttoned and he's wearing black leather trousers.

'Good God,' I say.

Caroline looks. 'Ah yes.'

'Yes?' I look at her amazed. Because, well… I mean you cannot just think you can say 'Ah yes' about Mick Jagger and get away with it, right?

She looks up, and says with a smirk, 'Well, it's a long story.'

I set my photographs down, grinning hugely. 'I have time.'

She throws her head back and laughs.

'Well, it was before he was Mick Jagger, you know?'

I shake my head. 'He changed his name?

'No, what I mean is, he wasn't a legend. He was a star, definitely, but back then fame wasn't what it is today. With the paparazzi, the entourage – it's more like a major corporation. Back then if you were young and in London, and knew the right parties, chances were you'd meet them. Rock 'n' roll was like I said, a movement, and everyone was invited.'

I look at her, not really sure I understand. 'So you knew him?'

'Yes, in a way we were sort of friends, I suppose.'

My mouth falls open.

So she hastens to add, 'We weren't great friends, but we had similar views and things, and mutual friends, so I'd get free tickets, and go to the parties afterwards – if we were in town.'

'Right.'

I don't quite know what to do with that, but I have to wonder just what views she shared with Mick Jagger.

'Do you think we should put it in the book?' she asks. 'It's not quite relevant, and I wouldn't want to give the wrong idea.'

I look at her. Bless her, she's quite serious. I mean… do fish swim? 'I think, you know, it would be of interest,' I manage, holding back my smile.

'I suppose. I mean, he was rather fabulous,' she says with rather a naughty cackle.

I look up in amazement. 'Caroline?'

She fakes an air of nonchalance, but there's a curious twinkle in her eye. 'Don't worry, darling, it was all very proper. I never would have done that to George.'

My eyes bulge. Was she implying that she could have… good lord. Now that was something. I try to just let it go, but of course I can't. 'Er… so was there, um, anything between you?'

She assumes an air of mystery, and raises her rather patrician nose in the air. 'Oh, you know, darling, it was so long ago, who could possibly remember.'

But from the small smile that plays about her lips, I have to wonder – was it something you were ever likely to forget?

'Don't worry, I won't put it in my profile,' I say.

She smiles and pats my knee. 'I know, but if you did that would be fine too – I don't believe in censorship. It just waters the thing down, and life, like good wine, should never be subjected to that.'

I look at her with dawning realisation. How often had I censored myself, or allowed myself to be censored, especially when it came to my writing. It was a constant battle with Janice, who, as far as I could tell, had two known speeds – gloss or sensationalise, and not much in between. The truth, though, is that real life doesn't work that way. People who died sometimes did have regrets. And sometimes the accountant is also a travel writer, and is friends with Mick Jagger. Real people are so much more interesting than forced one-dimensional characters, who were what Janice kept trying to make me write about. I resisted. By God I resisted. But Janice was one thing, allowing myself to censor other sides of myself was another.

'It's hard, though, to not—'

'Get in your own way?' supplies Caroline.

Exactly.

'Don't be hard on yourself… it takes time and age, I've found. It starts to shift at about forty.'

'Forty?'

'Yes, you just stop worrying about other people's opinions as much.'

'So there's hope?'

'Definitely.'

I go back to sorting the photographs with a smile, and for the first time I look forward to turning forty. After cataloguing hundreds of photographs that we place into piles dotted around the living room floor, it feels like we have barely made a dent, though we've been at it for hours. I've even stopped asking about some of the photographs. Just shrugged it off like oh well, then... was that Caroline with Twiggy?

Of course I have to ask that.

And yes. Yes, it was. Apparently Twiggy had been really lovely, she'd helped Caroline fix her make-up once when they were caught in a thunderstorm after a Beatles concert.

The Beatles.

I stare at her. Twiggy helped her with her make-up? Well, I suppose if you're friends with Mick Jagger, there's really nothing else that should be surprising.

After a couple of hours, Caroline brings in some wine and a plate piled high with houmous, olives, and strips of garlic and sundried tomato focaccia. Heaven.

'Sustenance,' she declares, and I laugh, although I insist that as her assistant I should be the one bringing the food. She raises her glass in salute and teases, 'Quite right, slacking on your first day already. Good help is so hard to come by.'

'I don't even know where the kitchen is, er, or the loo, really,' I say, trying hard not to giggle.

She looks at me in horror. 'Ria, we've been at this for hours. Good lord, please don't tell me you've been holding it?'

I laugh out loud. 'Caroline, I can assure you if I needed to pee, I would have just asked where the loo was.'

She looks at me appraisingly. 'You would, quite right.' She cocks her head to the side in thought. 'You wouldn't see that about you straightaway, but it's there.'

'What's there?' I ask.

She smiles. 'On the surface it's all rather sweet, but if crossed, there's a bit of fight and I daresay a few claws would come out,' she says, eyes dancing.

I can't suppress my smile. 'Not sure about that – but it's good to know that I don't come across as a complete wallflower.'

She looks stunned. 'Darling, you're not a wallflower.' Her face grows serious. 'Though you do strike me as a flower that's spent too long in the shade.'

I blink, my throat a little tight. Was it that obvious?

She gets up. 'Okay, come on, I'll give you the tour – bring your wine.'

I do as instructed. My boss actually pours me wine during the work day, could it get any better? I follow Caroline through the passage, where she shows me the bathroom, and down the corridor to a gorgeous Provençal country-style kitchen; the kind that I always promised myself I'd have when I was a grown-up. A pale blue Welsh dresser is stacked with beautiful white-and-blue patterned crockery on display. In the centre is a large wooden table; above it, a hanging rack displaying a range of shimmering copper pots, and a cream-coloured Aga sits by the window that looks out towards the kitchen garden.

'Coffee machine, kettle, tea… you can have anything you like so long as it's Earl Grey,' she says with a wink. 'And now for the cellar, very important.' She leads me down to a small wine cave beneath the kitchen, made entirely out of stone. It houses a few hundred bottles of wine, each arranged according to category and age. It's impressive; I touch the labels, amazed at how varied her collection is – there are bottles from all around the world. She tells me that whenever she travelled, she liked to bring back a bottle... mostly reds, though.

'I don't know why, but I just don't feel that you're a proper wine connoisseur when you drink white wine. It just reminds me of little old ladies sitting in a pub with their semi-sweet and a bucket of ice,' she says. 'Which, of course, makes me rather a bit of a pleb, or a snob, or both.'

I laugh, scanning all the varieties she has: Merlot, Cabernet Sauvignon, Syrah, Claret, Pinot Noir, Pinotage.

'Pinotage?' I ask. Not sure why, but the word seems familiar somehow.

She comes over and picks up one of the bottles I'm looking at. 'Fine choice... a South African wine, a signature of theirs. I tried it on my last trip there; we did a wine tour in Stellenbosch, such a gorgeous part of the country. This was from an old estate called Lanzerac. It's a strong wine, bold really, with a distinctly plum earthiness, but very palatable.'

While Caroline speaks, I realise, of course. The article. I turn to her. 'I think... the vineyard that burnt down. The son, Tom – this is what he's harvesting. The article implied he was a bit mad to do it,' I say, surprised that I remember that.

Caroline's smile falters, and her face shows a tinge of sadness. 'He's so like Jill. She would have done something wild and unexpected like that,' she says, her eyes glazing over in memory.

'Jill?' I ask, puzzled.

'My friend.'

I frown, then remember. 'Your friend, the one who went to India?'

'My best friend. Didn't I mention it? She was Tom's mother.'

THIRTEEN

'Jill is Tom's mother?' I ask, incredulous.

A shadow seems to fall over her blue eyes. 'Yes, she was.'

I note the past tense with dismay. 'I'm sorry.'

Caroline gives me a sad smile. 'She's been gone for nearly twenty years, and I still miss her every day. She was one of those friends that you know from the minute you meet will be a kindred spirit. The kind of friend that you never have to put make-up on for, or clean your house for because you see them so often. We met at university – she was studying classics, while I was studying accountancy. I used to sneak into the classes, and that's how I met her. She was on to me... accused me of being a closet nerd,' she laughs. 'We just instantly clicked, she loved travelling and had this really unique way of seeing the world, which was pretty much that she couldn't sit with the nine-to-five way of life.' Caroline shakes her head. 'Well, few really enjoy it, but I think with people like Jill it's actually just impossible. Anyway, she travelled and worked odd jobs and would send me postcards from all her travels. We planned a trip to India, and after I got cancer, we decided to just do it regardless. She was amazing. Later, she helped with my show. She didn't want to be in front of the camera – she was dreadfully shy. I still think it's a pity, we would have had such a blast on screen, but at least we all had the chance to travel together for a while. No one could have been more amazed than Jill herself that she ended up living in the same place for ten years, but she loved what she was doing, and there was Tom to think of too.'

'What do you mean?' I ask.

'Well, he was a bit of a surprise. Jill was, like I said, a free spirit. Didn't want to be tied down. She was determined to remain single, so of course she fell in love. It was inevitable. Though she and Gyes thought it was just a summer romance.'

'Tom's father?' I ask.

Caroline nods. 'She'd come to Crete to visit me just after we moved here. I was busy writing and researching my book, and Jill, itinerant traveller that she was, was incredible at finding the most beautiful places off the beaten track, and one of those was the old vineyard, Elysium. She set up a meeting with Tom's father, Gyes, and me to speak about the art of making Cretan wine, and joined us on a tour of the vineyard. Jill was very beautiful – charismatic too – and Gyes had been trapped in a loveless marriage for years. His wife, Constance, was a difficult woman; that's not an excuse I know, it wasn't a blameless love affair, but it was understandable. Gyes and Constance got married when they were barely out of their teens as a way to bridge two neighbouring farms, the move allowing Elysium to become one of the biggest wineries in the country. Although they were fond of each other, having grown up as neighbours their whole lives, when their parents suggested they got married, he'd resisted, as he only saw her as a friend. Then one night they had too much wine and Constance got him into bed. When she told him she was with child, he did the responsible thing. He never said that she trapped him into it, he really wasn't the type, but I don't think he would have married her if it hadn't happened.

He loved her, I think, in his own way of course, but there wasn't any passion. Gyes said that he'd thought that sort of ro-

mantic love was something out of a fairytale… till he met Jill
and it hit him like a thunderclap.

'I think they both thought it was a short but sweet affair,
though the truth was, by the end of it, Gyes fell in love and so
did Jill. I think he would have divorced his wife but Jill didn't
want him to do that, not when there was a young child involved
– Tony was around eight at the time.

'Jill went back home, pregnant. Later when Gyes found out,
he tried to get her to move here so he could see the boy, and
they could get married. He wanted to leave his wife for her but
she refused. She didn't want to wreck his marriage and destroy
Tony's home, so when Jill moved to London the following year
and began production on our show, he came out every year after
the harvest season to spend three months with Tom. Tom came
over, I think, a few times, but Constance didn't want him there.
The affair had been a blow and she didn't want the boy around.
She refused to divorce Gyes, she didn't believe in it. The trouble
was, she had been in love with him since she was a young girl.
The affair devastated her, and she just refused to acknowledge
Tom as his son – a decision she held onto, even though it made
them both miserable... you know the type.

'I thought it was a bit cruel. It wasn't Tom's fault. But Jill
understood. Gyes went every year also to be with Jill. He never
really got over her, and I don't think she ever got over him. Then
she got sick – it was just terrible. Such a shock, her body started
to waste away within months. I wanted her to come live with
me. I didn't give her much choice really, just went and packed
up everything and brought her out here.' Caroline pauses, her
voice shaking. 'But it didn't make much difference, a few extra
months is all. It was devastating for poor Tom, she was all he
had, apart from a father he saw a few months a year. His whole
life changed overnight, when he went to live with his dad. I'm

sure it wasn't easy – well, on any of them. Gyes's wife now had to look after her husband's love child – someone she'd vehemently denied existed till then. I worried about Tom and went to visit him as often as I could, inviting him to stay here if he preferred. He was strong, didn't speak much, but in time I think they accepted him on the farm. He was enthusiastic and helpful and over time he became happy there. Gyes was besotted with the boy and taught him everything. It helped that Tom was a natural – he had an innate love of the vines – unlike his older brother, who was a born businessman. When the fire claimed the vineyard, it was such a tragedy. My heart broke for Tom: after finding this new home, to then lose everything – including his father. I don't think he was ever the same again.'

'Did you see him, after the fire?' I ask.

'Yes. It was terrible. He'd aged overnight. He was the one who found Gyes, I can't even imagine what that must have done to him. Tony wanted nothing to do with him. I told him he could come live with me if he wanted, but he wasn't interested. Then after all the enquiries were over, next thing I knew he'd up and left. After that the rumours started.'

'Rumours?' I ask.

She raises a brow. 'That he really did do it.'

FOURTEEN

The week passed much as it did that first day: with wine, laughter and stories. It was hard to believe this was work.

It was the most fun I'd had in years.

On my day off, I decide to go out. Caroline, worried that she had cooped me up too much, had insisted that I venture out – explore. She rather ignored the fact that I quite enjoyed being cooped up. Still, I was vaguely concerned that I had come to a Greek island famed for its incredible beaches, and hadn't visited one yet.

Actually, that wasn't true. It was Caroline who was concerned. She'd said, 'I feel vaguely concerned that you have come to this beautiful island famed for its beautiful beaches and you haven't visited one yet.' So I go off for a walk, with the vague intention of heading towards the nearest beach.

I even bring a book with me. Some kind of romantic escapist tale that I'd found on her bookshelf. Caroline seemed to really approve when I'd asked if I could borrow it. I've even brought my beach bag – the one I bought on my first day in Chania, which until now has mostly held the bunch of old copies of *Eudaimonia* that Nigel gave me. Now, fulfilling its original purpose, it holds a towel, a hat and my book.

There. I can be normal.

Except… the thing is, all I really want to do is find that vineyard.

I want to see the burnt-out husk coming to life again, see the new vines. And although I don't want to think about what that means, I want to see Tom.

It's nearby. Just a twenty-minute walk. I checked. Look, I'm a journalist; it's what we do.

It is, however, twenty minutes in the opposite direction of the beach.

It's also five in the morning.

I should go to the beach. Normal people go to the beach. Perhaps not at 5 a.m., though.

The trouble is, since Christopher, I don't really know how to be normal any more.

It takes thirty minutes, walking uphill through the green and gold countryside along the mountain road in the Lefka Ori mountain range, with its bounty of wild herbs such as lavender, marjoram and wild thyme perfuming the air, and thriving vineyards on either side of the valley below. It's magnificent. I make the trek up, feeling like I'm hiking toward the clouds. A faded sign reads 'Elysium Wineries est 1002'. The long gravel pathway is bordered on either side by large, ornate iron doors that stand open wide, framing the entrance, where neat rows of newly planted vines beckon me in. I hesitate. What will I say if someone sees me?

Luckily, there isn't anyone around.

I slip inside the gates, grateful for the early hour. A faint haze shrouds the vines in the morning light, adding an otherworldly element to my clandestine activity. A low wooden fence separates the vines from the path. I step through the gaps and make my way through the vines. They're taller than I'd realised. In the quiet dawn I understand why they called it Elysium.

As I walk, my hands trail the dark green leaves and my feet crunch in the dirt. I see in the distance the remains of the farmhouse. The right-hand side of the house is blackened, several of the walls crumbled and half standing, and what remains of the roof is pitched. Beyond that I can see the rest of the land, the once charred remains now returned to dust.

I resist the impulse to visit the homestead. Even I can't make myself cross that boundary.

But I can't leave, either.

I'm not sure what it is, but here in this perfect imperfection I feel a sense of union. There's a part of me that feels that if this place could survive, perhaps so can I.

I make my way through the still vines and slip through a gap in the small wooden fence.

'May I help you?' a deep voice asks from behind.

I freeze. My eyes shut, and I feel my blood turn cold in sudden, total fear.

I don't need to turn to know who the owner of the voice is.

I straighten, hands trembling, and look up. The first thing I notice is his eyes; a blue so pale they look like bleached sky. I expect them to be angry, but they are looking at me with a mild expression of interest. He is tall and angular, in an athletic type of way, with a sharply intelligent face and dark hair. He is also extremely handsome. Intimidatingly so. I have the irrational desire to run away.

I urge my brain to join forces with my voice, to explain and rationalise my trespass, but fear has totally unnerved me and I remain mute.

Eventually, after his curious expression turns to confusion, I find my voice at last.

'I – I'm sorry,' I begin, thinking that is probably the safest place to start. 'I was just,' I swallow, 'so curious about the new vines and I was… in the neighbourhood,' I say, wincing as I consider my beach bag and the probability of that.

As if he heard my thoughts, he glances at my bag, but says nothing. Instead, to my relief, his eyes seem to soften, and he smiles, causing lines to form around his eyes. He gives me an odd look. 'So you came over to look?' he asks.

Then I do something really stupid.

'Occupational hazard, I guess.'

'How's that?'

'Journalist.' I grin.

He doesn't return the smile. His face seems to tighten. 'Ah,' he says.

As if watching myself from a distance, I hear myself say, 'Actually, I'm doing some work for *Eudaimonia* – the newspaper – and I was wondering if perhaps I could do a feature on you, and what running a vineyard involves leading up to a harvest.'

His face is inscrutable. He cocks his head without smiling. 'I'm happy for you to cover the harvest. It will take place in September, you're welcome to attend,' he says in the manner of someone who finds journalists distasteful but a necessary evil, 'but no profile, thank you.' His words are civil, but hold an air of finality. 'The paper has my details – you can contact me through them and we can arrange a time that suits. Is there anything else?' he asks in a way that lets me know that I am being dismissed.

I shake my head, wishing I could start over, and make to leave.

'Your name?' he asks.

I turn back to look at him, the vines creating a picture-perfect frame, while he stands, arms folded, looking all too much like the serious man from the article I'd read about him. The one that had brought me here, wishing I'd thought to say something else instead of the lie that had come out.

'Ria,' I say.

'Ria?' he questions, his mouth fixed.

'Laburinthos,' I answer somewhat reluctantly, feeling not that we had been introduced but rather that I had handed him a small piece of ammunition instead.

Humiliation.

It assaults me with every step as I make my way back down the steep path. I wish with every strained breath that I hadn't gone.

I'm not sure what I expected, but I should have realised that someone who had experienced what he had, whose life was tainted with awful conspiracy theories, would have a natural and abiding distrust for journalists.

Why in God's name had I done it?

I'm not this person. I'm not some ditsy idiot who gets herself into this type of mess. More than that, I hate liars. Why couldn't I have just told him that I wanted to know about his vineyard? That somehow, in my stupid grief-addled brain, his burnt-down vineyard seemed like... what? Hope? How could I have explained that? How could I have done what I did? Would Nigel even let me cover the harvest? Could I make him understand at least?

Suddenly, out of nowhere, a black car careens down the side of the road and for a second my heart dislodges itself from my chest. The car screeches to a sliding stop and I watch in mounting alarm as it begins to reverse. My heart stops beating, fear-stricken as the car heads straight for me. There is nowhere to escape aside from the sheer mountain drop, then suddenly to my relief it swings round and stops. I clutch my chest in fright, my mouth falling open when I realise. Tom.

He gives me a half smile. 'Brilliant – I caught you.'

I hesitate. For a brief second I wonder, for what? But he carries on, 'I'm sorry if I was a bit... strained. I realised as you were leaving that you wanted to find out about the farm and how it works – before the harvest.'

I blink. My heart is still thrashing in my chest. Seeing that he wants some kind of response, I manage a nod.

'So I phoned the editor—'

Oh God. I close my eyes. No no no.

'And he explained.'

I look at him, my heart in my mouth. But I'm on the derailed train now, no turning back. 'Explained?' I ask in a small voice close to a squeak.

'That you're staying in the area and would probably like to write a feature about the harvest.'

The rushing in my ears begins to quiet. Thank God for Nigel.

Tom is peering at me curiously. I mouth some sort of assent.

He smiles, a wide smile that takes over his whole face, his teeth white and even.

I blink at the transformation.

'Sorry about that, I thought maybe I'd catch you so we could arrange a time. I noticed you hadn't brought a car.'

His smile is infectious and, despite my shaking knees, I return it.

We arrange that I will come the following weekend.

He offers to give me a lift home. But I refuse. Really, I just want to get away. Have a bottle of wine, or throw myself off a cliff. Whatever comes first.

Before he leaves, he says, 'I'm Tom, by the way.'

As though there had ever been any doubt.

When I get home, I phone Nigel, finding the number inside the scrap of paper where I'd written it down when last we'd met, making a mental note to add it to my phone afterwards.

'Laburinthos,' he says in his booming voice. 'I'm impressed – in the area for five minutes and you've already sniffed out another story. I like it.' He laughs his loud barking laugh. 'The angle too. Find out how the farm works, cover the harvest… could be a really nice spread.'

I can picture him nodding to himself, pausing to take a slurp of coffee. He carries on, 'One of the island's oldest vineyards. You're right, it deserves a proper feature. Maybe even front page, we'll see.'

I gulp. Front page? Is he kidding? The closest I'd ever got to the front page was when the paper itself was folded over and the back page met the front.

I feel equal measures of relief, fear and excitement.

'So you're not angry?' I ask, only half joking.

He lets out another bark of laughter. 'Angry? Definitely not. No, I like a bit of initiative. Didn't think you young journos had it in you. Proper gumption, I like that in a woman! Definitely the best man, er woman, for the job. With your background, a profile of Tom would be really something.'

I don't have time to be moved by the compliment, all I can think is the line from Hamlet, 'ay, there's the rub. Remembering the way his face had turned to stone, I say, 'Tom doesn't want a profile, he was quite firm about it.'

Nigel snorts. 'Of course he doesn't, that's what they all say, but see if you can get him to come around. There's more to that story, Laburinthos, you and I both know it. I think it's our chance to find out once and for all what really happened. Ten years of silence… it would be good to find out the truth about that night, put it to rest.' He pauses, his voice sounding as if it's coming from far away. 'It would be one helluva story,' he says before hanging up.

I can't help but agree.

FIFTEEN

The next week I help Caroline sort through her letters. They're delicate; the papers faded and sepia-toned, some tied with ribbon, others with string. Addresses are made out in fine, slanted scripts, the stamps beautiful and exotic, some from as far away as Tunisia, Egypt, Cambodia and Tahiti. They number in the hundreds, and they're all addressed to Jill.

Seeing a lifetime of friendship reminds me of Tamsin, and that one friend who just speaks your language, like you've been adrift, never truly belonging till suddenly, *bam!*, there's someone just like you. We met at secondary school. One day, Mrs Bloom, our biology teacher, had come at me with her moustachioed mouth set in a firm line and asked me if I was learning anything. Her pointed look suggested she thought not and her black eyes seemed to pierce the frog I was refusing to dissect. I'd shrugged and said, 'Yes. Mostly how pointless and cruel it is to waste the lives of fifteen frogs to teach us something we could have learnt from a diagram.'

Tamsin's eyes had popped wide in realisation, and she put down her own scalpel right then. After I was sent to the head-mistress, I found her waiting for me outside, where she declared that from now on we were to be friends, just like that, and we were, too.

When I ask Caroline about it, she smiles, a sad smile. 'What-ever happened to me... wherever I went, it was all so that I could tell Jill about it. I couldn't wait to hear her reaction, see what she had to say. I still feel that way sometimes.'

Holding a stack of letters in my hand, I nod. I feel that way about Yaya all the time. She was always the person I told my secrets to, even more so than Tams.

I feel a pang of melancholy.

Caroline's eyes are full of understanding. 'You lost someone too?' she asks gently.

I bite my lip. Where would I even start?

She pours us a cup of tea, her cornflower blue eyes waiting, and I tell her about Yaya.

'She lived here?'

'Her whole life – until my grandfather died. After that she came to live with us.' Caroline frowns. 'So how did your father meet your mother?'

I grin. I'd heard the story countless times. 'He went to Oxford to study applied mathematics and they met one day while he was in the law library – I am still not entirely sure why he was there, but he saw her sitting in a patch of sunlight in the library gardens, a Biro in her mouth, while she twiddled her hair. By the time he had taken the book off its shelf and walked over to introduce himself, he was in love.'

'So your mum is very pretty?' she asks.

'Very, she's very elegant, a little bit prim, and Dad just loved that. When I met Yaya, I understood why: she had an effortless grace as well. I, on the other hand – with two sets of genes riding on it – skipped the pool.'

Caroline gives me a pointed look. 'Ria, you probably don't see yourself properly, because you're very elegant. You've got an old world sort of look about you. With your beautiful eyes and light brown hair and classic features – very Garbo, I must say.'

I blink.

'I always feel like I am that person who forgot to take off the price sticker from under her shoe or has mascara under her eyes. I guess I just don't have their... polish,' I finish truthfully.

'Well, you wouldn't,' she says, giving me a smile. 'You're a writer. It's a terrible curse to any sort of polished elegance, because just as soon as you've got your hair up in a chignon and fastened your pearls, your attention has been stolen by a bird of the imagination fluttering in the wind, before you know it, you've left the house with two mismatching shoes and forgotten your handbag.'

'Yes! That's it exactly.'

She laughs in response.

'But they aren't all like that, surely,' I say, picturing novelist Danielle Steele, who looked a little like the characters she wrote about – rather elegant and refined. I had a bit of a binge session on her books when I was twelve.

She disagrees. 'They are. You're just seeing the part of them they want you to see, but it's there. And you, darling, definitely have an "away with the fairies" look about you sometimes,' she says with a laugh.

'That's exactly what Christopher used to say!'

'Christopher?'

I pale.

Why did I say his name?

Why?

My heart starts to pound. Caroline just stares at me.

I swallow.

When Caroline's phone starts to ring, my breath comes out in sharp relief. I watch her dart off to answer and slump on the floor.

Later we make progress with the material for the first quarter of her memoir – a significant leap forward that Caroline feels deserves a bottle of some fine French wine. Her early years revolved around Paris, so it was a fitting tribute too. Still we haven't really scraped the surface. While we figured out mostly what we should use for the beginning and the middle, Caroline still needs to figure out the rest. It had taken a week to sort through the photographs and another week to get through the letters.

After work, during the twilight hours, I put together my profile of Caroline, thinking what a privilege it is getting to know her and write about her at the same time. I write about her friendship with Jill, one of those once-in-a-lifetime friendships. I cover Caroline's illness, and how it became the catalyst for her new life; how she became a travel writer, going around the world with George, till finally they found their home amongst the olive groves and fell in love with Crete, ensuring that Caroline would write one of the world's most beloved travel memoirs of all time. And I finish the piece by explaining that now she was finally telling her own story with over forty years of travel, friendship, loss and love in what was sure to be one of the most talked about and anticipated travel memoirs in years.

I'd been anxious about showing her what I'd written – a lot of it was deeply personal. She reads it, while I watch, her arm reaching out to grasp mine while she takes it all in. We both have our hearts in our throats when she finishes.

'I can change it—' I begin, worried.

But she shakes her head quickly. 'Not one word. It's beautiful.'

I'm moved beyond words.

I spend my evenings transcribing the letters and the travel memoirs Caroline had written on scraps of paper throughout the years. Of course, she would be horrified that this is how I choose to spend my time off. But it isn't work. Not really. It's like reading a really great book – only you have the author on hand to tell you just what she might have meant at a particular scene, or better yet, what happened next.

As I type these letters, with their rich memories, I think of Jill, the woman reading them. While I know that Jill travelled the world too, I can't help thinking of the older Jill; the one who had moved to London after she was pregnant, never realising that she had packed up her travelling shoes for good or what was in store for her. While the letters were one-sided – I daren't ask for Jill's, somehow it doesn't feel right to read her private thoughts, without her permission – I feel somehow that I know her anyway. Sometimes the letters would refer to their own travels together – learning to cook in Tuscany, riding elephants in India, staying in an igloo in Alaska. It was like being in another world. One so different from my own.

The email sat unopened for a week.

The one-word subject line an open wound that would never heal: Christopher.

Perhaps, when I said his name aloud, I'd invited it in: all that I'd tried to ignore. Because that night when I'd switched on my computer, and logged into my email, it was there. A missile, with Trish, Christopher's mother, at the helm, ready to explode all that I thought I'd built.

It was Thursday night when I finally opened it.

It feels like we didn't just lose him that day, we lost you too.

I slid to the floor, my breath coming in hard, painful.

SIXTEEN

May 13th is a very significant day for me, for none of the reasons it should be. It was the day I had looked forward to the most. It should have been the best day of my life. Instead, it was without a doubt the single worst.

The days before were bathed in excitement. My gown – perfect in its simple elegance – was vintage 1920s ivory silk and lace. It hung on a special hanger in Yaya's cottage and lent the room an old-world charm. In a shoebox next to it were beautiful cream flapper-style heels with a tiny diamante flower delicately stitched into the front – shoes that Yaya had surprised me with from her own wedding. The perfect *something borrowed*.

Christopher and I had decided to break tradition and have our photographs done before the wedding to take advantage of the morning light, having a moment to ourselves before the big day. We thought it was romantic. Later this would turn out to be the cruellest torment when the photographs arrived, capturing a life we would never have. But of course, we didn't know it then.

My mother and Yaya helped me dress – a gentler introduction to what I believed would be the main event, with all my bridesmaids and friends before the ceremony later that day.

Mum fixed my hair, brushing out the long loose curls, while Yaya helped me with my gown.

We met in Potter's Field, with its carpet of bluebells, arriving in two separate cars, to increase the suspense for when we saw each other. My stomach swooped when I saw him, relaxed and happy, waiting for me in the field, his smile lit from within, hair glinting burnished copper-brown in the dappled sunlight. His green eyes were filled with love as he held out his hand for me.

'You're beautiful,' he whispered, planting a secret kiss on my neck, his hand tracing the bare skin on my back.

We'd wanted it this way – just the two of us. A moment before all the madness.

Memory is a tricky, fractured thing. I know that the photographer stood nearby, occasionally telling us to stand a certain way, to look his way, but in my memories he isn't there at all.

The last photograph was of us with our arms outstretched, fingers just touching in parting, both looking over our shoulders as we made to leave. Sometimes I dream of that photograph and I always awake to a pillow wet with tears.

After our morning I returned home suffused with light. Hugging the moment to my chest, relishing the stillness before the day would officially begin.

Never once suspecting that anything was wrong.

You know how in films someone has that presentiment – some little feeling in their chest that things aren't quite right? Well, that's bullshit, because I had none of that. I'd just stepped into my bathrobe when I heard it. A blood-curdling scream that made my stomach clench in fright.

It was primal – terrifying in its raw anguish. I rushed out the door, my heart in my throat, my feet slipping on the wooden stairs as I raced outside, where a group of friends and family had gathered in front of the house in response.

Christopher's mother, Trish, was in the centre, her hand clutching a mobile phone. Her face deathly white.

Even then I didn't understand.

I rounded on the first person that I saw. It was my dad. His dark eyes met mine in anguish. 'Get Christopher,' I said, as I tried to rush towards Trish, not sure what was wrong, but knowing that Chris would know what to do.

Dad held me back.

'Dad, please I need to help her!' I insisted, my voice a mix of worry and exasperation. But he clutched my arm. 'Sweetheart… there's been—' his voice caught. 'There's been an accident.'

I blinked. Sudden fear gripped me. 'Oh my God, who, what happened?'

Dad opened his mouth. But no sound came out. I stared at him in terror. 'Where's Chris? Dad, we need Chris. Please, let's find him, he'll help.'

Where was he? I looked around frantically.

Tears tracked their way down my dad's face, his arms tightening their hold. Then other familiar arms wrapped themselves around my shoulders. I looked up to see Yaya, her dark eyes clouded.

'Yaya,' I said in relief. 'Please, we need to find Christopher – where is he? There's been an accident… his mother needs him.'

Her eyes pooled with tears. 'My darling, it was Christopher. There was—' She swallowed hard. I watched her throat, as she tried to find the words.

The world started to spin, even as my dad held me so tightly I couldn't move.

'But—' I said uncomprehendingly, 'he's upstairs, Yaya.' We'd just come home. Everyone stared, the way that people do when they're looking at a car wreck and can't tear themselves away, their faces frozen.

My dad closed his eyes and shook his head, once.

My throat closed.

My father's hands held me tight, as if he would give me his strength. 'He went with the boys to the pub for a drink, and there was…' His voice broke again. 'An accident... a drink-driver...'

I shook my head, wrenching myself out of his grip and away from him, and his mad words, even as terror clenched my heart. I shook my head wildly, hoping they would see sense. 'There's a mistake. Chris is upstairs, we just got home... he never went to a pub!' I exclaimed. Everyone's faces reflected the same thing. Torment. I looked at them all in an agony of exasperation and panic. Why wouldn't they listen? 'Look upstairs,' I yelled. But no one moved.

I blinked, my lungs like lead, trying to summon breath. This was all some horrible misunderstanding. Any minute now he'd come out of the spare bedroom... and everyone would see. It must have been… someone else. They were clearly misinformed.

I looked at my dad, my body shaking wildly. 'Dad, it wasn't him,' I pleaded, trying to make him understand. Why wouldn't they just go upstairs and look? 'Please, he's upstairs, just go get him – he's in the spare room.'

Yaya started to cry then.

I looked from her to my dad and turned to go. If I could get upstairs, then I could fetch Chris myself, then they'd see. Why couldn't they understand? Chris wouldn't have gone to a pub on his wedding day. How could there be a drink-driver at this hour in the morning? None of this made sense. Why didn't he just come down and clear this up? Surely he must be hearing this racket and wondering what was happening.

As I moved towards the house, a pair of strong hands caught me. I looked up. It was Alex, Chris' best friend, our best man.

'Alex!' I said in manic relief. 'Please get Chris – there's been a horrible mistake.'

Alex's face crumpled. 'Ria, I'm so sorry.'

'But… he's upstairs,' I said stupidly.

Alex started to cry. Hard. 'It was all my fault, I asked him… to come—' His whole body shook with grief. 'A last drink…'

I blinked.

It couldn't be—

Watching him sob, it hit me, the awful, ridiculous truth of it. My knees gave out. I couldn't see, I was drowning, and someone was screaming over and over and over again. I never realised it was me.

When I finally stand up, I have a desperate urge for a drink.

Christopher's mother's email had hit me hard, and it was hours before I was able to pick myself up off the floor. It was like I went straight back to that day.

All over again.

Mentally, I cringed.

Dr Rushma had said that I might. I can almost hear her soft, melodic voice in my head.

'You can stay in denial, Ria, pretending that it didn't happen, but it's not something that will remain buried forever. You need to talk about it, if you are ever to live with it.'

Dr Rushma was big into getting me to 'live with it', to accept what happened to me, so that one day I could move on.

I'd liked her, mainly because she didn't lie. She didn't give me those peppy little bromides that the other people in the group did, like 'time heals all wounds', or the very absolute worst one, that some moron said to me during one of our trauma group counselling sessions, which was 'everything happens for a reason'. Thankfully, someone in the group whose lithium dose wasn't on overload had thought to restrain me. I wasn't the only one who needed it.

After Chris' death I'd gone into a catatonic state. At night, though, I'd rent the air with my night terrors. After two months of that, my parents sent me to a clinic for a fortnight to recover. Though no one called it 'recovery' – that would have implied I'd come out the other end healed. The clinic was housed in the pretty Devonshire countryside, so pretty it felt like the worst kind of insult. I felt myself go quietly mad watching the ducks in the pond outside my window. I craved concrete and graffiti and anything that reflected what was going on inside of me. I couldn't stop thinking about what that idiot had said about fate. Like Christopher had to die.

I had so many other horrid thoughts in my head, I didn't need to add that one too.

My coping mechanism was to not speak about it. Any of it. No one seemed to understand. Except maybe Dr Rushma, and Yaya, who I knew had suffered her own grief when she had lost my grandfather and uprooted everything to move to a strange country. But even she didn't know what to say. There wasn't anything to say. Sometimes life is just crueller than you could ever imagine. Sometimes you do get to glimpse heaven, only to have God shut the door.

Everyone was horrified when I said that I wanted to go back to work. Especially Yaya.

'*Meli mou* – don't do this thing – there's no need, eh? And if yew want to be busy, we find yew work, no go back to the paper, and the writing all day about death.' She shook her head, her big ebony eyes filled with dread at what I was committing myself to.

But I had to. And in a horrible, inexplicable way, I wanted to. Writing about death meant that I didn't have to pretend to be happy. I could just do my job, my sympathy and tears a mark of respect.

Like Yaya, Dr Rushma didn't really approve either.

In one of our weekly sessions after I left the clinic she told me that she was concerned that I was doing it for the wrong reasons. She thought perhaps, after Christopher's death, that I felt like work was supposed to be hard.

I thought she was insane. She didn't understand. Part of why it was okay to write about it, or so I thought, was that these were my people. The people whom death had just visited.

It's only now that I can see that she was right. Rather than deal with the loss of Christopher, I had taken on everyone else's grief instead. And maybe more than that. Perhaps, as Dr Rushma had suggested, I was punishing myself. Pushing myself to do the thing I dreaded most. Like a martyr. I'd been through the 'what if' game for two years now.

What if we hadn't taken those photographs?

What if Alex hadn't felt the need to have that last single boys drink?

What if the local pub had thought to take away their patron's keys?

It was barely any consolation that the driver was charged with manslaughter. Or that he has now been eighteen months sober. Or that one of his 'steps' was to apologise to me, and that he had a name and it wasn't 'the drunken wedding reaper' as the papers called him, but Bernie Foster. A name that had no business ending the lives of people's fiancés when he should have been home on a Sunday doing the crossword, or listening to Radio 4. Perhaps I should have let him tell me himself how sorry he was, but I couldn't. I still didn't trust myself around him. I'm not sure I ever will.

I say a silent prayer of thanks that there's wine in my kitchen, thanks to Caroline. It's four in the morning as I pour myself a glass.

When Yaya died two months ago, it had brought everything back tenfold. The grief. The rage. All of it. My job – while constant in its regular torment – had begun to shift, feeling less like a noble calling and more like a noose around my neck. Whatever I'd hoped to bury had started to come out. And the funny thing was that, despite the pain, I was finding someone I'd thought I'd never meet again – me. The me who could smile at a sunset and not have her heart break. Who could laugh at a joke without feeling guilty for doing so.

There's no way, though, that I'll be able to get up and go to work, without having tonight's ravages broadcast across my face.

Could I call in sick?

A mad chuckle escapes me. Caroline would probably come over with some chicken soup. Hopefully it wouldn't be from one of the chickens in her roost. A horrible giggle bubbles at the thought. Just then, choosing to live on the same property as my employer seems possibly like one of the stupidest decisions I had made yet. I take a sip of wine, get up and do what I didn't think I could: I respond to his mother.

You haven't lost me. You never will. It's just taken some time for me to find me again. Love you.

Then I go to bed. Sometimes that's the best thing you can do.

Later that morning I wake up to the sound of loud, insistent knocking. My eyes feel as if they've been cemented shut.

I groan.

I'm so tired, I feel like I may throw up.

Although the half bottle of wine three hours before may have contributed to that as well.

I pull my pillow over my head and beg softly, 'Go away.'

She lets herself in instead.

'You okay, darling?' she asks, standing at the foot of my bed. I look up at her elegant curled hair, her fresh linen coat and concerned eyes, and groan again.

'You look awful!' she exclaims.

'Thanks,' I mutter.

'Shall I call the doctor? Is it serious?'

I shake my head. Which I regret instantly, my brain protesting in sharp needle-like stabs.

Is now a good time to explain that I have psychological problems?

Probably not.

'Migraine,' I say. 'Very bad.'

She clucks in sympathy. 'Have you been typing these all evening?' she asks with alarm, seeing the stack of letters I had indeed spent most of the evening typing.

'No – just a little, I'm a fast typist,' I lie.

'And now you've got a migraine!' she wails in despair.

I sit up, or try to. 'No, it wasn't that, I promise – really, I get them sometimes, there's no real cause.' She looks at me sharply, her hands clutching the letters.

'Please, Caroline – I enjoy it.' It's true. For the first time in years, I'm enjoying what I do. 'I just didn't get much sleep – and I've got a splitting headache.' This is true as well.

She gives me a sympathetic smile, her hand releasing the stack of letters.

'Shall I get you anything? Some painkillers?'

'That would be nice.'

I doze off.

When she comes back, she puts some ibuprofen by the bed, with a glass of water. 'There's more in the cupboard if you need it later. I'm just stepping out for the afternoon. Just rest, darling, that's the best – if you can go out I think that will be good too. There's my old bicycle in the garage if you'd like to do some errands. Jason, my last assistant, fixed it up, so it should be in order and there will be no work until Monday, understood?'

I nod before falling back asleep.

It's midday when I wake up, still feeling tender. I make myself a sandwich and sit on the little step outside the cottage to eat it, the bright sunshine like daggers to my eyes.

I find the bicycle in the garage. It's old fashioned, a real vintage collector's piece, painted cream with turquoise accessories: a leather Brooks saddle, matching handles, a little basket in the front. It's rather lovely.

I take a shower and decide to head to the library.

Caroline had mentioned that there was one nearby, known for its collection of English books and historical texts.

She had looked at me a little strangely when I asked her if there was any chance that they stocked old newspapers from the last ten years.

'Probably… more than likely. Although it may all be on microfiche.'

I shrugged. That would work.

We'd carried on working, but she obviously suspected my intent. I'd asked enough questions about Elysium and the fire to raise her concerns. 'Just be careful,' she'd said. 'Buried secrets, once exposed, don't go back easily, if at all.'

After a peaceful ride through the countryside, my notebook and laptop riding in the basket of my bicycle, I enter the peaceful sanctuary of the Ouranó Library, a small unimposing building that blends in with the mountain scenery. The librarian, who introduces herself as Nina Stasis, is in her mid-sixties and has a kind face framed by oval-shaped glasses. She shows me the old bound copies of the newspapers from the area – most of them are in Greek. She has a collection of old *Eudaimonia* copies too, but I know these won't be much use – when I spoke to Nigel recently, he told me that *Eudamonia* had only just launched when the fire broke out and they didn't cover breaking news stories like that back then, mostly travel news: as they'd grown over the years, so had their coverage. What he knew about the fire was what he'd already told me, based on his relationship with the family.

The library has free Wi-Fi as well, so I spend some time trawling the internet for anything useful.

I find a few old travelogues and reviews that speak of the vineyard before the fire –referencing the hospitality of the Bacchus family, their fine wines, and the way that Elysium seemed perched between heaven and earth – but nothing about its destruction later on, or the suspicions about how the fire started, or why the investigators had ruled that it hadn't been an accident. It's around that time that I regret my choice of ballet over Greek school. Yaya had threatened that I would need it more, but nothing at the time had seemed more important than wearing an ice-pink tutu. I know a little Greek, but not enough. I'm able to pick out every fourth or fifth word.

After an hour, I decide to try a different tack – I don't want to raise the librarian's suspicions by asking about Elysium – people in towns like this could be protective of their secrets – so I ask if she has any information on the history of wine-making in Crete.

She brings over another stack of books, in Greek, as well as an English brochure that offers the briefest overview and a map of the various wineries in the area, and their dates of origin. I sigh. Greek it would have to be, and I ask for a Greek-to-English dictionary, which she readily supplies, hiding a grin.

'Is for project?' she asks, as I make my way to a corner table by the window, armed with my stack of newspapers and books.

I nod. That, at least, is true.

An hour later I abandon the books – they all seem to end somewhere around the 1950s or before. It's the opposite problem with the newspapers, they're mostly from the last three to five years and I need to go back at least ten years.

The *Chaniá Ilio*, one of the more predominant Cretan newspapers, looks more promising. It's bound by year. I leaf through until I reach 2005 – that's around what I'm looking for. I check the folded-up article from *Eudaimonia* to be sure, but I needn't have bothered. I only have the year to go by, no month or date. I start at the beginning.

It's hard going; my Greek is worse than I thought. Language isn't like riding a bike: if you don't use it, it just goes and doesn't come back.

Well, that's how it is for me, in any case.

After about twenty minutes of peering at the small print, I almost give up when I spot it.

Just one word: *Elysium*.

It takes the better part of an hour to translate the article, with many cross-outs and having to thumb through the dictionary continuously, but I get there in the end:

Fire Destroys Thousand-Year-Old Vineyard

Story by Xena Alberos

An uncontrollable fire claimed the life of Gyes Bacchus, the owner of the thousand-year-old vineyard, Elysium, last night. Witnesses report that the fire broke out around 11 p.m., and spread quickly consuming most of the vineyard as well as the family's residence, the old farmstead Ston Ouranó. (I discover that this translates to 'In the Sky'.)

The cause of the fire is as yet unknown, although there have been reports that before the fire broke out some farm workers heard people fighting. Although this has not yet been confirmed.

It is believed that Bacchus, who is survived by his two sons Tony and Tom, died of smoke inhalation.

Iliana Kirosa, the girlfriend of Tom Bacchus, confirmed that Gyes Bacchus was found by his son. 'Tony and Tom were helping the men with the fire. Gyes had been there too, but at some point we realised he was missing. It was only later that Tom found and pulled him out of the barn where'd he'd been trapped, but it was too late,' said Kirosa.

The fire department believe Gyes Bacchus was trapped in the barn after a beam fell and blocked his way out. Investigations as to the cause of the fire are still underway.

As I uncover each word and transcribe it to my notebook, the article only gives rise to more unanswered questions.

It must have been so awful for Tom to find his father like that.

I startle as I feel a hand touch my shoulder. It's the librarian. 'I sorry – it's getting late, we open tomorrow,' she says kindly.

I give a guilty start, the clock on the wall opposite says 6 p.m. – I'd kept her past closing time. 'I'm so sorry!' I exclaim.

'Is no worry.' She tells me to leave the books on the trolley, she'll sort them out in the morning, and I follow her outside.

On my ride home, I stop by a little café in the village and order a carafe of wine and some food – a meze platter of stuffed vine leaves, souvlaki, houmous and pita. I'm starving. While I wait for my food to arrive, I look back over the article I'd transcribed. Was there something more there? More beyond the awful tragedy? I pore over my notes, but there aren't any answers. I have a feeling I've missed something. Something obvious. Something hiding in plain sight. Is it just that he'd had a girlfriend that no one had mentioned? What's odd about that? Nothing. When the food arrives, I take my time enjoying the combination of flavours. The diners around me are friendly but leave me alone, and I'm grateful for that.

It's only as I pour myself a second glass of wine that something begins to click. It's the name. Tom's girlfriend's name.

Iliana Kirosa. Hadn't I read it somewhere before?

I open my bag and extract the *Eudaimonia* article. Scanning, I find it early on in the article. I choke on my wine.

Bacchus is the half-brother of Tony Bacchus, whose wife is Iliana Kirosa, owner of the upscale resort Pleiades, in Elounda, daughter of the ex-mayor of the city of Chania, George Kirosa.

Tom's girlfriend? Now Tony's wife? Two brothers in love with the same woman?

SEVENTEEN

The next morning dawns with the scent of lavender, rosemary and marjoram lingering in my senses. It's the unique smell of the Lefka Ori, with its spring carpet of wildflowers and herbs.

After breakfast I go back to the library. I can't help myself.

I go even though I know it will make it harder. Even though in just over an hour I'm meant to be at Elysium for my interview with Tom. I need to find out if there's more: answers from the police investigation, or if anyone else thought it was strange that the two brothers had once dated the same woman.

I have so many questions, and not enough time. The only person I can ask would probably throw me out if I dared.

Nina, the librarian, greets me with a smile. She pushes up her oval glasses and says kindly, 'Is nice to see a young person at a library.' I smile back. The funny thing is that it takes me a second to realise she's talking about me. I don't feel young. But for the first time in years, I don't feel old, either.

I pull the bound copies of the *Chaniá Ilio*, the Cretan newspaper, towards me. Thinking that the follow-up story would probably have been printed within a few days, I start scanning the papers from the day after the last article. I'm right. Just two days following the first, a follow-up appeared. I bend to my task, impatiently looking up words I don't know, trying to make sense of the short piece. But it doesn't say anything about the cause of the fire, only the tragic news that the funeral of

Gyes Bacchus was scheduled for the following week, and that all members from the village of Ouranó, as well as many other neighbouring towns, were expected to attend. Included were a few well-known celebrities and dignitaries, as well as George Kirosa, the former mayor of the city of Chania, who would be flying in to attend the occasion.

I leave it there. I have fifteen minutes to get to Elysium on time.

The ride through the mountain path is tranquil, rich with the scents of wild mountain herbs: chamomile, wild sage and hints of lavender. I'm grateful for the exercise, although it doesn't lessen my anxiety. The last time I'd seen Tom, it hadn't gone as I had intended. I know that this time I have to do it differently. I ride my bicycle up the steep mountain path, through the open gates towards the vineyard, its beauty a balm for my unsettled nerves. There are a few people at work amongst the vines. An older man, with a craggy face, wearing a plaid shirt and a khaki outdoorsy hat, waves at me with a pair of what look like pruning shears, and goes back to work. I dismount and wheel the bicycle next to me as I follow the path up to the farmstead, my eyes drawn to the charred crumbled side, thinking of its beautiful name, *Ston Ouranó*. In the distance, I can make out two men working separately in the vines.

I wonder if one of them is Tom. I lean my bicycle against a small gate en route to the farmhouse, pulling my bag over my shoulder and making sure that I have my notebook with me. I walk towards the nearest vines, ducking below the short fence towards the men I had spotted working. As I get near, I see him.

Dressed in a white T-shirt and very faded blue denims, he's wearing a pair of gloves as he works between the branches.

'Hi,' I call.

He pushes his dark hair out of his blue eyes and looks up, puzzled; then realisation dawns. 'Oh God, sorry,' he says, wiping his hands on his jeans. He takes three long strides towards me to shake my hand. 'I completely lost track of the time.' He smiles rather disarmingly, showing perfect teeth; his eyes crinkle at the corners. It's a smile that is somewhat devastating to witness. I gulp, almost hoping he'll put it away.

I can't help wishing that I was wearing something other than the trousers, T-shirt and sandals I'd pulled on this morning in my race to get to the library, and I'm rather pathetically grateful that my hair is brushed and that I wore some make-up.

What I'm feeling isn't attraction exactly, but the natural urge to tidy myself in the face of such beauty.

'That's all right,' I say.

'Shall I give you the tour?'

'That would be great.' I follow him as he makes his way through the vines towards a long dirt path that cuts through the vineyard.

'We started with just five hundred square metres of land for the Pinotage, around eighteen months ago,' he begins, blue eyes scanning the field.

I turn to him in surprise. 'I hadn't realised you've been at it that long already.'

He smiles. 'Time moves slowly in the wine world, so as far as everyone – myself included – is concerned, I've barely begun,' he says with a wry grin. 'The first crop has been through the fermentation process, and is now nearly ready to be bottled – it was purely experimental, growing Pinotage here. We had to be sure of the soil and temperatures.'

I follow him to a hilly part of the vineyard that's planted with the dark plum-coloured orbs. 'Our second crop is bigger – over a hectare, and we've also planted Syrah as well – over there,' he gestures.

'So now you'll have two varieties?'

'Yes, eventually I'd like to get us back to what we once had – the seven feathers of Elysium.'

At my puzzled expression, he explains. 'It was the signature of our vineyard – seven different varieties: the Merlot, Syrah, Romeiko, Liatiko, Cabernet Sauvignon, and two Elysium blends – both secret. My father kept it under lock and key,' he says with a wink.

'But you know the secret?'

'Of course,' he says, assuming an air of mystery.

I have to laugh.

'Is that what you want to do – restore the vineyard to what it was?'

He pauses, and puts his hands in his jeans pockets, as he considers my question. 'Yes and no. I think for years that was my intention, I wanted what we had… but you can't go back,' he says, his face tight.

I nod. I know that only too well.

There's so much I want to ask about that, but I stop myself. It's clear that it isn't something he wants to discuss just yet – perhaps not ever.

'So that's why you decided to plant the Pinotage, to be different?' I ask. 'I believe it was considered a rather controversial choice?'

'Partly, I suppose. I also wanted to see if I could, how it would fare in our climate. We'd spoken about it years ago – and I just thought, well, why not?'

'We?' I ask.

'My dad and I.'

'So it was something that he wanted to try?'

'Yes – he wanted to try something new. The trouble with an old family-run vineyard is that it can be hard to do things differently. I think he wanted to push himself a little out of his comfort zone… So that's why I started with the Pinotage.'

I look at him, understanding. 'As a tribute?'

He laughs. 'Bloody stupid, though, if you ask me. It wasn't the world's best thought-out plan, particularly on an organic farm. Our first crop was only just short of a disaster.'

'Why, what happened – does being organic make such a difference?'

He starts walking again; I struggle to keep up with his long strides. 'Absolutely. We couldn't spray – we had to treat each vine individually. We also hadn't chosen the best location in the beginning, it was exposed to too much sun, the grapes turned to sugar. Half of them barely made it to term, and then they got infected.'

I gasp. 'But you still managed to save some of it?' I ask.

'Yes, thankfully, though not as much as I hoped. But with any luck by harvest we'll have about three hundred bottles. It's not a lot, but it's not a complete loss.'

I agree. 'Was it harder because you tried Pinotage?'

'No, not really – it's a fairly hardy grape. It's just that I wasn't used to it – didn't know what to expect. You have to develop a sort of relationship with the vines, and ours have just started,' he says with a wry shrug.

'I like that – like you're getting to know one another.'

He looks at me in surprise, his eyes alight. 'Exactly.'

'Were you always an organic farm?'

'No – not really. Our Merlot was organic, my dad's pet project, really.'

'So why did you decide to go organic now?'

'Well, it's more sustainable – better for the environment, as you avoid spraying pesticides and that type of thing, and it's cost-effective too. Elysium doesn't have the same resources it once had – so as we're starting small, I thought it would be a good idea to go completely organic.'

That made sense. 'But doesn't it make it more time consuming too?'

'Definitely, it's a vine-by-vine job now. You have to treat and pick by hand. That's all right, though – it means better quality wine, as we pick only when each grape is ripe. You're getting a much better product in the end, so it's worth it.'

I make notes as he speaks.

'Would you like to see the winery, and taste the Pinotage?' he asks.

I look up in surprise. 'Taste the Pinotage—' I breathe. I'm dying to taste the Pinotage, if truth be told. 'But doesn't it still need to mature?'

'Yes, but you can try it – a pre-sample before it's ready.'

I grin, that sounds great.

I follow him up the dirt path towards the main house, to a large building with massive oak doors that are standing open wide. 'This is where the magic really happens,' he says, leading me inside.

It's dark, cool and colossal. Towards the back a line of barrels stand in wait, and to the left of them is an assortment of large steel and oak drums, as well as a number of machines that I wouldn't have a hope of identifying.

'Right now the grapes are going through the secondary fermentation,' he explains. 'We've decided to mature them for the next seven to ten months in these oak barrels from Rhone,' he says, touching one.

My pen is moving furiously.

I touch the barrels with awe. 'It's like bottling art.'

'I suppose so – there's an art to making wine, a science too. When we get it right, there's a little of both.'

I smile. 'I like that.'

'So would you like to try some?' he asks.

'Definitely.'

He leaves to fetch some glasses, and when he comes back he pours some wine into the two glasses and swirls it about for a bit, then hands me the glass.

Before I take a sip, I take a breath, scenting the contents: pleasant, warm and mildly identifiable. In some ways it's an aroma I recognise, I just can't place it. I'm not sure what I was expecting – perhaps to see half-pulverized grapes – but it looks and smells like wine.

I take a sip, then another. It's even nicer than it smells, which is surprising; wine usually works the other way for me. It's rich to the taste, a full body, I suppose, not being that familiar with wine tastings or terminology. And there's a faint, almost cherry undertone – cherries that have been soaked in liqueur and covered in chocolate.

'What do you taste?' he asks.

I look up, realising that I have my eyes closed. I feel a faint flush creep across my face, seeing him staring at me so intently, his blue eyes searching.

I swallow. 'It's rich – richer than I expected – but warm too, if that makes sense. It goes down easily. It tastes a little like… the Lefka Ori,' I say, suddenly realising why it smelt familiar. 'There's a faint scent of lavender, and marjoram, but it tastes... a little like liqueur-soaked cherries.'

'Wow.'

I bite my lip, embarrassed. I'm probably all wrong.

'You've got a really refined palate,' he says. 'You're right, the Lefka Ori is definitely in the wine – chamomile, lavender, marjoram – wild herbs, we call that the "terroir", the essence that gets bottled in the wine. And the cherries,' he smiles, 'that's the barrel – they're from France. They were used to make cherry brandy. Keeping the taste pure is one of the reasons we've gone organic too.'

'It would affect the terroir if you weren't?'

He dips his head in ascent. 'Definitely – chemicals can really affect the taste. What's hard, though, is that when you decide to go fully organic, like we have, it can sometimes mean a less streamlined product, as we've gone preservative-free.'

'I can imagine – so is that what makes a winery organic, when it is preservative-free?' I ask.

He shakes his head. 'It's such a contentious issue – technically you can still be organic according to some so long as there's no spraying. But I'm a bit of a purist, so I figured if we were going to call ourselves organic, I wanted it to reflect on every level, including the fermentation process.'

I'm impressed.

It shows integrity, and something else too – character, I suppose. Here's someone who isn't afraid to put in the time, even if it means more work. That isn't something you really see a lot of nowadays. I suppose I shouldn't be surprised. My first impression of Tom had been that he was determined – I saw that in the article I'd read in *Eudaimonia* – but it hadn't told the full story. It had shown his resolution, his commitment to resurrecting his family's legacy. What it hadn't shown was how alive it made him. It was compelling to witness.

I look away, and take another sip. 'I think I'll be first in line when it's ready – three hundred bottles should do me quite nicely,' I say, only half joking.

His eyes dance. 'I might just take you up on that offer.'

I feel my cheeks flush again.

A loud crash outside makes me jump. Tom hurries to see what has happened, and I follow in his wake. I can hear raised voices, and one of the farm workers races over – an older man, his swarthy face a picture of concern. 'I tried to stop him,' he shouts.

There's an unmistakable screech of tyres against gravel, and the sound of a car coming to an abrupt stop: the brakes squealing, and the heavy sound of a car door being slammed shut. In the cloud of dust that follows, a man with a stocky fighter's build, poured into a tight and expensive suit, tears at Tom, bellowing in rapid-fire Greek.

Tom stands rooted to the spot, his face like stone.

The man, his dark face a hair's breadth from Tom's, shouts, 'You dare to speak to the papers! To show your face here!' You think… what… that you can just come and fix everything, brush it aside and everyone will forget what you did?'

Something in Tom seems to snap. 'What I did!' he says, outraged. 'So it's back to that? For once in your over-privileged life, Tony, take some responsibility for what you did… stop blaming everyone else. And you're right, I am the only one who dares to show my face here.'

Tony raises his fist to punch Tom, but the old man lurches forward and separates them, placing a burly arm on each. 'Stop, stop – your father wouldn't want this,' he yells.

Tony's face flushes an even angrier red. 'My father would be here – if it wasn't for him!'

The old man shakes his head sadly. 'Tony, that's not true, it was—'

Tony cuts him off short, addressing Tom. 'No one wants you here, don't you understand? You ruined my family. This—' he opens his hands expansively at the vineyard, 'was never meant for you. You were the mistake he should have left behind. Look what it cost him, cost us all when you arrived.'

Tom looks as if he'd been struck. The old man waves his hands, as if to strike Tony's words from the air. 'Is not true, you're brothers – it's Tom's birthright as much as yours, Tony, that's what your father would have wanted.'

Tony's eyes go dead. 'His birthright?' he scoffs. 'He's a bastard – he has no right to anything. All he knows how to do is take.'

Tom narrows his eyes. 'I never took anything that didn't want to be taken.'

Tony's face colours, an angry rash of red appears and he pushes Tom. 'You leave her out of this.'

Tom scoffs. 'Really – why, when it's you who always makes everything about her? Why don't you just for once admit it – even to yourself – and stop blaming everyone else for what you did?'

Tony shakes his head, his lip curling in contempt. 'Consider this a warning – get out, go back to where you slid in from or—'

'Or what?' says Tom.

'Well… accidents happen, don't they, Tom? Isn't that what they called this before anyone knew better? Let's just say that this one will be guaranteed.'

Tom leaps at Tony, and the two brothers hit the gravel with a thud, rolling about the sand, each trying their best to dismember the other. It jolts me out of my shock. I rush over and try to help the old man separate them. 'Stop it!' I scream.

Tom backs away from Tony, his face a mask of anger, his eyes clouded. 'The only one of us who needs to go is you. Go before I make sure the only way you'll leave is to crawl,' he spits out through gritted teeth.

Tony's eyes flash in anger; he looks from Tom to the rest of the workers, who have all flocked around Tom. He sneers and says, 'You've got them all fooled, haven't you? Just remember who you're working for – what kind of a man he is, someone who did that to his own father. Don't think he won't do it to any one of you.'

The old man shakes his head and edges closer to Tom. 'Tony, don't be like this, it was an accident.'

Tony's black eyes bulge. 'That fire was many things, Kokes, but an accident was not one of them.'

Tom, his jaw clenched, says, 'You're a fool, Tony, a blind fool.'

Tony begins to lurch at Tom, but Kokes grabs him and shoves him into his car. 'Go – just go.' And to my disbelief he does, giving one last glare before departing, leaving the air littered with a trail of dust and squealing tyres in his wake. Tom stands in the middle of the dirt path, and without warning strides off, walking a road that none of us dare to follow.

I pick up my notebook, which I hadn't realised I'd dropped, and put it in my bag. Feeling unaccountably sad, I make my way back to the farmhouse and pick up my bike, my mind full of unanswered questions.

When I get home, I pull all my notes out of my notebook so that I can spread them across the floor, then make myself a cup of tea.

The day is warm, the sunshine pouring in through the cottage window, bringing with it the scent of the Lefka Ori, which would forever remind me of Elysium, of the young wine and all its promise – all of which now seems balanced on a precarious knife edge of hatred between two brothers. I can't get the fight out of my head. Or Tom's stricken face.

I don't know what to think about the scene that I witnessed. It's clear, though, that time has changed nothing.

I can't imagine what it must have taken to start over, when so many people insisted that he didn't belong. Or how he'd found the will to come back.

I still don't know what to think about what or who had caused the fire. All I know is that it is far from over, and even though I know that Tom probably doesn't want to dredge up the past and discuss what had happened – it's still there, no matter how hard he tries to leave it behind.

It's after dark when I see the message on my phone. I look up from the timeline I've drawn of the events of the fire and all the unanswered questions I have.

My eyes widen. It's a message from Tom: *'Got your number from Nigel Crane. Sincere apologies for how it ended. Can you come tomorrow?'*

I sit cross-legged on the floor, the phone clutched in both hands, my notes spread around me, wondering just how much farther down the rabbit hole I'm prepared to go. And if there's any hope of turning back. And even if I could, would I want to? But I already know the answer to that.

My response is short, but immediate: *'Be there at 9 a.m.'*

EIGHTEEN

Tom is waiting for me outside the farmhouse when I get there. I lean my bicycle against the stone wall and take a deep breath, feeling a little tense.

As I draw near, he doesn't lose his serious expression; his face taut, he dips his head in greeting, his blues eyes unfathomable.

'Coffee?' he asks.

'Please,' I say.

I follow him as he walks around the farmhouse, my eyes trailing the faded soot on the walls and the burnt-out husk of the rest of the old homestead. He leads me around a wall towards a large blue wooden door into a rustic farm kitchen. I take a seat at the big wooden table while he places a coffee kettle on the stove. 'It's just standard Greek coffee, I'm afraid,' he says.

'I'm used to that.'

He looks at me with a probing stare. 'You're Greek?' he asks.

'Half – my father. He married an Englishwoman and defected to Reading,' I say with a half-smile.

'Ah,' he says. 'So we have that in common.'

'Your father also defected to Reading?' I tease.

He snorts in an amused way, but it relaxes him a little.

I smile. 'But yes, you're right – we both had Greek fathers…' I say, wondering if he'll speak about his father. He dips his head in agreement. The silence stretches out before us, gone was the easy conversation we'd had the day before.

He busies himself making the coffee, then hands me a steaming mug filled with the thick, tar-like liquid. I smile appreciatively. 'Thanks.' I take a sip; it is very strong, but good.

'Look, about yesterday—' he begins. He hasn't taken a seat, but is standing at the edge of the table, facing the door, his hands clenched.

'It's fine,' I reply.

His hands move through his hair, a gesture of impatience. 'It's far from fine – I haven't seen that...' He pauses, no doubt about to call Tony something vile but controls himself. 'My brother in years.'

I take a sip, then say casually, 'Well, I thought it went rather well.'

His mouth falls open. Then slowly he starts to laugh. It transforms his face, lines appearing at the edges of his eyes.

He wipes his eyes. 'God, I needed that,' he says, taking a seat opposite me and giving me an electric smile. My stomach does a little dive, and for a second I can't breathe.

That smile should come with a warning, I think. Like 'hazardous for your health' or 'will cause irrational sixteen-year-old self to re-emerge'.

Right. Okay, focus. I take another sip. Bloody hell, even indoors those eyes were freaking blue.

OKAY. No. *Something else.*

Thankfully, Tom speaks.

'So, I'm sorry about yesterday, that's really what I wanted to say,' he says, looking apologetic, giving me a bashful look. 'That and... er, about the article...'

Ah. He's concerned that it would land in the paper... fair enough. Perhaps if I'd been Kimberley it would have, but there are enough bloody Kimberleys in this world. I reassure him that the article won't mention the fight.

He looks relieved.

'Were you always like that?' I ask.

'What do you mean?'

'You and your brother.'

'Pretty much. We didn't really grow up together. I'd come for a few visits as a kid, and he was… polite, I suppose. He'd say hello, but then I wouldn't see him again for the rest of the time. He's a couple years older. This was before my mother died – when I moved here. After that, things got worse.'

'He resented you?'

'I think so. My dad made sure that we both felt included, and for a little while we didn't exactly get along but we were headed that way. Then about a year afterwards, Constance – my dad's wife – got sick and Tony started to blame me.'

'Blame you, why?' I ask in dismay.

Tom rakes his hands through his hair again, the action causing it to stick up wildly. 'She felt ashamed, I guess – having her husband's bastard come to live with us. She was a proud woman… quite tough, someone who found it hard to forgive, or to look past mistakes. I suppose it made her bitter.'

'She was cruel to you?' I ask, appalled.

He laughs, a sad, cracked sound. 'No, not really. I mean, she wasn't cruel or anything… she just didn't want me there.'

I have to disagree – indifference can be its own special brand of cruelty.

'She said as much?' I ask.

'No. But she just kind of withdrew, even before she got sick, so we'd never see her.'

'You sound like you pity her,' I say in disbelief.

'Do I?' he says, his thoughtful blue eyes meeting mine. 'I suppose I do. It must have been awful living like that – so full of anger.' He looks away then, and I wonder if it was something he'd come to realise himself after the fire. He takes another sip of his coffee. 'Ugh – cold,' he says, getting up and tossing it aside. 'Shall we go for a walk? I can show you the rest of the vineyard.'

I nod, following him outside.

'Must be something to wake up to a view like this,' I say, taking in the sweeping vineyard that just then was bathed in a lemon-coloured glow. Surrounded by such tranquillity, it seems impossible that there's a more sinister story beneath the surface.

'I missed it,' he admits, and starts walking towards a large hill up ahead.

'When you went away?' I ask, following him. Today he's keeping more of a languid pace, no doubt making allowances for my shorter legs.

'Yes. It was tough – for a long time it felt like I didn't have a home. I suppose, for a while, I didn't, really – after the fire,' he explains.

I'm amazed that he's volunteering so much. I'd got the impression the first time we met that he would be reticent – reserved, even. As if he's reading my mind, he says, 'You're easy to speak to, you know. It probably makes you a good journalist.'

I cringe.

'What?'

'I'm not really a journalist. Well, not in the traditional sense...'

He looks at me, perplexed. 'What do you mean?'

'I am... or at least was... an obituary writer,' I admit, wondering why I'm telling him this.

He stops stock still. 'You're kidding?' His eyes are wide.

I give a sheepish look. 'Nope, afraid not – for three years, three very long years,' I say.

'No doubt. That must have... I can't even imagine. Did you come here, to Crete, for a new job?'

'Oh no.'

'No?' he asks.

I blink. 'Well, no. You see, what happened was – I was on my way to work one day and then… I just couldn't, you know.'

He nods. Yet I wonder if he really did get it. If your job was to work somewhere like this, did you ever really get those days? I mean, really?

'So what happened?'

'I got on a plane instead.'

His eyes bulge. 'You skipped the country because you didn't want to go to work?'

I laugh. 'Well, yes… and no, not actually – there were a lot of other things too. My yaya – my dad's mum – she passed away and she was always on me to do something… anything else, especially after—'

'After?'

I take a breath. I was about to say 'after Christopher died'. I'm shocked that I almost had.

'After… She knew how miserable I was at work,' I finish lamely.

'Was it awful,' he asks, 'writing about death all the time?'

'Sometimes…' I start and then stop myself. 'Actually, yeah, pretty much awful most of the time. The worst was if I got something wrong.'

He cringes. 'I can imagine. Sort of like you've ruined someone's life, I suppose.'

I look at him in disbelief. 'Exactly!'

Then, because I don't want him to think I'm incompetent, I say, 'Not that I got it wrong often, it's just that sometimes with the grief, things could go a bit… you know—'

He holds his palm up. 'Everyone makes mistakes,' he says simply.

I smile. 'Not according to my editor.'

'Well, then he's an idiot.'

'She.'

'Same goes.'

I grin.

'So now you work for Nigel?' he asks.

'Yes. Well, not exactly. I'm freelancing. I've got another job that pays the bills – it's actually sort of lovely, really.'

'Oh, what do you do?'

At that moment I remember that he knows Caroline. I wonder if I can keep her out of it but decide against it. I'm not prepared to lie any more than I already have. As far as he's concerned, Nigel assigned me his story, he doesn't know of my own interest in his life, of the research that I'd already done. If he knows that I'm staying with Caroline, would that change anything? It's too late to wonder, though: it's not something I'd really be able to keep under wraps.

I take a breath and answer. 'I'm helping a travel writer – Caroline Murray – finish her memoir. I'm her assistant.'

His eyes widen in surprise. 'Caro – really?'

'She said she knows you.'

He considers me for a moment, his face inscrutable. 'She's an old family friend.'

I dip my chin. 'She's great.'

'A bit of a legend.'

I smile, thinking of her and a certain rather fabulous musician. 'You have no idea.'

He raises his eyebrows. 'I can only imagine. How's she doing?'

'Really good, you should come by and visit.' As soon as it's out of my mouth, though, I wonder if he thinks that I'm trying to see him again. To be honest, I'm wondering about it myself. To cover up, I continue, 'I'm sure she'd love to see you.'

'It's been a long time.'

'You haven't seen her since you came back?'

He shakes his head. 'It's been hectic, I've been meaning to.'

I look at him, biting my lip. 'You said earlier that you left – after the fire, where did you go? Why did you come back?'

'On the record?' he asks.

'I'd like it to be.'

He sighs. 'I didn't really leave after the fire – well, not for a year, anyway. But things got messy, the estate was tied up and there was no way for us to rebuild right then. I was completely broke.'

'But couldn't you have got a loan or something?'

'Not really. The banks wouldn't have given it to me anyway.'

'Why not?'

'They weren't likely to give a loan to help rebuild a vineyard to the person they suspected of starting the fire.'

I stop. 'But who did?' I ask, surprised that he would share that information with me.

He scoffs. 'Everyone. You name it. I was the prime suspect, you heard Tony yesterday.'

I can't help but agree. He'd all but accused Tom of obliterating his home.

'But… they cleared you?'

'They couldn't find any concrete evidence, if that's what you mean. But one of the farm workers placed me by the outbuilding, and later that's where they found what was used to start the fire.'

I exhale. 'Had you been there?'

He dips his head in assent, his face wretched.

At my expression he shakes his head. 'I didn't start the fire, but I'd been very close to whoever started it. I kept going through a "what if" scenario. You know, what if I'd spotted them in time?

What if I'd got there sooner? But I'd been a bit distracted that night, and I didn't have a good enough explanation of why I was there.' He pauses as if he's about to say something else but then continues, 'The judge said it wasn't enough, so I was let off.'

'That must have been awful.'

'It was bad enough losing my dad, but everyone thinking that I'd actually try to destroy my home. That – well, it nearly killed me,' he says candidly.

'I'm so sorry,' I say, meaning it.

He gives me a tight smile.

'So what do you think happened?'

He looks at me seriously and says, 'Off the record?'

'Sure.'

His eyes cloud. 'There was only one person who could have done it.'

My eyes widen. 'Who?'

His hands ball into fists. 'Tony.'

NINETEEN

'Tony?'

'Yes,' he says simply. 'He was there... I saw him that night at around the same time that they placed me by the fire. We'd had an argument.'

'Did you tell the police this?' I ask.

'Of course, but it was just a mudslinging match. No one could corroborate what I said, so no one investigated properly. Apparently he had no motive,' he says, his mouth tightening.

'And you did?' I say, exasperated. 'It was your home too – why would you have a motive to destroy it, yet Tony didn't?'

He snorts. 'Apparently bastards always have a motive.'

My heart goes out to him. It's horrible to think that in this day and age people could still think that way. 'They never even looked into it?'

'He had an alibi apparently.'

'He did?'

Tom shrugs, but doesn't elaborate.

I look at him, not sure what to say. It wasn't fair. But then when was life ever really fair?

'Well, he has to live with what he did – that can't be easy,' I say, remembering how angry Tony was and how his anger oozed from him, so tangible it tainted the air.

'That's the thing – he can't admit it. Not even to himself.'

He's right. It did seem that way.

I have to ask, even if he doesn't want to speak about it. 'You said earlier that you were having an argument on the night of the fire?'

He nods, but doesn't volunteer anything further. So I ask again, 'Why – what were you fighting about?'

Tom's face goes dark. 'Who knows, we were always at each other's throats back then,' he says, his mouth compressed into a grim line.

I let it go. It's obvious he doesn't want to talk about it, but I know with certainty that there was more to it than he let on. It wasn't likely that he would forget what they'd fought about – especially on a night that had caused them both to lose the only home they'd had.

I look at him, the unspoken words lying between us, and know with sudden clarity what they'd argued about. Or whom.

TWENTY

'Loved the Caroline piece,' comes Nigel's booming voice down the line. 'Nicely handled. I'll send you a cheque in the week,' he says in his customary clipped tones.

I'm sitting on the steps to my cottage, the door wide, inviting in the cool evening air after a full day's work.

'I'm so glad you like it,' I say, surprised and pleased that I'd be getting paid. It hadn't occurred to me, to be honest; I'd just been thrilled to get a chance to write about something besides an obituary for a change.

'We'll be running it in the next edition. Any updates on your other project?' he asks, his voice deepening further, stressing the intrigue.

'We did the interview over the weekend,' I say.

'The weekend, eh?' I can envision his bushy red caterpillar eyebrows rising meaningfully.

I shake my head. 'Well, there was a lot to cover on the vineyard... and how it works...'

He laughs his big booming laugh. 'I'll bet. Any luck on finding out what happened there? The real story?'

'Sort of – his brother showed up yesterday.'

'Tony?' Nigel breathes.

'Yup.'

'How'd that go?'

'Well – rather as expected, I think.'

'At each other like dogs?'

I chuckle. 'Pretty much.'

'Ah well, there's always been a bit of bad blood there.'

'He threatened Tom – said he'd better leave or he'd take matters into his own hands.'

'Like what, do you reckon?'

'Another fire, I should imagine.'

'Good lord, let's hope not.'

I have to agree.

'I said I wouldn't print any of that,' I say, suddenly worried.

'Ah,' says Nigel. 'Pity. Would be good, maybe a little too sensational, though.'

I smile. Got to love that about Nigel, for all his boom and bluster he remains a gentleman.

'Keep me posted, and good work again on Caroline's story, really,' he says before ringing off.

I smile. It is perhaps one of the few times I have ever received praise about any article that didn't start, 'Lovely story *but...*'

It was the nature of the beast. Writers couldn't be overly precious about their work – not for long anyway. Still, it was nice to have someone say something about it that didn't come with a 'but' attached.

My eyes are tired from staring at the screen working on Caroline's typewritten manuscript pages, sustained with endless rounds of coffee. I'd protested that the assistant was meant to do all the coffee making, but Caroline had insisted.

After my third cup of the day, it had suddenly dawned on me. I'd narrowed my eyes at her suspiciously.

'Caroline, is there something you want to tell me?' I'd asked, accepting the cup with narrowed eyes. It had been several weeks and I'd yet to make her a cup of coffee. I'd only made her a single cup – on my second day. Now that I think about it, she'd been rather keen to have someone make coffee – her advertisement had even said as much.

Caroline was a study of nonchalance.

I'd probed again. 'Caroline?'

She bit her lip and looked out the window.

I frowned, realising. 'I make bad coffee?'

She hung her head. 'You make bad coffee,' she agreed.

'How very unGreek of me.'

She snorted in amusement. 'Although… okay, I'm just going to say this because I've been here for close to twenty years so I can. The Greeks, you know, are an incredibly talented and wonderful people who have brought the world a lot of joy, culture and history.'

'But not great coffee?'

'Sorry, darling, but we need to thank the Columbians and the Italians for that.'

'And the Ethiopians, I suppose,' I said, to be fair.

'Ethiopians,' she agreed, 'but not the Greeks – or Turks really, who put them onto the stuff in the first place.'

'But I like Greek coffee.' I protested.

'Ah yes, but there's an excellent explanation for that.'

'Which is?'

'Well, you're Greek.'

Good point.

We'd finished up a few hours earlier, Caroline insisting that we start implementing real finish times from now on. I'd be going back in a few minutes, though, for dinner. She'd seemed rather impressed that I could make baklava. 'Now really – that's another one of the gifts the Greeks gave us,' she'd joked, when I promised I'd show her how to make it.

We'd fallen into the habit of eating dinner together a few nights a week, which I really enjoyed. She was brilliant company. It would be nice to tell her that Nigel liked the profile I'd written about her.

I watch the fading light and consider what Nigel said about the fire, and how he'd called that the real story. I realise he had a point: no matter how hard Tom worked to resurrect Elysium, or start over, he was stuck. Stuck in the past, in that night ten years ago that had ripped their family apart, and he couldn't move forward until they found out what really happened.

It was something I was all too familiar with myself. I'd lived there so long, unable to accept what had happened to me, to Christopher. I had held myself prisoner in that place for years.

But I'm not captive any more.

And if nothing else, I can help Tom do the same by trying to find out what really happened. Somehow, that has become important.

'So you want to keep the filo sheets from drying out by covering them with a damp towel,' I say, while prepping a baking pan for the baklava. Caroline is staring at me, slightly in awe.

I'd given her the task of chopping up the almonds, while I set about making the syrup, more than a little thrilled to finally be using Caroline's beautiful farm-style kitchen and her cream-coloured Aga.

'It's all about the layers,' I say, while I stir the sauce. The lingering scent of cinnamon and honey reminds me of the summer sun, and Yaya.

It was always summer in my memory. I'm not sure why. Winter – well, that came later, and never really went away until I arrived here in Crete, I suppose.

'Was this one of your grandmother's recipes?' she asks, dipping a spoon into the sauce, blowing on it for a second and putting it into her mouth, her eyelids closing in ecstasy.

'It is. My fondest memories are of us in the kitchen baking. It's the first time I've made something since she passed,' I say, noting this with a curious lack of pain.

Her eyes are full of understanding.

'More vino, darling?'

'Please.'

'Italian?'

'Surprise me.'

She winks. 'Okay, be right back.' She shoots off down to the cellar, then comes back with a dusty bottle. 'Let's see if you guess this.'

A bit like Tom, Caroline is rather impressed with my ability to distinguish different flavours in the wine. She's taken it upon herself to develop my wine education, and I've been enjoying the experience.

She pours me a glass, and waits.

I sniff the contents, swirling them about, pretending to take rather exaggerated breaths so that she laughs aloud.

'Expertly done,' she says, her face deadpan.

I grin, and take a sip.

'Liquorice?'

'Close,' she says, impressed. 'Fennel.'

'Some kind of berry.'

'Strawberry,' she concurs.

'Wood smoke?'

'Oak matured, yes.'

'Pretty awful.'

She takes a sip and wrinkles her nose. 'Agreed.'

She sets the bottle aside, mentioning something about it having rained at the wrong time for that particular vintage, and opens up another bottle of the Greek wine we'd been having earlier.

'Consistently good' is my verdict.

'Another victory,' she agrees.

We layer the baklava by pouring the nut and syrup mixture on sheets of pastry and repeating the process until we cut diamond shapes into the thick golden syrupy mixture and pop it into the oven.

'You're a marvel,' she says.

'I bet you say that to all the girls.'

'Only the ones that bake,' she teases.

We take a seat at the long oak table with its assortment of mismatched chairs; Caroline explains it was part of her eclectic shabby chic look.

'Really?'

'Well, no – I broke one, then I bought another, and liked the look so I kept it going.'

I giggle. I like it, but then I like it when things have a story, some character. It was one of the things Trish, Christopher's mother, and I had bonded over very early on. Her house is a collection of items with a story to tell. As an interior designer, a big part of her job was trying to get her clients to look beyond the Ikea catalogue. We'd gone antiquing together a lot – and loved the old brocante fairs the most. We'd even travelled as far as Normandy once, just the two of us roaring around the French countryside, the perfect girls' weekend. The two of us rose with the sparrows to trawl some field and getting rather excited when we found old French linen, especially when it was monogrammed – part of someone's wedding trousseau. We always convinced each other that this dresser with its Queen Anne legs and doors that needed to be repaired was essential, that mirror with its faded gilt trim would look perfect in the hallway, etcetera, and would come home loaded with treasures.

'Look at all that loot,' Chris would say, shaking his head and wondering just where we'd fit it in our box-sized London flat, but Trish and I always made a plan, some trick to make it work.

God, I miss her.

Caroline waves a hand in my face. 'Where did you go?' she asks.

'A field just outside Devon. Early morning brocante fair.'

'Get anything good?'

'An 18th century chamber pot.'

'Ah.'

'Despite its rather prosaic use, it was rather exquisite. I used to go brocante trawling a lot with my fiancé's mother,' I explain.

Caroline pauses mid sip. To her credit she doesn't blurt out 'Your fiancé?' but keeps her composure.

'By choice?' she asks, with a quirk of the lips.

'Oh yes. God she was great, like a female version of Chris, really.' I say with a small, sad smile.

Her eyes are grave and she touches my arm, eyes widening in comprehension. 'He passed away?' she asks sadly.

I manage a nod.

'I'm so sorry, Ria.'

And she is. Her eyes brim over when I tell her everything, about how it had happened, how I'd fallen apart, and then losing Yaya, and that despite how awful that had been, how it had changed everything.

Like a bone, sometimes to set it properly it needs to be broken again, so you can begin to heal.

In journalism we are taught that the best sources are closest to the story. It hadn't escaped my notice that Caroline, with her insider's knowledge of the Bacchus family, may offer insight into the strained relationship between the two brothers, and more specifically their relationship with Iliana Kirosa. I didn't really know how to bring it up, without raising her suspicions, though.

About a week later, a ready-made alibi presents itself in the *Eudaimonia* newspaper, in the form of my article on Caroline.

Caroline rushes into the cottage to show me the piece, which she says rather excitedly is placed in a prime position on page three. 'I mean, that's where the nudie picture would be if it was a tabloid, so it's top real estate, if you think about it,' she says with a wink.

I laugh. I'm sure the fact that it's Caroline, one of Britain's most beloved travel writers, responsible for the swollen band of English expats who made Crete their home, probably has just a little more to do with its placement.

I smile as she hands me the paper. Apparently she'd ordered an extra copy for herself. I'm quite touched really that she thinks so highly of the piece – this is a woman who had her own show on the BBC, for goodness sake. But Caroline isn't like that, she really takes joy as and when it comes. And it's really sweet that her joy has more to do with the fact that my name is on the piece than hers.

My eyes fall to the right and I spot a face that I recognise, standing next to a new hotel that just opened up.

I frown. I can't quite place her. I must be staring hard because Caroline leans over, and sniffs. It's a sound of disdain, and not at all like her free-spirited friendly self.

I unfold the newspaper and then see just why Caroline sniffed. I do the same. Even though, to be fair, I really have no right.

'Heiress Iliana Kirosa Opens New Five-Star Beach Resort' reads the headline, followed by a larger-than-life photograph of her with Tony, both of them dressed to the nines, captioned: 'Former mayor of Chania's daughter Iliana Kirosa with husband, Tony Bacchus, open their latest five-star resort, Thalassa in Elounda'.

'She's beautiful,' I say. Because she is. She has dark slanted eyes, black hair like watered silk, and a curvy Kim Kardashian-type of figure.

Caroline's lip curls up.

I raise a brow. An unspoken question.

She pulls a face. 'She's beautiful, yes. It's just… I rather can't stand her,' she admits.

'Do you know her?' I ask, hoping that she knows at least something about her relationship with Tony – and Tom, for that matter.

'Oh yes.'

My eyes widen. She sees my unspoken question and counters, 'Well, no. I mean not very well, actually. But what little I know is enough.'

I understand this: thinking of Kimberley, knowing her any better could hardly make me loathe her any less. It's Newton's law, really. Every action of hers elicits an equal and contrary reaction in me. You can't argue with physics. All right, you can. But you'd very rarely win. So instead, I ask, 'Why?'

'Difficult to say, really. It's just this feeling I have – that something wasn't quite right.'

I frown. 'In what way?' I prod.

'She was very beautiful. Quite spoiled, liked the limelight, though that wasn't what… concerned me. A little vapidity is perhaps to be expected in someone so mollycoddled, it's rather—' She makes a little self-admonishing sound. 'It's silly… and perhaps I was just imagining it…'

'But?' I press when she doesn't go on.

She looks heavenwards. 'I got the feeling that she was leading them both on… both brothers, Tony and Tom.'

'Wow,' I breathe.

'I know, nonsense, I'm sure.'

'Not really.'

'Oh?' she asks.

'No. I think that something happened between them.'

Caroline's eyes widen. 'Why do you think so?' Then she narrows her eyes. 'Ria, have you been digging?'

I cringe. 'Yes.' Then admit, 'I'm doing a story… for Nigel.'

'You never!' she exclaims. Then in total contradiction she cries, 'I knew it!'

I hang my head.

She narrows her eyes. 'You've been going to the library.'

'I've been going to the library,' I admit.

'And visiting the vineyard.'

'And visiting the vineyard.'

'I knew it! Did you ever go to the beach?'

I hang my head again.

'So that's where you've been running off to on your days off.' If anything, she sounds rather pleased. I take heart from this.

'You're not cross?' I ask.

'Cross! Good lord, darling, why would I be cross?' she says, eyes puzzled.

'Well…' I start. 'He's Jill's son…'

Caroline shakes her head. 'Exactly. It was a terrible tragedy and the worst of it was what happened to him afterwards.'

'I know. He told me a bit about it.'

'He did?'

'Yes,' I admit.

'I'm amazed. He's quite taciturn, at the best of times. It's good that he has someone to talk to.'

I suppose she's right.

'Did – did he say anything about Iliana?' she asks.

'No.' I hesitate for a second but then make a decision. I reach into the drawer of my desk and pick up my notebook. 'But I found this,' I say, showing her the passage that I had transcribed the other day. The one that referred to Iliana as Tom's, and not Tony's, girlfriend.

She looks at my notes, and frowns. 'But that could just be a—'

'A mistake, yes. I thought so too. That is, until Tony showed up at the vineyard threatening to destroy Tom.'

'What!' she exclaims.

'He did. And while they went at each other like dogs, Tony mentioned her…'

'Really?'

I nod, although truth be told they hadn't actually mentioned her name, but then they didn't need to. It was written all over Tony's face.

'That's terrible. Awful when a woman comes between two brothers.'

I agree. 'I think they never had a relationship really, not from what he told me.'

'Of course, you're right. Even from the start Tony shunned him – saw him as an intruder. But for a while when they got older, it did look as if things might change…'

I thought of what Tom had told me and have to agree.

'So you're going to do a story?' she asks.

'A feature, on the vineyard and the harvest in September.'

Caroline gives me a look. 'And that's all?'

'Yes. Well, no. Nigel thinks that we should dig a little deeper too – try to find out what really happened.'

'Nigel thinks, eh?'

'Yes. Although I just may have helped him along with that thought,' I confess.

'Ah. And here was me thinking that you were more of a writer than a journalist,' she teases.

I shrug. 'It's like spilt wine on silk – you can wash all you like, some stains are there to stay,' I admit.

She grins. 'But seriously. Just be careful – I meant what I said the other day, about buried secrets, once brought to light they don't go back underground.'

I hope that her words won't turn into an ominous portent. One that risks alienating Tom, and prising open a wound that he doesn't want open.

The next afternoon, I head for the village on my bicycle, the scent of wild lavender mixed with the briny scent of the ocean filling my senses. The honey-coloured town is like something out of the Cotswolds, with its picture postcard quaintness, little shops and cobble-lane paths. It's suffused in sunshine and warmth, and every shop stall welcomes summer in with a bountiful display of bright red begonias and shocking pink trailing bougainvillea.

I feel my shoulders relax; Caroline's words about buried secrets seem far away here.

Leaning my bicycle outside the post office, I pop inside. I'm fetching a parcel that Caroline's publisher had sent through, a box of the thirtieth anniversary edition of *Falling for Crete*, with a new cover and introduction by Caroline. It's great marketing for the new memoir, which will be published the following year.

The only trouble is the package is huge, far bigger than the cute little basket attached to my bicycle. I'm cursing myself for not bringing Caroline's car, which she'd said I was more than welcome to use whenever I needed it, the huge box in my arms. I should have just asked the postie if I could have come back a little later; instead I'd signed for the parcel and headed out with the vague plan of fixing it behind my bicycle seat with some rope from the hardware shop. It was not looking good. The box kept slipping as soon as I got the one rope end under it, only for it to slide onto my knees.

'Bloody hell,' I mutter for the fifth time, when the box lands on my kneecap, making me wince with pain as I shift the box back in place.

'Need a hand?' I whip around to look, only to have the box land straight on my foot. I swear, rubbing my foot.

'Sorry! Are you all right?'

It's Tom, his electric blue eyes filled with concern. I stare at them, thinking, good lord, I mean you can't just bring those out on the unsuspecting public. I blink, then give him a rueful look. 'I'm fine, stupid really. I should have brought the car.'

He grins, showing those amazing lines around his eyes. 'Tell you what, why don't I give you a lift? I've got the van, I was stocking up on some supplies for the farm so there'd be space for all three of you,' he says, indicating the box and the bicycle.

I laugh. It would be churlish to refuse. 'Thanks, that would be brilliant.'

We put the box and the bicycle in the van, which says 'Elysium Wineries est 1002' on the side, along with a falling feather motif.

'I like it, really captures the idea of Elysium,' I say, referring to the feather. 'Was it always part of the branding?'

Tom shakes his head as he climbs in and we back out onto the cobble path. 'No,' he laughs, to my surprise. 'I added it when I reopened the farm. It's me being a bit of a sentimental fool, I suppose.'

'What? Why?' I ask.

'Well, when I came here as a kid, this place really did seem a bit like heaven, you know. Up in the mountains, the sea, all of it. But then when it burnt down and Dad passed, well it wasn't any more. So I added the fallen feather, as kind of tribute to what had happened.' He ran a hand through his dark hair, giving me a sad smile.

'I like that.'

Tom smiles. 'You busy today?'

'Not really, just a few chores around the house really.'

'Anything that can wait?'

I nod. 'Sure.'

'Do you feel like coming with me to see what used to be the north farm? We could pop into the café and get some sandwiches on the way.'

I look at him, feeling an unexpected little flip in my stomach. Get a grip, Laburinthos, I tell myself, he just knows you're interested in the vineyard, that's all. Which is true, isn't it? So I ask, 'The north farm?'

'It was where we grew the Merlot. It was sold off after the fire. There were rumours that a developer was thinking of building holiday accommodation there but my vintner heard that they've pulled out of the deal, so I'd like to go and see if the land is ready for sowing.'

'I'd love to see it,' I say, meaning it.

'Great,' he says, with an easy smile that I return.

We pop into the little café I went to the other night, and get two takeaway deli sandwiches, mine with sundried tomatoes, artichokes and buffalo mozzarella, Tom's a giro sub that looks heavenly.

I put the sandwiches in my bag and we head towards Elysium, past Caroline's olive grove towards a stretch of land near the sea that goes on for what seems like miles. Tom parks the car on the side of the road and I follow after him as he makes his way towards the now barren land. Up ahead I can see a little 'for sale' sign and take heart.

Tom walks a few feet then kneels down, gathering some of the dusty earth in the palm of his hands. He looks up at me, mid crouch, and nods. 'It's ready,' he says, while his gaze tells me he's far away.

He gets up and walks some more. I leave him, knowing all about old ghosts: some roads you really do need to walk alone.

I take a seat in the old vineyard, trying to picture what it must have looked like before the fire. As if reading my thoughts, Tom comes and sits beside me and says, 'This was the oldest and biggest part of the old vineyard, the vines went on for miles, right to the edge there.' He points to a patch of mountain overlooking the sea.

'It must have been magnificent,' I say.

He nods. 'It was.'

'And now it's ready… what did you mean by that? How do you know?' I ask.

'The fire didn't just destroy the vines, all the nutrients in the soil were destroyed as well, what would have grown out of that ground would have been, well, disastrous. But now… it's healed.' He smiles.

'It's been waiting.'

I look at the ground, feeling a sense of wonder. There's a kind of magic in that.

'So you'll buy it back?'

Tom folds his lips together in thought. 'I'm going to try.'

I stare at him, moved. 'Sometimes that's all you can do,' I say.

He nods, then reaches over and gives my hand a squeeze.

It's such a small gesture, but my breath catches in my throat. I look at him; his blue eyes look so serious. I can't seem to look away. He hasn't moved his hand. I swallow, and tear my gaze away. Removing my hand from his, I reach inside my bag and say, 'Let's toast it…we don't have any wine but our sandwiches will have to do,' with a small laugh, handing him his, willing my hand to stop shaking.

For a second, he just stares at my trembling hand; he seems about to say something. He's staring at me so intently, I bite my lip, but he just takes the sandwich.

The moment seems to pass and he says, 'I'm not sure if there's anything to toast yet… I might not get it. Let's just say I'm not the most favoured client at the Ouranó bank.'

'Because of the fire?' I ask.

He shrugs yes.

'That's so unfair. Is there anyone else you can try? Somewhere that's, well…'

'Not overly familiar with the rumour mill around here, you mean?'

I nod.

'Yes. There's some old family friends who might be able to help with a loan. I'll see.'

I can't help wondering who they could be, but don't ask. We finish our sandwiches and later Tom takes me home.

I summon the nerve to invite him in to see Caroline, but her car isn't here. Tom jumps out and helps me bring the box inside Caroline's house. I expect him to say that he needs to get going, but he makes no move to leave, so I find myself offering him a coffee, from Caroline's impressive machine.

'That would be great,' he says, following me into Caroline's farm-style kitchen, his eyes taking in the room. 'God, this brings back memories,' he says.

'I can imagine,' I say, thinking of him, and his mother, Jill.

I hand him a cup of coffee and our fingers touch. There's a frisson, and I take my hand back fast.

He frowns, setting down the cup. 'Look, Ria,' he begins.

I swallow and quickly try to change the subject. 'You know, this is my favourite room in the house. There's a cellar just below, have you been?'

He looks at me for a second, then shakes his head. 'Um, yes, when I was a kid.' He laughs suddenly, closing his eyes in memory, 'Just reds though, if I recall.'

I chuckle, 'Yes! Caroline said that she doesn't feel that you're really a wine connoisseur if you like white wine.'

He snorts. 'That sounds like her.'

'Do you agree?' I ask, my eyes amused.

'What do you think?'

'Mmm… no,' I guess.

'No,' he agrees, eyes alight.

He's staring again. I look away, set my coffee cup down and say nervously, 'Would you like a tour?'

He shakes his head, 'Got to get back, do my sums,' he says.

'Ah, yes,' I say, walking him out. 'Good luck.'

'Thanks.' He opens the car door, then says, 'Have you been to the farmer's market yet?'

I shake my head. 'Is it good?'

'Very. It's this Sunday, if you want to go. I could come fetch you if you like?'

'Oh,' I say, a little taken aback, wondering if I should decline. But why should I? It's just a friendly outing, right? I shouldn't overthink this. He's waiting for an answer, so I say, 'Um, yes, sounds lovely, around nine?'

'It's a date,' he says with a grin, before driving off.

I'm left standing in front of Caroline's house, my mouth opening and closing at his words. Is it a date? Do I want it to be a date? God, I'm sure it's just a figure of speech. He didn't mean a date, date did he?

On my day off I go to the library again. Nina is happy to see me and, quite against the rules, while I'm poring through one of the heavy tomes of bound newspapers, she brings me a cup of tea.

'You're my saviour,' I tell her sincerely.

'Milk? Sugar?

'Just one spoon of sugar, thanks.'

She switches on the lamp next to me. 'If yew need make copies, yew can do them in the back room, no problem. Is old machine but it works, mostly,' she says with a wry smile, her palm doing a little wave.

I stutter my thanks. It will be an enormous help, particularly as my Greek is so rusty that hours are likely to pass before I get to the gist of any article that happens to mention Elysium. At least this way I can take some of my research home.

Two hours later, using makeshift bookmarks (torn scraps from my notebook), I'm standing by the hiccoughing photocopier, a relic from the eighties that emits odd humming noises. I'd managed to find a number of references, deciding to open my search pool to two years after the fire, just in case anything interesting comes to light.

I'm hopeful, even though I'm quite sure most are reiterations of what I know already, but there's a chance that something will come to light.

I'm not sure why I think that I can find something that no one as yet has uncovered. But I have to try.

One advantage that I have on my side – one that my mother said as a barrister she never failed to appreciate in proving a case – is time.

Watching the papers lurch out of the machine, I have to hope that time will be on my side.

That night I lie in bed, a grilled cheese sandwich for company and a pot of tea on the floor, my eyes straining from the minute script I've been transcribing. I rub my eyes in fatigue. The first three articles hold nothing new, just the information that investigations are still underway. Four hours and three dead ends. One had seemed hopeful, it mentioned Elysium at least, but then it was only in relation to Iliana Kirosa, and it turned out to be about a rather high-stakes robbery at La Mer, the jewel in her collection of five-star beach resorts. The crime had been dubbed 'The Monet Escape', as someone made away with not one but two paintings by the French master from Kirosa's private collection in the dead of the night. While fascinating – and I had to wonder just how much even one Monet must have cost, let alone two – it was still a dead end. I turn to the next sheet, mustering my resolve with a generous bite of my sandwich and groaning in pleasure as the salty cheese hits my tongue. I'd popped in at the market on my ride home from the library and impulsively bought the cheese and a slab of olive-studded ciabatta. My newfound appetite was still a bit of a revelation: a happy one, though. My face has lost that grey, gaunt look it had held for the past two years, at least.

My eyes scan the page through their haze of fatigue, which quickly snaps to attention when I realise that this article is referring to a police report – one that seems to indicate for the first time the suspicion that the fire wasn't an accident.

I sit up straighter, swallowing heavily in my haste. Almost choking, I take a gulp of water and begin transcribing furiously, managing to get most of it translated in under fifteen minutes, a new record.

Arson Destroys Elysium?
Story by Xena Alberos

New evidence has come to light regarding the fire that claimed the thousand-year-old vineyard in Ouranó, Western Chania, two weeks ago. Investigators uncovered the remains of an accelerant that was believed to have started the fire. This new discovery has led Lead Inspector Stenalis to rule out an accidental cause for the fire.

'Lab testing confirmed that the fire was the result of petrol – and with the positioning of the bottle, it seems likely that it was a deliberate action,' said Stenalis.

In a further twist, twenty-two-year-old Tom Bacchus appears to have been near the scene at the time. One of the investigators confirmed that Bacchus has been brought in for questioning. 'At this stage we cannot confirm or deny his involvement, other than to say that he was identified near the scene minutes before the fire broke out,' he said.

However Stenalis maintained that for now, no one should jump to any conclusions. 'Our source mentioned that she had seen him within 50 metres of where the fire broke out – at this stage that could mean anything, for right now we will only be questioning Bacchus on his whereabouts

on the night of the fire, and hope to get this resolved as
quickly as possible.'

I set my notebook down with a frown. They hadn't resolved it, though, had they? It's still unresolved today. I tap my pen against my chin, thinking hard. It's just a hunch, but when I'd spoken to Tom, he'd mentioned that one of the farm workers had identified him there that night. I'm quite sure he'd said that it was a man. While, according to the article, Stenalis had revealed that his source was female. It may mean nothing at all. There were sure to be many female farm workers at the time. Yet somehow I doubt it. Maybe it's just an overactive imagination, but I think I have a good idea of who Lead Inspector Stenalis' source may just turn out to be.

TWENTY-ONE

'You're concerned,' I say.

I look up from my desk the following Saturday to find Caroline's troubled blue eyes peering at me. Her face is framed by a wide sunhat.

'I'm concerned,' agrees Caroline.

I pause mid-type, my finger poised over the letter J, to look at her.

'It's just a bit of transcribing … nothing to worry about,' I say, in a placating tone.

She nods, but by the way she's standing in the doorway, it looks like she has some kind of plan.

'I have a plan,' she says.

'Does that basket have anything to do with it?' I ask, pointing to the one at her feet.

'That it does.'

'Ah,' I say. 'Let me guess – does it involve the beach, perchance?'

She grins. 'Well, darling, if Mohammed won't go to the mountain… we'll just have to drag him there.'

'But I'm almost finished with the letters.'

She narrows her eyes. 'Your eyes are red. Have you been crying?'

I hang my head.

'How far did you get?' she says, referring to the letters that I'd been transcribing.

'Just after she was diagnosed.'

'Right – well then we definitely need to get out. I mean, darling, if only so that when someone asks you what it was like living with a travel writer and helping her compile her memoirs, you can say that you saw more than the inside of her garden flat.'

'Ah, I see – so what you're saying is that if I don't get out and see the island a little… you will look bad?'

'Yes. Glad we cleared that up. Hopefully you'll make more of an effort in that department now that you know my reputation is at stake here?'

'Yes, I see, it certainly puts it into perspective.' I hit 'save', and say, 'Okay, I'll go.'

She narrows her eyes. 'Good, I'm coming with you.'

I look at her in astonishment.

But she just challenges me with her eyes. 'Do I need to re-mind you of what happened the last time you said you were going to the beach?'

I shake my head. Good point. It's how I'd got myself into this mess.

'Look,' says Caroline, 'I just wouldn't forgive myself if you came all this way to Crete and you didn't even see Elafonisi.'

I look at her, thinking of the perfect white beach that goes on for miles, aquamarine lagoon as far as the eye can see. It does sound rather wonderful.

'You're right. I've been wanting to see that. Let me get my things.'

'Meet you by the car,' she says, her smile wide.

I slip on my bathing costume – the one I'd bought in Chania when I first arrived. It's a one-piece with blue and white stripes that go over just one shoulder. It's the first time I'll be wear-ing it. I pull on a pair of shorts and a T-shirt, and throw my towel in my beach bag. I stop at the desk, wondering if I should bring some of my research with me but decide against it. I pick up *Sense and Sensibility* instead. You're never alone when you're with Jane.

An hour later, we're lying on our beach towels.

'Hit me,' Caroline says.

'You're sure?'

'I can handle it.'

So I read her the part where Colonel Brandon tells Elinor the dark truth behind Willoughby and the mistress he abandoned.

Caroline pauses, drawing circles in the sand. 'Poor Marianne – dodged a bullet there in the end... Again!'

I grin. 'The "Edward is not married" scene?'

'Please.'

I oblige. I need very little encouragement. Shameless.

We pause over the long scene where Elinor, the straight-laced, sensible Elinor, finally comes undone on hearing in a fabulous twist that Edward, who had been trapped in an engagement to a woman he didn't love, didn't in fact marry Lucy Steele. And that when she'd learned that a Mr Ferrars had married Lucy Steele, it was actually his brother who had done the deed.

Caroline sighs in satisfaction. 'Perfect twist... even I didn't see it coming.'

I agree. 'When you first start reading it, you swear the passionate story is about Marianne and Willoughby, but it's the repressed love between Elinor and Edward that is so moving.'

'I'm ashamed of myself for not giving Jane more of a chance, that I've taken this long to discover her.'

'You've been making up for it, though – you've read them all in a month!' I exclaim. It had come as a surprise to me one evening to find that Caroline had never read Jane Austen before. She'd come into the cottage to drop off a batch of olive tapenade to my delight, and had spotted my beaten-up copy of *Sense and Sensibility* on the kitchen table. I'd had it since I was sixteen. Whenever I feel a bit low, I pull it out of my bag, its ever-ready resting place, and read a line or two. It always offers a bit of comfort.

'Austen?' she'd asked, making a face.

Which had the unintended effect that we spent the next three hours in a hot debate. It soon came to light that Caroline, despite growing up in the Lake District, had somehow managed to avoid reading any of her books. She told me that she wouldn't read Austen on principle.

I argued, how could she have a principle against something she'd never tried?

She riposted that she didn't need to try laughter yoga to know that it sounded a bit daft and disrespectful.

I countered with just two words. 'Mr Darcy.'

I had her. It is a truth universally acknowledged that Mr Darcy is one of the most iconic male characters to come out of English literature. To deny Austen is to deny Darcy.

Caroline conceded. I was rather pleased, if a little startled, to find her knocking at my door at three in the morning with red-rimmed, yet opened eyes. A true and complete convert. Caroline then read everything Austen ever wrote in record time, chastising herself for her misplaced snobbery.

She slathers on some more sunscreen and says, 'Yes, but see – you've had a lifetime of loving them.'

'Well, I was lucky. I discovered Jane before I discovered Charlotte, see.'

'You were lucky,' she agrees.

The Charlotte in question being Charlotte Brontë, who rather famously disliked Austen's work. To love Charlotte, one often felt one must dislike Jane. Personally I love them both, in the way the night could appreciate the day; both please the senses but for different reasons.

'So which is your favourite?' I ask. 'Don't say *Pride and Prejudice*,' I warn.

She looks pained. I roll my eyes. 'It is *Pride and Prejudice*?'

She sighs in mock anguish. 'Such a cliché. I know. But—'

'Darcy?'

'Darcy,' she agrees. 'I mean, Darcy is such a, well—'

'A man?'

'Yes.'

He was that, no arguing there.

Then, just for a second, I wonder what type of man Tom is – an Edward, someone repressed, gentlemanly, ready to do the right thing? Or a Darcy, not afraid to defy everyone, including himself, and go after what he really wants?

I hide a grin: no question, Darcy definitely.

I spend an eternity in the water, floating on my back as I contemplate the pure duck egg blue sky, my mind curiously and wondrously free. When my thoughts turn to Chris and Yaya, it isn't with the usual accompaniment of pain. It was good to get away.

Later we lunch on the beach. I dip a wedge of pita in houmous, drizzle lemon juice over it and set a garlic-infused beef kofta strip on top, and pop the concoction into my mouth, groaning in bliss as the tang of the lemon combining with the salt of the beef hits my tongue.

'It's so good,' I moan, reaching for another. 'Last meal definitely.'

'I'm partly sure I moved here because of the food,' she agrees.

She tops up my wine glass. 'That, and that no one thinks it odd when you drink wine on the beach.'

'Or are semi-nude,' I say.

'Or that,' nods Caroline, casting a glance at a pair of nubile ladies lounging topless nearby.

Afterwards we walk the endless stretch of beach together, my sandals swinging in my hand, in that comfortably relaxed state that only a combination of good wine, company and sun can achieve. We stroll past a five-star resort, with its beach restaurant spilling over the white sand, complete with blue-and-white umbrellas.

Caroline sees them before I do.

She's sitting with her face in profile, long dark curls tumbling down her back.

Iliana Kirosa in the flesh.

Next to her is Tony, dressed in a dark grey suit. His face trained on Caroline and me, his expression hardly welcoming. It's too late to turn back. Caroline, with her usual poise, greets them graciously, shaking hands all round.

'So wonderful to see you again, Caroline,' says Iliana in a warm molten voice, the result, no doubt, of years of gratuitous oiling.

'Tony.'

'Caroline,' says Tony with a thin smile, which grows even thinner when he notices me, and recognition blooms.

Caroline introduces me as her assistant, 'and journalist – Ria Laburinthos.'

Tony's eyes snap to attention. His expression darkens as he considers me.

Iliana says, 'Speaking of journalists… we read such a lovely story about you the other day in the *Eudaimonia*, about your new book.'

Caroline smiles. 'Thanks so much, it was a lovely piece. In fact, it was Ria who wrote it, she's a freelance writer for *Eudaimonia*.'

'That must be interesting work,' says Iliana politely.

'Very.' Then rather recklessly, I say, 'Speaking of interesting work... I'm writing an article on Elysium.' This comes as a surprise to everyone, including me.

Iliana looks sharply from me to Tony. His face hardens. 'So that is why you were there,' he says flatly.

Iliana frowns, and Tony explains. 'I went there to speak to him about his... ridiculous plans to resurrect the old farm and things got a little heated.'

I raise an eyebrow. 'A little heated?'

Tony glares at me.

Iliana doesn't say anything about the incident, she just gives me a thin smile and says, 'What is your article about?'

I almost tell her the truth. Almost. But thankfully common sense intervenes. It wouldn't do to raise her suspicions, particularly since she has so many connections. Nigel is a man of honour. But I'm no stranger to the politics of the media world – it would be ill-advised at best to give her any qualms. So I reply, 'The new harvest – how the farm is doing now.'

Tony waves his hand dismissively. 'You'd do better to forget all about it – save yourself the trouble. That bastard knows less about making wine than he does about farming potatoes.'

'Tony,' admonishes Caroline.

Tony scoffs. 'It's true. After everything that he did, to come back and start over with those African grapes and dare to call it "Elysium", it's an embarrassment. Frankly, Ms Laburinthos, I wouldn't waste my time.'

I feel a sudden sharp sting of anger that I can't suppress. 'I'm surprised that you would feel that way about the Pinotage – I was under the impression that this was always something your father wished to try himself. In resurrecting the vineyard, Tom decided to plant it as a tribute to him,' I say, knowing that I risk his wrath, but I can't help myself. He's wrong, it's anything but an embarrassment.

Tony stands up quickly, his hands balled into fists. 'That's what he told you? That he was – fulfilling some dream of my father's?' He takes a step towards me, his eyes black and full of rage. 'No, Miss Laburinthos, quite the opposite – he killed my father's dream, when he killed my father,' he hisses. 'That's the story you should really do – why this arsonist bastard is not behind bars, and how it is possible that he dared show his face here and actually think that he could "resurrect" the thing he destroyed.'

Iliana pulls him away. 'Tony – enough.'

But Tony is unmoved. He tears himself away and storms back towards the hotel.

Iliana watches him go and turns back to us. She's oddly calm. 'I would appreciate this not going any further than among the three of us.' She gives me a pointed look. 'I'm afraid that Tony has still not come to terms with what happened… he still blames Tom, even now… I'm sure you can understand.'

There's something in the way she says it that makes me wonder. 'You don't?' I ask.

She gives me a searching look. 'I don't what?'

'Blame Tom?' I ask.

She stands up, her lip curling slightly. 'I must be going as well, it was good to see you again, Caroline.' She turns to leave but then looks back at me, her eyes sharp, the polite veneer suspended. 'My family and our discussion here today is not to be used in your story, I hope I have made that clear,' she says in the manner of someone who is well used to issuing orders and expecting them to be obeyed. She walks away without another backward glance.

The next morning Tom arrives to take me to the farmers' market. When he smiles at me, I get inside his car feeling like a swarm of bees have taken up residence in my stomach.

It doesn't help that at every turn I seem to be getting pulled further into his life. Our friendship certainly complicates things... especially with me researching the fire. Though I can't help wondering if that's all that it is.

Luckily Caroline isn't here this morning. While I know she'd love to see him, I'm not ready to expose our friendship to the light. I enjoy his company, his passion for what he's trying to do. It doesn't need to be more than that.

'You okay?' he asks.

Oh god, was he speaking to me? I blush. 'Oh yes, sorry, mind was somewhere else.'

He laughs. 'Thought that was just me.'

'What?' I ask, confused, as we head towards the centre of the village, driving past the coastal road, the ocean a deep electric blue, the mountain pass full of the colours of spring and the scent of wild herbs. It's another beautiful day in Ouranó.

'Well, everyone is always accusing me of being somewhere else. I'll start thinking about the vineyard, what needs to get done, that sort of thing, and check out without realising it, can't seem to help it sometimes.'

I laughed. 'Oh! I do it too... My mum always said that she knew I was going to be a writer because one minute I'd be there, the next, *poof!* gone... making up more adventures about the rabbit who lived next door. He solved crimes, you see.'

He grins. 'Really?'

'Yes, I had a whole serial going, which I illustrated myself. Christmas presents for friends and family.'

He looks amused, 'How old were you?'

'Seven, though the rabbit's adventures continued until I was at least nine.'

He laughs. 'Do you still write stories?'

I shake my head. 'Only non-fiction ones now, but, you know, so often truth is stranger than fiction.'

'That's true,' he agrees. 'I can only imagine the stories you must have heard writing obituaries.'

'You have no idea.' I amused us both by telling him some of the rather weird and wonderful stories I'd heard over the years, including one about a circus performer from Poland who was so good at fake accents and imitating others that he was recruited by the British government as a doppelganger for a Nazi officer that they had imprisoned.

'He then went on to be marooned off the coast of German South-West Africa, for two years, when the U-boat he was travelling in was torpedoed, and he became stranded with one of the most influential Nazis in Hitler's army. For two years he pretended he was the officer he was impersonating: even though it was just him and the other Nazi, he never let on who he was.'

'What? And then?'

'He waited till he was on British soil then he told the government all he'd learnt… including, apparently, where Hitler's bunker was.'

'You're joking? That can't be true, can it?'

I laughed. 'Honestly? I don't know. His wife swore that it was. She was the only surviving relative. Only she was living in a home and had been diagnosed with dementia, so I suspected not, but then a little while later I came across an old newspaper article in the forties that spoke of a young Polish man who'd been marooned in German South-West Africa, along with a Nazi officer who was taken as a prisoner of war. So who knows? Maybe it was true. Of course, Janice, my boss refused to run it…'

'Wow,' he says, 'Imagine if it was true. How did you find that article, the one about the marooned officer, that must have been pretty hard?'

I shrugged. 'I'm good at finding things.'

He gives me a strange look then, and I feel a sudden trickle of apprehension, hoping he doesn't suspect that I've been looking into his life. But it's just my guilty conscience because the next thing he says, 'That's brilliant, I'm really impressed.'

We pull up at the town centre, which is buzzing with people. There are so many cars, which I'm surprised at. 'Where are all these people from?'

'From the neighbouring villages, Chania town… people come from miles around to this market.'

In a minute I see why. Everywhere I look are stalls full to bursting with some of the most tempting morsels on offer: fat juicy olives, sun-ripened tomatoes glistening in oil, farm fresh cheeses so wispy and soft they look like little white crested clouds. There's Greek lamb on spits. Houmous. Pita. Then there's the bread, every kind imaginable: golden ciabatta that perfumes the air with its scent and the sound of its perfect crunch; sourdough; baguettes. My mouth starts salivating just looking at them. And that's just the food. There's wine too. Homemade, rich Cretan wine that slips down as easy as water.

Tom and I sample everything, and I come away with fresh cheese, pita bread and some of that gorgeous home-grown wine.

'Traitor,' he tells me, mock serious.

'Well, this has nothing on yours… but I've got to have something to tide me over until my investment matures.'

'Investment?'

'Those three hundred bottles you're making for me.'

'For you?'

'Just about,' I grin.

'Well, okay then, have your home-made wine if you must,' he says shaking his head.

'You like it,' I say, narrowing my eyes at him suspiciously.

'No,'

'Liar,' I tease.

He laughs. 'Okay, you got me. I do. Even though it's not regulated or anything, I love that people here make their own wine in their backyards. I can't help it, I'm half Cretan, it's in the blood.'

I nod, grinning. 'I knew it.'

His eyes crinkle. 'Mmm. Can't seem to keep any secrets from you, can I?'

'Nope,' I tease.

'Tom?'

We both turn. A pretty young woman with long dark hair and deep black eyes is looking at Tom in surprise. Her eyes dart to me, then back at him.

'Maria? Hi, it's… um, nice to see you again,' says Tom.

She just looks at him for a minute, her face tight. 'And you.'

'This is Ria Laburinthos. Ria, this is Maria Kostigavas,' he says introducing us.

'Laburinthos? You don't look Greek,' she says, giving me a somewhat condescending look.

'Just half,' I explain.

She snorts. 'Like him,' she says, her shoulder stabbing in Tom's direction. She eyes us with suspicion, like we're in on some secret felony. Worse, she seems saddened by it, and gives Tom a look full of hurt.

I look away, feeling embarrassed. When she leaves, I ask, 'What was that about?'

Tom looks a bit shamefaced. 'My ex,' he explains.

'Oh?'

'Did not end well.'

'Ah.'

'Long story, but essentially it's the first time I've seen her since we broke up.'

'Sorry,' I say with a grimace, but I don't press him for more information, though of course I want to. We carry on looking at the stalls, but our easy conversation of earlier is gone. When we head back home I can't help wondering at the accusing look Maria had given me, or the inexplicable bubble of guilt I can't help but feel.

TWENTY-TWO

'You have been asking questions about Elysium?' enquires Police Chief Carlos Mino, a man who, despite having his chinos belted just below his armpits, ostensibly to disguise his expanding girth, is a forbidding figure in the late afternoon light. 'About the fire?' he says, black eyes sharp from behind the large wooden desk where he sits. Behind him the open window displays dark clouds that swathe the Lefka Ori mountain range in a pewter mist.

I nod, clenching my hands in my lap to stop me from wringing them, uncomfortable under his penetrating gaze.

I'd wanted to speak to Inspector Pano Stenalis, who ten years before had been the lead inspector on the case, the only person who might be able to shed light on what really happened. But when I'd called at the station, I'd been given the usual run around. Using *Eudaimonia* as an excuse had carried some level of authority, though I couldn't help but wonder if that had been a mistake, as upon my arrival I was directed into the chief of police's office, an unexpected and, I suspected, ominous step in my unauthorised investigation.

'You are doing a story on the harvest, is that correct?' he asks with a frown, leaning forward.

I look up, surprised. He had done his homework. I wonder if that was all it was. 'Yes, though as you can imagine there are many unanswered questions surrounding the story as well. I had hoped to speak to Lead Inspector Stenalis.'

He steeples his hands onto the mahogany desk. 'Questions?' he asks, choosing to ignore my query after Inspector Stenalis. 'Such as?'

'Well... what really happened that night? How the fire started, if any new suspects have come to light?'

'I'm sure this is all a matter of public record, Ms Laburinthos – it was all in the police report that was filed and closed some seven years ago already. Perhaps you haven't had a chance to read it yet?' he says, his eyes narrowing.

I bite down my irritation. Public record? Is he kidding? I'd searched everywhere and the only references I'd found to it were in the *Chaniá Ilio* articles. Rather than risk his ire or mine by pointing out the obvious, I hedge. 'I have – although I'd be happy to see it again.'

'Perhaps, Ms Laburinthos, you were hoping for a translator here at the police department? Someone who can be taken away from their busy work, to sit with you and break down a case that was closed many years ago? You must forgive me, but we are not like the big police departments in London that have the resources and taxpayers' money to sit and have a cup of tea with every person off the street who happens take an interest in our work.'

Wow. My feeling towards Mino went from mere dislike to active hatred in one fell swoop.

I raise my eyebrows, offer him my most mocking smile and speak in admittedly less than perfect, though adequate, Greek. 'I assure you, Mr Mino, I do not need a translator. However, you do have a point, considering the many questions that have sprung up from the report – which, as you have so adroitly pointed out, is a matter of public record. As a journalist who acts on behalf of the public, it is my job to ask those questions. I'll agree as well that in London the police force understand this and takes the time to be civilised about it – if that is what you meant in reference to tea.'

Mino's swollen face seems to swell even further with anger; he turns purple as we glare at each other. After what seems like an eternity, he manages between gritted teeth, 'Well, then how can I help you, Ms Laburinthos?'

'I was hoping to ask Inspector Stenalis a few questions, as some things came to mind after I read the report.'

'I will be happy to answer any questions you have.'

I shrug. I would prefer to speak to Stenalis, but a lead is always better than none, even if it is with a sanctimonious bastard.

'My questions are really about the source who identified Tom Bacchus on the night the fire broke out.'

'The source,' he repeats with a sardonic expression.

'Yes, according to my research it says that a woman identified Tom Bacchus as being near the west barn at just minutes before the fire broke out.'

Mino steeples his hands together again, resting them on his expansive girth while he leans back in his chair. Classic bastard posing. 'That is, of course, a mistake,' he says, rather casually.

I look at him in disbelief and begin searching in my bag to show him a copy of the article, stating the time in black and white. Mino waves a hand for me to stop, opens a document in front of him, flicks through a few pages, and then all but shoves the report under my nose. 'Tom Bacchus was identified on the night of the fire, you are correct, but the source was a Mr Portcullis – the old, now retired wine master for Elysium Wineries.'

I stare at the report, frowning. 'My research indicates that Inspector Stenalis – who I believe was the lead investigator on this case – spoke to a woman who identified Mr Bacchus.'

Mino scoffs. 'Perhaps that is why you have encountered a problem. The lead inspector on this case in the very beginning was Mr Stenalis – you are correct – however when he was transferred to Iraklion, I took over the case. Furthermore, Mr Stenalis never spoke to any witness as far as I know, as it was I who was first on the scene and spoke to Mr Portcullis, whose testimony was thrown out due to lack of evidence, and the case was closed, unresolved.' He looks at me above his steepled fingers. 'How did you come to believe it was a woman?' he asks with a frown.

'From an article in the *Chaniá Ilio*.'

His eyes light up. 'A journalist misreporting the facts – oh la! Well, it wouldn't be the first time – pity, had you gone straight to one of your "representatives of public interest", as you called yourself, you could have saved yourself the bother,' he says with a lazy drawl.

I sigh. Obnoxious as he is, he has a point.

Though I do wonder at it – it seems a really strange mistake to make. While journalists do get their facts wrong sometimes, this is something else – a fabrication, and that's a bold accusation, to be sure.

'Is that all?' he asks, standing up.

I stand. 'Yes. Actually – would it be possible to have a copy of that report?'

'Certainly, I'll ask my secretary to make you a copy before you leave.' And with that he sees me to the door and bids me farewell, with one last jab. 'Ms Laburinthos, let me leave you with a little piece of advice. I don't know what you hope to uncover with this investigation, but the facts speak for themselves – while Mr Bacchus managed to avoid prosecution on a technicality, the case for us was closed. I think while you may wish for something not to be true, based on your emotions, having met the handsome young vineyard owner, and no doubt told yourself some romantic little story, it's always better to look at the cold facts, past the pretty face – if you can.' He gives me a patronising look.

I clench my jaw. Somehow I manage not to commit an act of violence, and choose not to comment on his sexist remark, saying benignly, 'You're right. I think it is always best to examine the facts. All of them.'

The trouble is, I mean it, but just not in the way he imagines as he shuts the door in my face, his smirk firmly in place.

The black clouds that had been threatening all afternoon unleash a torrential downpour as I make my way back to Caroline's car, the last parting shot for the day. I climb inside, the report cradled under my arm, the dark sky creating a blanket of shadows, putting me more in mind of London than Crete, particularly with the surprising icy chill that came with it. I shiver miserably, and switch the heaters on to warm my frozen fingers. The weather, I can't help but notice, accurately symbolises my current mood.

Perhaps if Mino hadn't been so insufferable, I might be ready to let it go. To admit to myself that my investigation has led to a dead end. That one journalist's error – whatever had caused it, an ordinary mistake or a deliberate subterfuge – has ensured that any hope that I have of resolving this mystery is in short supply. But I'm not ready to give up, not yet, even if everything is suggesting that perhaps I should. I've come too far, and discovered so much more of myself along the way, to give up now. Not just that, but there's just no way I'm going to let that smug bastard Mino have the last word on this.

TWENTY-THREE

The heaters don't work, and it takes forever to get home. The lashing rain, combined with the steep mountain path, make for nervous driving, to say the least. That, combined with the chatter of my teeth for company, has resulted in a pounding headache.

When I finally pull into Caroline's driveway, I have one thought and one thought only: warm bath.

Okay, perhaps two thoughts, really: wine and bath.

I park the car and make a dash for my cottage, opening the door to its warm, inviting interior with audible relief.

I've just pulled my soaking wet T-shirt over my head when a knock at my door causes me to moan in frustration.

If it wasn't raining, I would just ignore my visitor, who was no doubt Caroline, feeling concerned about my welfare.

I groan. Couldn't she have waited just half an hour? Half an hour and I'd be warm and toasty and numb from wine instead of cold.

With heavy heart and heavy feet, I open the door, only to have my heart lurch into my throat.

It isn't Caroline.

'Hi.'

'Um, hi,' I say in surprise.

'You're wet,' says Tom, his blue eyes laced with concern. For some strange reason he is standing outside my cottage door, looking ridiculously handsome in a pair of dark blue jeans and a navy V-neck sweater, while stating the obvious.

'Well, it tends to happen when you get caught in the rain,' I manage to quip, despite the fluttery feeling that has taken hold of my stomach.

His eyes are unfathomable. 'Of course. I was just at Caroline's. I came by to see her, and I didn't want to leave without saying hello.'

He wanted to come say hello. I blink, feeling rather touched by the unexpected warmth on such a cold day. 'That was kind of you.'

He smiles.

Good lord, that smile again.

'Would you like to come in?' I offer, knowing that he's probably just being polite, but to my dismay, he says, 'Why not?'

As I move aside, watching him fill my little cottage with his foreign maleness, I can think of a few choice reasons. Namely the fact that I look like a drowned rat, and that my little cottage looks a lot like some dodgy private investigator's office, my desk littered with all my research. Research that has everything to do with him and his family, which I'd have a hard time explaining. The word 'stalker' involuntarily pops into my brain and I find, to my utter horror, that I'm blushing.

I make my way surreptitiously to the desk to straighten my work, hiding my face, and shove everything in the drawer, grateful that most of my research was sitting in the beach bag by my bed.

'Would you like some coffee?' I ask, teeth chattering slightly from the cold.

'Tell you what, why don't you have a shower and get into some warm clothes and I'll make us a coffee – I'm sure I can find everything in there,' he says, pointing to my small kitchen.

'Thanks,' I say with a wide, grateful smile.

'Don't mention it – I feel the need for some real coffee after Caroline's weak British slop.'

'Well, then we're a pair – apparently I make the worst coffee this side of Christendom.'

'Well, to be fair, you probably do.'

'Hey!' I say in mock outrage.

'It's not your fault, you're Greek.'

'So are you,' I say, pointing out the obvious.

'Half. That is how I can acknowledge this weakness that I share as well,' he says with a grin.

I'm still giggling when I close the bathroom door and start the shower.

There's something oddly comforting yet unnerving at the same time about having him here in my private space, especially as I had spent countless hours over the past few weeks wondering about him and what happened. To have him actually here in the flesh was more than a little strange.

I take a super fast shower – so much for my leisurely wine-fuelled soak – and pull on a pair of jeans and a jersey – my wardrobe, limited as it is, doesn't run into the 'what to wear in case strange and ridiculously handsome men come over unexpectedly' category.

That's probably for the best.

I towel-dry my hair and give it a quick comb, screwing it into a messy topknot out of the way. I hesitate for just a second by the bathroom mirror, looking at my pale skin and dark eyes before I give in and apply a coat of mascara, some blusher and a dash of a plum-coloured lipstick.

When I come out, Tom is sitting at the small kitchen table, his long denim-clad legs and Converse trainers stretched out in front of him. To my surprise, he's reading Caroline's article.

I hesitate, knowing that it references his mother; it couldn't be easy reading about her.

He looks up when I come in, setting the paper down. 'Your coffee is over here,' he says, handing me a mug.

'Thanks,' I say, taking a seat opposite him.

'Is that why you came – to Caroline's, I mean,' I say, indicating the paper.

'It was a good excuse, really,' he says truthfully.

I frown. 'Did you need an excuse?'

'I suppose not. But it's been years… and I left quite suddenly.'

'I'm sure she understood.'

'Did she? I suppose she may have. Still it wasn't right… to just leave.'

He's looking at the paper, and I feel like I can read his thoughts. 'Your mother wouldn't have approved?'

He gives a small smile, his eyes sad. 'No, probably not. You did a good job,' he says, pointing to the article, from the paper that is open on the desk, where a picture of the two women as young girls accompanies the piece.

'Well, from everything I've come to learn about her, I think she would have understood the need to get away more than anyone,' I say, thinking of the woman with wanderlust in her heart.

'Of course you're right. I suppose I'd forgotten that – seeing her only as my mother, especially in the end when she got sick. I'd forgotten that she'd lived another life… To be honest, it was a wonderful reminder.'

I can imagine. I tell him about Yaya, and how hard her death had been for me, and yet how wonderful it is to be reminded of her here in the place that had made her who she was.

When the rain stops, we open up a bottle of wine and sit companionably on the little step outside, the open door inviting in the scent of rain-washed olives, lavender and thyme.

I breathe it in. 'When I was little, Yaya would tell me that Crete had this incredible scent, but it was hard to imagine it where I grew up, which mostly just smelt of rain, wet earth and the country. Not a bad smell, to be sure, but not a herbal bouquet like this.'

'I know. I missed it when I was away.'

'Where did you go?' I ask.

'Everywhere, I suppose. London at first, then Oxford to study.'

'Oxford?' I ask, curious. Although a part of me isn't completely surprised, really. He had that refined something about him that many Oxford men seem to have, like they'd come out of another era – elegant was probably the word. But masculine too. It was rather a killer combo. But then I'd always been attracted to the intellectual type. Christopher used to love teasing me, knowing that few things could charm me quite like him explaining a complex algorithm. It was a rather weird fetish, I admit.

'What did you study?'

'Microbiology.'

'Really?'

'Yes, but I couldn't see myself doing it.'

Neither can I. I can't picture him stuck inside a lab.

'But I stuck it out – and afterwards I spent a rather degenerate year in Paris, reading French philosophy at the Sorbonne, followed by several even more degenerate years travelling the world. I'd always end up by a vineyard, though. Couldn't seem to keep away. Napa, Australia, Spain, France... At some point

I realised that it's where I belonged, and when I wound up in Cape Town I decided to stop running from it, put my life on track and did a degree in oenology and viticulture.'

'Wow,' I say. 'So… degenerate years?' I'm intrigued.

'Very,' he says mysteriously.

'What exactly defines a degenerate year?' I press.

He rubs his face, almost bashfully. 'Well, the usual I suppose. Drinking heavily, never sticking around the same place twice, parties, recreational drug use…'

'Women?' I tease, though with his looks I know what the answer will be, and as soon as I say it I wish I hadn't. I don't want to know. Even though I have no right to feel that way.

His face turns serious. 'Yes.' His eyes have that haunted look again. 'I'm not like that any more… and even then, it wasn't really me,' he says, putting his hand on my thigh.

The small, intimate action makes me flinch involuntarily. Tom looks at me intently.

My heart starts to thrash against my chest, the rushing sound in my ears so loud it's deafening.

'I hope this doesn't change what you think of me.'

I shake my head, but can't speak. His hand is still on my thigh, he starts to lean over and I panic.

'Ria?' he asks in concern, when I start trembling. I shoot up, away from his touch. My breathing is sharp, edged with pain. 'I'm sorry,' I say, feeling the hot tears form. 'It's just—'

He stands too, his face serious. 'It was a long time ago, I promise.'

I swallow what feels like glass. 'It's not that, Tom, truly—'

It's true, it isn't; it's everything in between, all the things that I haven't yet told him. About why I'm really here, and about Christopher. How do I even begin? How can I tell him, and not have him look at me the way I'd been looked at now for two years? I'm tired of people's pitying looks, the way their eyes skim past mine – the way people do when they've seen a car wreck. I don't want that. Not from Tom.

My chin starts to wobble and I look down. 'It's not you, I'm just not… ready.' As soon as I say it, though, I wish I could take it back. I know he won't understand.

'Right,' he says, his face impassive. 'Well, I'll see you,' he says, turning to leave.

'Tom,' I say, 'I need to explain – it's really not you.'

'It's okay,' he says with a tight smile. 'It's nothing, let's just forget about it.' He looks at me, his face softening when he sees my naked despair. 'We can be friends, if that's what you want,' he says, and steps out into the night before I can protest.

I watch him leave with a mounting sense of loss, my throat constricting over the words that I just can't say. I don't know why I reacted the way I did, why his touch had made me panic the way it had. It wasn't Christopher, or if it was, I didn't want it to be. All I know is that Tom was wrong; it isn't okay, and it isn't nothing, not even close.

TWENTY-FOUR

Twenty minutes. That's all it took to change my fate. While I'm no stranger to the way life can turn on a dime, even I'm amazed at how easy it was to track down Xena Alberos, the journalist from the *Chaniá Ilio*. The internet is a marvellous thing. As are newspapers that list their staff on their Contact Us page. For there she is in black and white, a grainy picture highlighting her serious, dark-eyed gaze, below which is her direct telephone line, and the fact that she's now the paper's managing editor.

I note the change of title with some interest, hoping that it will play in my favour.

When she answers with a short clipped bark that announces 'Alberos', I start with my usual brand of polite enquiry, letting her know that I'm writing an article on Elysium, and the new harvest, asking her anything she may recall about the fire that occurred there ten years before, and if she wouldn't mind discussing it with me.

Politely, but with an edge of impatience she doesn't bother to disguise, she lets me know that the articles are available to purchase on the website or can be accessed for free through the public library. And while she's sorry, she really doesn't have the time to sit and discuss a story from ten years ago, as she has a paper to get out.

I wonder if I'm dealing with someone from the same school of stinging fish as the likes of Kimberley, so mentally I roll up my sleeves and change tack. 'I have read them, which is why I am phoning.'

'There is nothing more I wish to say on the subject other than what was put in the paper,' Alberos interjects. 'I'm sorry, but I really do not have the time.'

Something within me snaps. 'Ms Alberos, it's funny that you mention time – I suppose you were saving time when you mis-reported the facts?'

'I – w-what!' she splutters in outrage.

'Precisely, what indeed. Perhaps you'd care to explain, as on the second of March 2005 you reported that a woman identified Tom Bacchus to Lead Inspector Pano Stenalis of the Chania metropolitan police as being near the west barn minutes before the fire broke out.'

'That is correct,' says Alberos.

'Is it? Well, not according to the police report, it's not. You see my predicament?'

A deep sigh follows. 'Ms—?'

'Laburinthos,' I supply.

'Ms Laburinthos, I don't appreciate your allegation, particularly as it is easily proven false – not only by the report in question but by Stenalis' testimony as well, all of which I have on file. We at the *Chaniá Ilio* are not like you tabloid journalists making up celebrity gossip for the purposes of entertainment.'

I choose to ignore that dig. 'The report in question, Ms Alberos, states that the lead inspector for the case was, in fact, Chief of Police Carlos Mino, who identified the source as a Mr Portcullis, the wine master for Elysium.'

'Impossible,' she flares.

'I have it here in black and white.'

'That I doubt. Mr Portcullis could not have identified Tom Bacchus that night, I can assure you.'

'How can you be so sure?' I ask.

'Because,' she breathes out in a huff, 'he died the day before.'

My head reels in mute shock, but Xena Alberos continues regardless. 'So unless it was a ghost who gave testimony, it could never have been Mr Portcullis.'

'He died?' I repeat dumbly. 'But how would you know that?' I ask, puzzled.

An annoyed sigh. 'He was my uncle.'

'Oh!'

'Who told you it was him?' demands Alberos.

'The chief of police himself. It's also in the report he filed.'

A long silence follows. 'I'd like a copy of that report,' she demands.

Not so fast, I thought. She isn't scooping me on this story, not now. 'First, if you don't mind, can I have a copy of yours, as well as the testimony from Inspector Stenalis?'

Perhaps she got the hint because a minute later they're sitting in my inbox, as well as a friendly piece of advice: Tread carefully, call if you need me.

This unforeseen vote of confidence is followed by two mobile phone numbers – hers and, to my surprise, that of Inspector Stenalis.

TWENTY-FIVE

I don't know why I'm doing this. That's a lie. I do know, I'd known since the night he'd come to my cottage that I'd probably end up doing something like this.

Something stupid, something I'll regret and wish to God I could go back in time to change. Something that even years later will end up making me cringe. I suspect even when I'm an old lady and I have Alzheimer's... even then I'll probably still remember this, and want to curl up and die.

Because the worst part of it is that I've spent most of Sunday morning preparing for it. From the freshly baked bread to the sun-ripened tomatoes straight from the farmers' market, and the lemon cake I made to the hand-picked bottle of summer's most perfect rosé.

I'm even wearing a dress. The new yellow and grey sundress that I bought when I first arrived.

I've been humming to myself all morning, packing the basket, excitement bubbling in my stomach, choosing at the last minute to take Caroline's car instead of my bicycle, as I don't relish the idea of getting caught in another thunderstorm on my way home.

Perhaps I should have called. Or at least texted. But I wouldn't know how to start.

Yaya had always said that actions spoke louder than words, and in this case I'm taking her advice to heart.

It occurs to me as I drive, the window rolled down, the picnic basket with its blue-checked cloth on the seat beside me (courtesy of Caroline's kitchen – she uses it for the eggs), that there is a possibility that he isn't home.

He could have gone out for dinner or met a friend. It's Sunday afternoon after all.

But I don't think so. Call it intuition, or whatever, but I know he'll be there.

I don't know what I plan to say. 'Sorry' seems a good place to start. At the very least, I owe him some explanation for what happened the other night.

To let him know why I'd reacted the way I had because I know that he probably thought it was because of his past. That I didn't trust that he'd changed. But I did. I understand, perhaps more than anyone, what grief can do, how it can rip you up and tear you apart and make you do things you'd never normally do.

I know as I drive in, the vineyard's blue doors standing wide, the afternoon bathing the sky in pink magenta, the faint sparkle of the sea in the distance, that he has changed.

How wrong I am.

I park the car at the back of the farmhouse, swallowing my fear as I head towards the house, the basket slung over my arm, cheered to see that there are lights on in the kitchen window.

As I near, I see them.

A young woman, whose lithe curves are poured into a pair of skinny jeans, her long flowing black hair cascading down her back. Tom is standing framed in the light of the kitchen, when she pulls his face towards her and kisses him. He pulls away and places a hand on her shoulder.

I stand, rooted to the spot.

It's Maria. The woman he'd told me was his ex.

Perhaps it's the sound of my own heart plummeting but they both turn to look at me. Tom's face looks stricken.

I feel ill, take a step forward, a bitter smile in place, wondering if I have it in me to pretend that I'm here for some other reason.

But when he moves, my heart starts to thrash, panic overtakes me. I shake my head wildly and flee, jumping into my car and reversing as quickly as possible down the drive, my humiliation dark and suffocating in my throat.

I don't go home.

Somehow I just can't. Instead I drive down towards the sea road, in fear that he'll come looking for me at Caroline's and try to explain. What had he to explain anyway? Nothing had happened between us. And the other night, well, that could have been anything. Though he did say she was his ex. Still, he had a right to change his mind. It's not like there was anything between us. Hadn't I made that clear?

Still, perhaps I shouldn't be surprised. The angry blush on my cheeks tells me that I should never have trusted him at his word. When someone has had a past like he did, what was I expecting? I'd got caught up in his sad story and beautiful, haunted eyes.

I was a fool.

And the worst part of it is that I can't blame him.

Not really. We hadn't made any promises to one another. I'd read more into the other night than there was.

I park my car along the road and head down towards a deserted-looking beach, taking along the bottle of wine for company. I pass a lively tavern filled with people enjoying the last of the sun, my head down, hoping to pass by them as quickly as I can, feeling more alone than I had since I came to Crete.

I breathe easier on the beach, walking along the sand, away from everything.

I don't know what I feel.

Beyond the shame and dismay over what I'd done. It was all so new, not just because it was the first time in years I'd felt something or what could have been something for someone else. Or that it was the first time in two years I'd really felt something other than being trapped in a torturous waiting room, in the cycle of work and home and hardly being able to bear my life.

And yet here I am, feeling sorry for myself over some man.

If I didn't feel so ridiculously sorry for myself, I'd laugh.

The thing is, I've never really experienced this before. Christopher and I had met on my first day at King's College, I was running late for my first philosophy lecture, going in circles trying to find room number 7686B.

I'd walked the length of the corridor and back, and kept passing a rather tall guy with dark blond hair, big green eyes and a wry smile leaning against the wall, a pair of blue Nike trainers crossed at the ankles.

'You won't find it,' he'd said.

I'd looked at him with a raised brow, hot and bothered from my trek across the campus.

'What?'

'Room 7686B.'

I looked at him. 'Why not?' I'd asked, partly wondering if this was part of the programme, some weird philosophical test that, to be honest, I was in no mood for.

'Well, look,' he said pointing at the room in front. I read the number by the door, 7686A, and next to it, room 7687.

'If it did exist it would be somewhere there,' he said, pointing to the black wall between the lecture rooms. 'And, unless we find Hagrid, I'm not sure how we'll get in.'

'Hagrid?' I asked, then slowly started to laugh. 'Oh! You mean like Diagon Alley?'

He winked.

For a second I was tempted to tap on the third brick.

'Do you think it was just a typo?' I asked, looking at the closed door belonging to 7686A.

'Probably.'

'Should we go in?'

He shook his head, green eyes dancing. 'I was thinking… maybe it's a sign.'

'A sign,' I said, my hand perched over the handle. 'Like what?' I shifted my heavy textbook-laden bag over my shoulder.

'That we're meant to be somewhere else.'

I looked at him in confusion. 'Like where?'

'I dunno, like… in a coffeehouse. Like that one over there.' He pointed casually to the window opposite, which showed the sweeping library lawns outside and the students' café across the street.

I brushed my hair out of my face, and said, 'Well, you know… if it really is a sign, then I think we must.'

He smiled, green eyes alight. 'Oh, it's definitely a sign.' And he crooked his elbow out for me to follow.

We never did find classroom 7686B. But we did find love, and from then on we were rather inseparable. Best friend, class clown, boyfriend. It had been so easy with Chris. I never had to worry if he'd phone or where our relationship was going because the answer was yes and everywhere.

Falling in love with Chris was easy, he was like a big shaggy Labrador, the life of the party, the one everyone wanted to be around, like flowers turned towards the sun.

His presence brought out the best in everyone. From my somewhat crotchety mother to Yaya, who was known to give a girlish giggle every time he asked for a little more moussaka, or when he decided to also call me *meli mou* like she did, to my feigned annoyance. Even my rather scary roommate Dorothea, with her pencil-straight black hair, who was studying applied mathematics and muttered equations in her sleep in the manner of something out of *The Exorcist*, who you were never ever permitted to call anything other than Dorothea, liked Chris. She even permitted him to call her Dorrit – the only one who dared. I tried it once and thought that my head might explode from her scathing look.

But she adored Chris, despite his inferior studies as a robotics engineer; she dismissed it as gaming, which to Chris was more of a compliment than anything else. Their friendship was built to last from the very start when he agreed with her that the Jordan Curve Theorem was indeed obvious.

When she didn't see his suede jacket (don't ask) slung over the back of my desk chair, her face would droop more than usual, and I'd have to break the news to her gently that he was pulling an all-nighter at the library for an exam.

She'd flush, ever so slightly, her corpse-like pallor coming to life. 'Well… good, then I can get some work done for a change.'

But I knew she never meant it.

'He'll be back tomorrow – he said he needed to unwind, he's going to bring along some light reading along the lines of the Kepler conjecture.'

She hid a grin. 'Whatever,' she said, but I could tell from her small, pleased smile that she was glad.

I'm not sure if she was in love with him, it was hard to know with Dorrit, but by the end of that year, we were all three friends. She was even a bridesmaid… or would have been.

I close my eyes for a second, thinking of Dorrit. She'd taken it badly. Very badly.

Poor Dorrit.

I open the bottle of wine, take a sip and watch the surf crash.

Wishing, rather insanely, that Christopher was here, so that I could ask him about all this.

But of course if he was I wouldn't be in this mess.

TWENTY-SIX

'You climbed Mt Kilimanjaro?' I exclaim in awe, looking at the picture of Caroline at the summit, her smile brilliant, dressed in a rather lurid neon pink and yellow parka with a fur-trimmed collar and, rather true to form, a glass of champagne in her hand.

'Darling… it was the eighties, everyone was doing it.'

'And the champagne?' I ask curiously.

'A bad idea at that altitude, it was just sparkling apple juice. Champagne, like Paris, is always a good idea, unless you're climbing a mountain. We must remember to put that into The Book,' she says with a wink.

I look at the pile of notes and half-written bits of manuscript scattered across the writing den. 'Yes, just in case anyone else decides that's a good idea. Important to get the word out,' I say, my face deadpan.

She pops a grape into her mouth. 'Precisely.'

Progress on The Book had been made over the last two weeks and it looked like we'd be on track to finish it before the end of the year.

Still, even now I'm finding out things about Caroline that I never thought I would.

Like the fact that she took a year off to follow the migration of a herd of elephants – her favourite animals, apparently – across the Savannah, and that she narrated the series for the BBC.

'Wow, our very own David Attenborough,' I'd said.

'Ah, yes, a dear, dear friend.'

Well, of course he was.

After the Tom debacle I'd thrown myself into my work, grateful for any distraction. I couldn't have looked for it in a better place.

Like the other day when I found the letter from Oprah. We were listening to Louis Armstrong sing 'Blueberry Hill' on one of her (signed) and original LPs. Yes.

'You're friends with Oprah?' I'd said, flabbergasted.

'Don't be silly. My God, it's Oprah…' she'd scoffed, which I thought was rather sweet and a little funny, as Caroline seemed to be friends with, well, everyone. But even I had to agree… I mean… Oprah.

'May I?' I'd asked, looking at the letter, addressed in Oprah's own hand.

'Of course.'

When I was done, I closed it reverentially. 'Beautiful.'

'I know.'

'So she picked your book for her book club and made it one of the books of the month? What was that like?'

'Like the moment Edward finally tells Elinor that he's not in fact married… and he's up for it if she is.'

I snort. 'Ah, though I'm pretty sure he never said it like that.'

'Not the way I read it,' she says, with a lascivious wink, so I laugh.

Afterwards I'd wondered if we should share the letter in the memoir, then agreed that something this treasured would only remain so if we didn't.

'Speaking of amazing,' says Caroline, proffering me some dolmades and calamari, which I took from our floor picnic eagerly. I tried not to think of the last time I'd planned a picnic, though perhaps Caroline read my mind. 'Young Tom came around here again last night, I think he rather hoped that you'd be here, but once again he left disappointed.'

I sigh. It was the third time he'd come. I'd have to give him credit for his persistence.

I bite my lip. 'It's… arggh! I just can't see him, not yet.'

Maybe after a year or so… when I've forgotten how stupid I'd been and what an idiot I must have looked running away.

'Darling, that's what I told him.'

My face pales. 'What – what did you say, exactly?' I demand.

'Nothing… just that maybe you needed to cool down.'

'Argghhh!' I groan, stuffing my face into the nearest pillow. 'Caroline!' I gasp, peering at her with one eye above my pillow.

'What?' she asks, with an air of studied innocence.

'You were meant to say I'd gone out! Anything, anything else but that.' I squirm uncomfortably. I'd overreacted about seeing him kiss someone else, when we weren't even together, and now he thought I needed to … calm down. God, what a bloody nightmare.

She smiles devilishly. 'I knew it!'

'Knew what?' I ask.

'Something happened between you! What was it?' she asks. For the third time this week.

'I don't want to—'

'–talk about it… I know, I know. But you're forgetting one very important thing.'

'Which is?'

'I'm DYING to know. Plus, darling, you know, I'm old, it's not good for my health. What if I died in my sleep and you never let me know? I couldn't let you do that to yourself, your conscience would positively eat you alive. Really, I'm just thinking of you.'

I chuckle, giving her an exasperated smile. 'So you're only thinking of my moral welfare, is it?'

She looks at me with amused eyes. 'Yes.' Then. 'Did you kiss?'

'No!'

'Oh?'

'Well… almost.'

'Oh!'

'But then I started crying.'

'Oh.'

'Will you stop saying "oh" like that!' I exclaim.

'O–kay,' she says. 'But darling, why are you avoiding him then – did he not understand?'

I shake my head, and put my face in my hands, cringing as I remember. 'No, it wasn't that. I haven't really told him about it, and it was just a surprise when he… although he might not have actually been trying to kiss me, I jumped up so fast.' I swallow, the sudden awful thought making me grow pale – God, how much worse could it get?

'No, he was,' assures Caroline.

I look at her, my heart pounding, 'How do you know – did he say something?'

'No, not about what happened, but I just know.'

I'm not so sure.

'But that's not that bad – you should go speak to him, let him know about Christopher, and that maybe you could start as friends?'

I shake my head. 'Tried that. Let's just say it didn't go so well.'

'Oh?'

'He was—' I am about to explain about the woman I'd seen him with, Maria, his so-called ex, about the stupid basket I'd prepared and how I'd fled, but then stop myself. It sounds ridiculous, but I don't want Caroline to judge him, not when there isn't anything going on between us in the first place. It hardly seems fair.

TWENTY-SEVEN

25th of August Street.

That was where I'd find what I was looking for. Or at least some of the answers I'd been searching for.

The lyrically named path was the pedestrian pass along the old Venetian harbour, with its assembly of old fishing boats and yachts, which serves the bustling metropolis of Iraklion, the capital city of Crete.

It's the meeting place for my rendezvous with the elusive Inspector Stenalis, which, I had to agree, sounds better than 'Meet me at the docks', which is what we were doing, I suppose. The distinction, coming from Stenalis himself, unsurprisingly doesn't ease my mind.

I'd called Inspector Stenalis the night before, and a gravelly voice had answered with, 'Ah. The English journalist, I wondered when you'd call.'

I'd frowned, then realised. 'Alberos?'

'She filled me in,' he agreed. 'So when would you like to meet?'

'Meet?' I hadn't expected that. But then again, it made sense, you couldn't be too careful. 'As soon as possible,' I heard myself say.

I heard him mumble a word of assent, and he suggested that I come to Iraklion, suggesting that I could speak to him while he worked on his boat.

I'd taken the coastal road, grateful that it was a Saturday, though no less busy. Summer in Crete, I was discovering, was a bustling place to be.

I know which boat it is straightaway. An old-fashioned wooden yacht – beautiful, with a glistening navy blue hull and polished wooden trim.

Stenalis is already on board, and as I near I can see him bent over as he sands the deck. He is tall with black hair threaded with grey, wearing a pair of dark jeans, sneakers and a blue golf shirt. Somehow I'd expected chinos, or some kind of sailing garb.

I call out 'hello' and he greets me with a nod, his head cocked to one side as if in thought. Perhaps I'm not what he was expecting either. He holds out a hand so that I can jump on board, and leads me towards a small table in the helm, offering me a seat on a blue-and-white-cushioned bench.

'You brought it?' he asks.

I hand over Mino's report.

He studies it with a frown. Then emits a low whistle. 'I should have known.'

'What?' I ask, watching him scan the document. But he holds up a hand and carries on reading.

He closes it with a shake of his head.

'So it was… a fabrication, this report?'

'Parts of it, yes. Three points as far as I can tell.'

'Three?' I ask.

I'd uncovered just the one myself: the witness, Mr Portcullis. I hadn't realised there were more.

'Well, the first is the report itself. A police report doesn't usually dismiss the initial investigation done by the first officer on the case – in this instance, done by me. Whereas this report claims no other authorship, except Mino's. In fact, it states that he was the one who took the witnesses testimony, implying that he was the lead inspector on the case from the start, when he was only assigned the case after I was transferred to Iraklion.'

That makes sense. Though it doesn't explain why Mino would choose to lie. 'The second – has to do with the witness?' I ask.

'Yes – Mr Portcullis was a friend. He died the day before the fire broke out, so there's no way he would have been there.'

I shake my head. This confirms what Xena Alberos had said, but still. 'Why lie about it?'

'The witness who came forward to me asked to remain anonymous to the media – but her testimony had to be filed in our official report.'

I close my eyes.

'Your witness,' I say. 'It was Iliana Kirosa, wasn't it?'

He looks at me in surprise, and agrees. 'She said that she'd seen him just minutes before the fire broke when I'd taken her testimony. Later she told me she saw him by the west barn. It seemed a bit strange that she didn't mention that the first time around, but she stuck to her story. We had to wait for forensics to do its investigations, particularly after we found two partial prints.'

'Fingerprints?' There had been no mention of that at all in the report – or in any of the articles I'd found.

'They found them on the petrol can that was used to start the fire, early on in the investigation, actually. But processing them takes longer than one imagines – and we expected to get the results back within the next six months. By then I was moved to Iraklion on a homicide case. I'd heard that the evidence was insufficient and Tom was cleared. I thought about it from time to time of course, as I said, Costas Portcullis was a friend of mine, and it was sad to think of the vineyard burning down, but I believed that the Chania police had done all they could. I didn't really give it much thought beyond that until I heard that Tom Bacchus had returned to resurrect his family's vineyard. I'd thought that he had guts to return there and restart when so many people believed that he had started the fire in the first place. Now I wonder.'

'So they weren't Tom's prints?' I ask.

'I don't know. As far as this report states there were no prints, which means that someone went to a lot of trouble to disguise the fact that evidence was found – but I intend to find out.'

I sit back, stunned. I hadn't realised it went this far.

I'm beginning to understand why I'd been ushered into the chief of police's office mere hours after I'd made the call. Someone didn't want me finding out more than I should.

I frown. 'Inspector Stenalis—' I start, hoping to impart some kind of warning.

But I needn't have bothered. He pats my arm. 'Don't worry – I've got friends who will be discreet, a few favours I can call in.'

I feel relieved.

'But I advise, Ms Laburinthos, we keep this to ourselves for now.'

I have to agree, even as Caroline's warning about buried secrets that won't go back in the ground races through my head again.

I drive home with questions darting around my brain, more than I had to begin with. Like how far back this went? How deep was the cover-up? And why? Why go to such lengths to say the same thing – what was the point? Aside from getting rid of the fingerprints, the only real cover up was that Iliana was the witness. It's only as I drive into Ouranó that it occurs to me: perhaps that was the whole point after all.

TWENTY-EIGHT

'Have you got a frock?' asks Nigel in lieu of a hello, even more cryptically clipped than usual.

'Er – why?' I ask in confusion, taking a seat on my little step in the cottage, my mobile pressed to my ear.

'There's a bit of a meet and greet for sponsors, that sort of thing. *Eudaimonia* are going – part of the annual *Guide to Good Cretan Living* ball that they have on for the idle and monied… would be nice to have a woman representative there for once.'

'Sounds interesting,' I say.

'Er…' he starts. 'There's another thing.'

'Yes?'

'Do you think Caroline would want to come?'

I look at my phone in surprise, barely able to contain myself. Careful to keep my voice neutral. 'I can ask.'

'Good, good. I'll wire you all the details,' he says before hanging up.

I hang up, and have to laugh. Did Nigel have a crush?

A few minutes later I open the email and go a little pale.

The *Guide to Good Cretan Living* welcomes you to its annual moonlight ball.

Date: 30 May
Dress: Black tie
Time: 8.00 p.m.
Where: The Boathouse, Xrysi Akti beach, West Chania

Bloody hell. Black tie?

Bloody Nigel.

I look out towards the long expanse of countrywide olive groves, and rolling vineyards – where the hell was I meant to find an evening gown here?

I decide to consult an expert.

I find her inside, sitting at her writing desk, a glass of sherry in her hand, eyes closed as she listens to Etta James.

'I need to find an evening gown.'

She opens one languid blue eye and looks at me. 'You do?'

'Yes. Actually, it turns out… you may need to as well.'

She takes a sip. 'Really? Are we also in need of a pumpkin carriage and some glass slippers – or just the gowns for now?'

'Just the gowns,' I concur.

'Well, that's a relief. No pumpkins until October at any rate.'

I grin. 'Nigel has invited us both to the *Guide to Good Cretan Living*'s annual moonlight ball.'

'Ah.' Then both her eyes open, and she blinks. 'A ball? Good lord.'

'Exactly.'

'I see your predicament.'

'I rather thought it was a shared horror.'

She nods, and then smiles widely. 'Well, it can't be helped… there's really only one thing we can do.'

'Which is?'

'Go shopping,' she proclaims. 'Definitely.'

'So you'll come too?' I ask happily.

'Darling, why ever not?' she says with a wink.

I have to agree. Surprisingly, for the first time in years, I'm looking forward to getting dressed up.

Not only that, but I'd been told that Xrysi Akti beach is gorgeous, the perfect location for a beach-style gala event.

Now, however, two days later, it turns out that there's a much more important reason for me to go. One I find out only after meeting Stenalis at a nearby taverna in Ouranó.

He'd been cryptic on the phone, saying that he'd prefer to meet me in person and I'd readily agreed.

I head to the Yasou Bar after work, realising that it's the same taverna I'd passed on the night I'd seen Tom kiss another woman and had come to the beach to drown my humiliation; the irony was not lost on me. I can't help but wonder, as I head inside, whether I'll find out something more about Tom today, something else I'd rather not know.

The restaurant has subtle blue-and-white accents, complemented by French country-style woodwork, yet I barely register its attractive appeal, my attention claimed by the sight of Stenalis sitting outside on the balcony, his expression thoughtful as he nurses a beer.

'Laburinthos,' he says, when he sees me.

What was it with everyone using my last name?

'Inspector,' I greet him.

Thankfully, he cuts straight to the chase.

'I'm going to cut to the chase,' he says.

'Good,' I say, hiding a grin.

A waitress comes past then and takes my order. It takes all my strength not to chase her away. I order a scotch, thinking I may need it later. When she finally leaves, Stenalis gives me a lopsided smirk. 'I'm sure you can understand why I felt it would be better to meet in person,' he explains.

I nod. A subconscious part of me is holding my breath, not knowing what I'll do if it turns out that Tom had been responsible for the fire after all. Though if he had, I can't help but wonder why the cover-up.

Stenalis takes a sip of his beer. 'It wasn't Tom Bacchus.'

I exhale the breath I hadn't realised I'd been holding. Somehow needing to hear it again, I ask, 'You're sure?'

'Quite sure. His fingerprints were not a match for those we found on the petrol can. We collected prints from everyone who worked at the farm and none matched.'

'Oh,' I say, deflating. I'd hoped that we could have a suspect, a real suspect at least. 'But then surely we can still find out who it was?' I ask.

'Well, no. It doesn't work that way. The fingerprints need to already be in the system for us to make a match. If we haven't got them on file, we can't know whose prints they were. '

The waitress comes over with my scotch. I down it in two. I shudder – vile. I hate the stuff. But I needed it. Had we come this far only to encounter another dead end? I swirl my empty glass and consider. Actually, that isn't true – this new information is exactly what I'd been looking for. It clears Tom. That isn't a dead end at all, far from it. Surely that's enough to reopen the case?

I shake my head and give Stenalis a wry smile, thinking aloud. 'You know, I'm surprised. I think a part of me really did think it was Tony,' I say, shaking my head.

'Tony?' asks Stenalis, his frown deepening.

'Tom's brother. The way they were at war for most of their childhood. I – well, there's a theory that they were both in love with the same woman. Which, if it is true, could have only bred even more animosity. A powerful, well-connected woman, who had the resources and political connections to help skew things so that it looked like it was Tom.'

Stenalis is staring at me intently.

'It's just a theory…' I say, self-consciously.

Stenalis leans forward, his black eyes luminous. 'But a good one. I think you may be right.'

I splutter. 'What?'

'My suspicions are the same. As I told you, everyone who worked at the farm was taken for fingerprints.'

'So then we're out of luck,' I say, in disappointment.

He shakes his head. 'You're not hearing me… I said everyone who worked at the farm, not everyone who lived there. The family weren't booked for fingerprints.'

I gasp as I realise. 'You're joking!'

He takes a sip of his beer and scoffs. 'I wish I was.'

I stare at him, my mouth agape. 'But how could they just leave them out?'

Stenalis shakes his head, leaning back in his chair. 'We tested Tom along with the other farm workers because he was a suspect and it was established that he, like any of the workers there, may have held a grudge against the family.'

I shake my head. 'But you didn't factor in Tony as well – someone who would have as much of a grudge as Tom?'

'He had an alibi.'

I remember that Tom had said as much. 'Iliana?' I say.

'No.'

'No?' I say incredulous.

'That would have made me very suspicious, as she would have had to have been in two places at once. It was his mother.'

I gasp. Somehow I'd forgotten about her. She'd hated Tom from the beginning. It wouldn't be a stretch to imagine that she used this event to point a finger at Tom.

He nods. 'She must have lied. Something didn't add up, she was… delirious. Rambling. I didn't quite trust her word. Later when I went over her testimony I gave instructions that the whole family be tested as well, I assumed that they'd actually done it but there are no records, and the trouble is, we don't have his fingerprints on file.'

'But in light of this new evidence, can't we just call him in and Iliana—'

'And Iliana.' He agrees. 'We'd have to do it properly, she was there too. But considering how this case was handled, and how the facts were buried, it wouldn't be wise to start accusing anyone of anything until we can be sure. I wouldn't want to take the chance that the evidence gets tampered with again, or run the risk that this time it really is made to look as if it was Tom after all.'

I gasp. 'They could do that?' I exclaim.

'They pretended that a dead man gave testimony, and buried evidence. I'm sure that they, as you call them, would do anything. It's why we've got to keep this to ourselves for now. Tom's a wildcard, there's no telling what he'd do if he found out that his name could have been cleared ten years ago.'

I blink as I digest that. He's right. This is much bigger than I thought, and much more dangerous. As much as a part of me wants nothing more than to head over to Tom right now and tell him that he's innocent, I can't. Another more horrid thought occurs to me. Was I potentially placing Tom at risk with this? I hope not, because I can't turn back now, not now when it looks like we may find out what really happened.

Perhaps Stenalis can sense what I'm thinking because he says, 'Don't worry. I have a plan. One that, if we pull it off, will blow the lid off this whole thing. Are you in?' he asks in a rather bad American accent.

I nod, a small grin forming. 'I'm in.'

TWENTY-NINE

On the day of the party, Caroline and I head into Chania like a pair of excited schoolgirls.

After a breakfast at one of the harbour-side tavernas, we hit the shops.

As Caroline knows Chania rather well, I'm pleased to have her as my guide, as I wouldn't know where to start to find the equivalent of an upmarket boutique here.

Caroline is adamant that such places do exist, and takes me to a small dress shop in a hidden street near the old town. The shop is about as big and as wide as the span of my arms out-stretched and has the name Spanzerona emblazoned on the window in a funky curly script.

There are three racks filled with beautiful dresses, but I find the one of my dreams on the mannequin.

It's sheer, a dusky beige material like thinly spun cobwebs, shaped like an inverted tulip, with tiny black seed pearls that travel from the skirt to the bodice, ending in gossamer thin straps.

It's a dress like a night full of stars. I can't help casting a wish.

The sound of a violin welcomes me as I walk along the white sand path lit on either side by lanterns, towards a Bedouin tent, facing the surf and garlanded by fairy lights.

It looks like something out of a film or fairy tale.

I'm greeted by one of the organisers standing by a podium, who checks my name off the list. I enter the tent to find a large stage dominating the room, where a jazz band is playing and people are already dancing, dressed in cocktail gowns and tuxedos. Beyond them the surf crashes outside.

I wish again that Caroline had come with me, but she'd had a last minute meeting with her editor in the city and would meet me here as soon as she was done. There are few things lonelier than being in a room full of people all by yourself. To steady my nerves, I take a glass of champagne from a tuxedoed waiter and make my way towards the back.

Within seconds, Nigel's booming voice calls my name and I turn round and greet him in relief.

'You look lovely,' I say, looking at his neatly brushed red hair and smart suit.

'That's my line,' he says with a twinkle, clicking his heels and making his bushy auburn brows dance.

I laugh. 'My apologies. This is wonderful,' I say, indicating the gorgeous beach setting, the warm night and the jazz band dressed in white suits, who had begun playing Billie Holiday.

Caroline will love it.

'Not too shabby,' he agrees. 'Come,' he commands, tucking my arm under his elbow and leading me to a rather formidable group of well-clad men and women who are standing in a circle.

He smiles at a woman in an expensive black gown with short brown hair. 'Ria, this is Kate Mondsworth-Greene, the chair of the *Guide to Good Cretan Living* and her daughter, Kimberley.'

I turn sharply and face not just one but two pairs of identically gimlet eyes.

'Ria!' exclaims Kimberley.

Her black hair is parted severely down the centre and she's dressed in a rather short sequined dress. She looks at me through squinting eyes; they are, I suppose rather nastily, missing their home behind their window of square-framed practicality.

'Kim,' I say, because I know she hates it when anyone calls her that.

'What are you doing here?' she asks rather bald-facedly. 'Are you out?'

'Out?' I ask with a frown. Then realise with sudden, awful clarity. Bloody Janice. No doubt she'd told everyone that I'd gone to a clinic. Again.

Nigel and Mrs Mondsworth-Greene look at her quizzically.

I take a breath and ask, 'Of journalism?' Deliberately misunderstanding her question. 'Actually, I'm—'

'One of our top writers,' supplies Nigel. 'She's quickly become one of our best freelancers. If I could just prise her away from Caroline Murray and make her full time, then I could be sure of doubling our reach.'

'Someone say my name?' says a refined voice, and everyone turns to see Caroline, who sweeps into the group, the picture of glamour and style, her blonde hair up, wearing a gown of midnight and gold that beautifully offsets her honeyed skin.

'Nigel, darling,' she says, greeting him first, while she snakes a hand over my shoulders. 'I'm glad I came, if only to prevent poaching.'

'Now, now, children, no fighting,' I say. 'There's enough of me to go around.'

Kimberley looks nonplussed. She has a right to be taken aback, I'll admit, as having someone praise my work was something we were both not really quite used to.

But I'll damned if I'll let her know that.

She blinks. 'So you came here... Janice said that you'd gone to an insti—' She cuts herself off.

I give her a wry smile. 'She would.'

'Janice Farland?' enquires Mrs Mondsworth-Greene in strident tones. 'Did you also work with her?'

I nod. To my astonishment, she purses her lips. 'Well, whatever she said, I'm quite sure it was rather horrible. Bloody terrible woman.'

My mouth falls open slightly.

'Mother,' says Kimberley, looking embarrassed.

Mrs Mondsworth-Greene just rolls her eyes. 'Well, it's true. I'm sorry to say it, but I think if people were a bit more honest about her, then perhaps they could have got rid of her years ago.'

I look at Mrs Mondsworth-Greene in a new light, especially when she sighs in a way I recognise. 'I've been telling Kimberley to leave for years.'

I shake my head. People can surprise you. I smile at her. 'Yaya – my grandmother – used to say the same thing to me. I finally took her advice this year.'

She smiles at me. Then her eyes seem to widen. 'You used to write the obituaries, right?'

I no longer feel the need to qualify it. 'I did.'

'Well-written it was, too. Isn't that what you always used to say, Kimberley?'

My mouth falls open. 'You did?'

She looks at the floor and nods.

I shake my head, amazed. I always wonder at people like this. Why make a big show out of being nasty if underneath it all you were actually nice?

'For an obituary, anyway,' concludes Mrs Mondsworth-Greene.

Then again, not that surprising.

A hubbub of noise breaks out and I turn in time to see the glamourous form of Iliana Kirosa dressed in an emerald green floor-length gown with a slit straight to the top of her thigh, entering with Tony at her side amidst a small flurry of hangers-on.

I take a steadying breath.

Game on.

I have no idea how I'm going to manage it. So many things could go wrong. So many people are here. I have only the slimmest chance of pulling this off, but that's enough.

I'd got by with less than that before.

My eyes scan the room and hit upon Stenalis, blending into the shadows, a tray of champagne glasses at the ready. His head tilts once; we're on.

I dip my head, thinking of how I can orchestrate a meeting with Iliana and Tony, when luck favours me. Nigel hails them in his booming voice.

Iliana turns, her face stretched in a practised smile that wavers when she notices me.

She greets everyone with a perfunctory air kiss and a cat-like smile. When she gets to me, however, she raises a brow and says, 'My, my, we do seem to be seeing you everywhere.'

'Seems that way,' I say.

'Spanzerona?' she says, indicating my dress. 'Journalists must do well for themselves.'

'We do all right.'

She gives me a Cheshire cat smile and says in perfect English, 'I can imagine. Especially ones who tell such tall stories.'

'Tall stories?' I say. Making everyone turn and stare at us.

'Oh, silly me… English isn't my first language. I meant long stories… like the lovely article you wrote about Caroline.'

Everyone starts laughing. Nigel, bless him, even takes the time to explain, but I know that she had perfectly understood what she'd said. More than that… it was intended as a threat.

When Stenalis heads over with a tray of champagne, I hold my breath, not daring to look at him. I keep my eyes focused instead on Iliana, sagging in relief when she takes a glass, not bothering to look at the man who offered it to her.

I look from Iliana to Tony, who had stood by while Iliana made the rounds like her own personal bodyguard. He'd greeted everyone with barely a glance and hadn't even acknowledged me. I don't care about that, I only care that he takes a glass too. I watch in dismay, though, as the tray comes round to him and he declines with a shake of his head.

I suppose I should have known that it wouldn't be that easy.

But there's no way I'm letting Iliana go without getting that glass.

I fake a stumble and crash into her, causing her to topple slightly and slop champagne onto the bottom of her dress.

'I'm so sorry,' I say while she shrieks in outrage.

'Here,' I say, handing her a handkerchief from my purse, and holding my hand out for her glass, which she shoves towards me with one hand, while reaching for the cloth with the other.

Careful to take the glass at the stem, as instructed, I apologise again, but she only snorts before stalking off towards the bathroom, Tony following in her wake.

'You okay?' asks Caroline.

I smile. 'Oh yes,' I say, a slow grin forming. 'Very okay.'

She frowns in puzzlement, but before she can ask her attention is captured by Nigel.

I choose that moment to make a quick escape towards the kitchens, where Stenalis is waiting. I hand over the glass, which he pops into a bag. 'One down,' he says with a wink and stashes it out of sight.

I shake my head. 'Just one more heart attack to go.'

'Thankfully we have reinforcements,' he says, glancing towards the back of the dance floor, where a tall woman with a long crop of curls and a curvy figure stands in a waiter's uniform. She looks a bit like an Amazon.

'That's Alberos?' I say, shocked. 'She – she's kind of kickass,' I say in awe. She looks like a bloody Greek Lara Croft.

'That's what she said about you.'

'Really?'

He nods, elbowing me in the ribs.

I smile. Maybe tonight I was, just a little.

'It might have been something about kicking your ass, though,' he teases.

'Ah well, she may have to if this doesn't work.'

His face grows serious. 'It will.'

'And if we get it – how long will it take to run the prints?' I ask.

'Should be about a week – I have someone who will work on it night and day.'

I blink. If we pull this off we could solve a ten-year mystery, and change Tom's life. That was a lot to ask for in one week. I touch Stenalis' hand. 'I'm sorry, but I have to ask… what if they let Chief Mino know? Can you be sure that your people in the department can be trusted?'

'Let's just say I've secured a way to ensure that that doesn't happen.'

I give him a look of surprise.

'Some damning evidence… something that this particular person most definitely wouldn't want his wife to know about.'

My eyes bulge. 'Like what?'

'Nothing to worry yourself about… and nothing illegal either. I can't speak for Mino but most Cretans pride themselves on their honesty and integrity.'

Now I really want to know, but Stenalis is immoveable. 'You'd better go – we don't want anyone to grow suspicious.'

I leave, making my way as discreetly as I can towards the jazz band, where Tony Bacchus is standing and brooding.

He seems to come out of a reverie when Alberos approaches him with a tray of whisky.

'Whisky?'

Tony shakes his head, but as I make my way over to him, he seems to change his mind, and takes a glass, holding up the amber-coloured liquid as a barrier.

'Tony,' I greet him, 'I was wondering if I could ask you a question about the upcoming harvest at Elysium.'

His black eyes snap. 'I believe my wife and I made our feelings very clear on that subject.'

'I see. I was under the impression that your commentary at the time was off the record, I'm delighted to discover otherwise,' I say, with a wide smile.

Tony's face goes puce. He slams his drink down onto the table next to him. 'It is not on the record, do not include me in your story at all,' he grits out, before storming away, his hands balled into fists.

'Nicely done,' says Alberos from behind.

I turn, and laugh. I seem to have a knack for pissing people off. Granted, with Tony it didn't seem that hard. But at least we got what we need. She gives my arm a squeeze before leaving. 'Let me know when you know.'

I nod. A few minutes later Stenalis gives me a wave goodbye, the two glasses neatly tucked away in an evidence bag. As I watch him go, I realise we are all in this together now and, in just one week, we'll finally know what happened.

I take a glass of champagne from the nearest waiter and make my way outside to a small balcony that offers an impressive view

of the star-strewn night, the sound of the band playing an old
Etta James song sweet in my ears.

'Ria?'

I turn, and my heart stops. Tom is leaning against the rail-
ing, with an air of casual grace, dressed in a slim-fitting black
suit and white shirt and tie. He gives me a small smile, his eyes
crinkling at the corners.

My stomach does a little flip. 'You look wonderful,' he says,
his eyes holding mine.

I blush, but do a twirl anyway, so he can see the back.

'Wow.'

He moves closer, too close, and whispers in my ear, causing gooseflesh to erupt all along my arms. 'I think it's the most
beautiful dress I've ever seen.'

I step back, my heart pounding slightly. 'Thank you.'

He touches my hand. 'Ria, about the other day.'

I cringe.

He cringes back.

'Ah, Tom, can we rather not? I was an idiot.'

'You? God no, you were great. It was me. I can explain—'

'Tom, please,' I say, embarrassed. 'There's no need. I mean,
the truth is we hardly know each other,' I admit, perhaps even to
myself. The trouble is... I feel that I do know him, so embroiled
am I in his story, his life.

He shakes his head. 'God, Ria, that makes it worse. Especially after I told you about my past, and that Maria and I broke
up – which we have, I promise. You must have thought I was
the worst kind of ass – trying to kiss you one night, then only to
have you see me with my ex.'

I smile a bit like an idiot. 'So you were going to kiss me, then?'

He looks thrown. 'Of course I was.'

'Oh,' I say. A bit too pleased, really.

'Well, I thought that's why you jumped away...?'

I close my eyes. 'Tom, actually, that's the thing. It's me that needs to explain.'

He shakes his head. 'Ria, it's fine. I mean, I know I'm no picnic, we can just be friends if that's what you want. But I want you in my life. I haven't – there hasn't been anyone that got to me quite the way you do, perhaps ever, really. Maria is an old girlfriend... we broke up months ago, and she hasn't er...' he says, not quite knowing how to say politely that she hasn't got the message. 'We dated for a short while after I came back to Crete, but it wasn't serious. She's an old family friend, one of the few families that believed in me, but there was nothing there, I just didn't feel it. So I called it off a few months ago. When we ran into her in the market... Well, she came over because she wanted us to start up again...it's why she kissed me, hoping I'd change my mind.'

'And did you?'

'No, of course not... I wouldn't anyway, but especially not when I'm interested in someone else... In you. I'd hate to lose you because I was an idiot... I tried to push you... only to then have you think that I'm some kind of lying bastard.'

I look at him intently, a lump forming at my throat. I believe him. I think somehow I'll always believe in him. Somehow I always have, from the day when I saw his story in *Eudaimonia*. From the first time I saw his haunted face.

'Tom, I don't want to be friends.'

He stares at me, his face tight. 'Right,' he says, and begins to leave. I touch his arm. 'Not just friends.'

His eyes widen. 'Ria,' he says, touching my arm.

I touch the hand he placed there. 'Tom, first I need to explain.'

'Do you want to take a walk on the beach?' he asks, pointing to a small set of stairs to his left that lead to the beach.

'I saw a bottle of champagne back there that we could appropriate,' I say, pointing to a small table at the back.

He grins in return, and fetches the bottle in two long strides. He takes off his shoes and socks, ties a knot in the laces and flings them over his neck, then rolls up his trouser legs. He looks unbelievably devil-may-care and sexy.

It's a bit, well, unnerving. In a fluttery tummy sort of way that I'm trying and failing to ignore.

We walk along the lantern-strewn beach, almost touching.

'So we're just going to drink out of the bottle,' he says, offering me the first sip.

'You'd be surprised… It's sort of my new thing.'

He laughs. 'What – you?' he says, taking in my dress, and my hair – which if I do say so myself is looking much more polished than usual.

'Oh yes, I'm a woman of mystery.'

'Well, you've got me there,' he winks.

I laugh. Though the truth is, as far as Tom is concerned, I am a bit of a mystery, I suppose.

We walk companionably for some time along the surf.

I'm reminded of the last time I'd visited the beach at night and how much things had changed, even in such a short time.

'Tom. The reason that I jumped away the other night—'

'You don't have to explain.'

'But I do.' I set my mouth. 'Tom, I told you about how my grandmother passed away and that it was the push I needed to get away, finally,' I say, echoing Yaya's words. 'But I never told you why I needed that push… or about Christopher.'

Tom stares at me, but doesn't say anything. So I continue. 'He was my fiancé and he died in a car crash on our wedding day, two years ago.'

Tom gasps, then takes my hand.

'I stopped believing in anything good after that. It was the cruellest twist of fate. He was this incredibly lovely, loveable guy, the life of the party, the one everyone wanted to be around. Even my mad roommate Dorrit – who hates everyone – loved him,' I say. 'Then, just like that, because of some drunk idiot on a Sunday, he was gone.'

Somehow I keep myself from crying.

Tom looks thunderstruck. His blue eyes fill with sympathy, but he lets me speak. So I carry on, telling him things that I'd never told anyone else. 'I just got stuck. Writing about death day in and out, while every day wishing I could die instead. Then when Yaya passed she left me a letter. It was so like Yaya to leave something like that for me. She told me that she'd loved my grandfather more than life itself, and when he died she'd thought of ending it. She'd come to live with us in England, moving far away from her home and her life here, and she'd thought that she couldn't go on missing her husband so much. Until a little girl crept into the corners of her heart and filled it, and she found her reason to live again. She told me that I needed to come here to live again so that I could find that life could go on. That, like her, I could find that the second half of my life, despite the pain that had gone on in the first, could be worth holding on for, and that the beauty I found would be heightened, made more precious because of the first.

'She was right,' I say. 'But then Yaya, as Yaya would have said, was rarely, if ever wrong.'

Tom grins, and wraps his arm around me so that I lean in close.

'So now you know,' I say.

'I think I knew or suspected something like that from the first day I met you. It was like… I don't want this to sound ridiculous, but it's like – I recognised something in you.'

'Like we belonged to the same club?' I said.

His eyes are full. 'Something like that.'

We sit down, sharing the champagne, and Tom puts his jacket over my shoulders when I shiver.

'Tom, I have to tell you something else.'

He looks at me. 'There's more?' he asks in disbelief.

I shake my head. 'No, not about me. It's about you. What you said just now, about us being part of the same club—'

'I think you said that but it's what I meant, yes?'

'Well, the truth is I felt that way even before we met.'

He looks at me with a quizzical expression, and I explain about finding the story in the paper on the plane and how I'd wanted to see the vineyard, how I'd felt that if it could survive what had happened to it, there was hope for me. How I still felt a little like that.

'So you asked if you could do a story?' Tom asks.

'No,' I laugh, 'I just… showed up at your door. Nigel covered for me.'

'That cheeky bugger – he really did,' he says, and gives me a hug.

'You're not angry?' I ask.

'Ria, why would I be angry? That was one of the best things that has happened to me in a long time, when you came there with your little shorts and your bloody huge eyes.'

'My huge eyes?'

'Yes, those. Stop that, it isn't fair. You'll give an old man a heart attack.'

'You're kidding – when you've got those,' I say, pointing at his blue eyes. 'Yes – and that,' I say as he starts to smile. 'That should come with a warning.'

'What?'

'Really? Like you don't know that you should be in an advert for toothpaste or something? It's unnatural, no British men have teeth like that.'

'Half Greek.' He shrugs as if in explanation.

I grin.

'So you saw my picture in the paper and couldn't resist coming to meet me?' he teases. 'Now that I wouldn't have figured.'

'Hah!' I mock smack him. 'Not you! I wanted to see the vineyard!' I exclaim.

'Uh-huh, I'm sure… my vineyard.'

I laugh and kiss him on the cheek.

He raises an eyebrow, takes my face in his hands and kisses me. Desire, warm and glittery, like a thousand shooting stars spreads through me, and I kiss him back, like I've never kissed anyone before.

It's some time before we break free. I feel the loss even as I pause for breath.

He entwines his hand in mine, turning my hand over in his, his finger tracing an old scar. I wonder if there will come a time when he will know every line and every scar I have.

He pulls me close and we kiss again. This time longer than the first, but etched with a deeper desire, one that could easily have found us making love in the moonlight. I break away, not quite ready for that. Not just yet. He passes the champagne for me to sip, and holds his arm out so that I can snuggle close.

THIRTY

At sunrise we walk back along the beach, the empty champagne bottle swinging in Tom's hand. 'You hungry?' he asks.

'Starved,' I admit.

'Come,' he says, pulling me along.

'Where are we going?'

'Just up ahead – a little café I know along the waterfront. They make the best apricot Danishes in the world.'

'But Tom, it's barely dawn – no one will be open now.'

'She will, trust me.'

I follow as he sets a fast pace up the beach towards a line of cafés, tavernas and waterside shops.

A sweet little blue and white café with a striped awning stands on wooden planks, with a sweeping view of the sea; a faded sign on the side reads 'Breeze In Café'.

'Cute name… But it's closed,' I say, noting the locked door.

'The lights are on,' he says, pointing at the window, where a faint glow suggests that there's someone inside.

Tom knocks on the door.

'Tom!' I say, somewhat nervously. What if someone comes and shouts at us?

'Don't worry,' he says as the sound of shuffling feet draws near and the door opens with a loud creak. A short, elderly, plump woman with curly grey hair stands in the pale light, dressed in comfy slacks and slippers, with a large floral-patterned apron around her waist. She has flour on her brown, wrinkled hands.

'Tom!' she exclaims, clapping them together, large black eyes brimming with delight.

'Aunt Therese!' he greets, giving her a hug.

'But you look so dashing! Where-a you been?' she asks in a heavy accent that melts my heart.

'To a party, with a pretty girl,' he says with a grin.

'I can see that!' she says, giving me a big smile.

I smile in return.

'Therese – this is Ria.'

'Nice to meet you,' I say, shaking one of her floured hands.

'And you,' she says. 'I've been telling Tom to find he-self a girl...'

Tom runs a hand over his mouth. 'Therese... please, let's just this once try not to embarrass me?'

Her beetle-black eyes dance mischievously. 'Okay. I'm good.'

I stifle a laugh. 'Therese is my aunt,' he explains. 'My father's sister.'

I look at him in surprise. I'm glad that he has someone besides Tony to call family.

'So where-a you been?' she demands, short plump hands on hips, eyes narrowing. 'I don't see you for weeks. Nothing. No word. Like you drop – *poof!* – off the face of the earth.'

Tom gives her a sheepish smile. 'I've been working.'

'Pah – work, work, work. That's all he do,' she says, looking at me and shaking her head. She elbows me in the ribs. 'I the only family he got. But does he visit? No.'

She straightens her five-foot self and gives me a rather lascivious look. 'But... maybe not all work?' she says with a naughty cackle.

'Aunt Therese...' Tom says.

She suppresses a smile. 'Okay, okay. You hungry? I make you something?' She raises a brow. 'Danish?'

He grins. 'We'd love some.'

'Okay – go sit, I bring.'

'Can I help?' I offer.

'Pah. Sit, sit please.' She smiles, evidently delighted to see her Tom with a girl. We take a seat on the little red and white patio outside. 'She's lovely,' I say.

His eyes dance. 'Bonkers. But yes, quite lovely, she is without a doubt one of my most favourite people in the world.'

A few seconds later she comes bustling in with a fat blue coffee pot, three cups and an assortment of mouth-watering patisseries crammed onto a plate.

'You made these?' I say, eyeing the perfect golden squares topped with a glazed apricot.

She nods.

'Therese is the best baker in Chania. People come from miles to try her patisseries.'

'Pah,' she says, negating his words, though her eyes twinkle from the compliment.

Taking my first bite, which sinks into sweet apricot and layers of mouth-watering pastry, followed by the creamiest vanilla custard in this world, I have to agree with Tom.

'I'd travel to the moon for this,' I say, sighing in ecstasy. 'So I see this is part of your evil plan. Introduce me to the best baker in Chania on our first date. Nice move.'

'I certainly thought so,' he agrees. 'Don't hate the player…'

I laugh. Then reach for another. You cannot be polite when confronted with pastry like this.

'Your first date!' exclaims Therese, clasping her hands, the apples of her cheeks rosy red.

Tom shakes a finger at her. 'Behave.'

'Okay. Okay.' She hoots. 'But—' She can't seem to help herself. 'It must have been a good one, no? Yew still on it.'

I giggle. There is no point denying it. It is without a doubt the nicest date I've ever had.

Particularly as it's been topped off by meeting someone who reminds me rather wonderfully of Yaya, which is, if anything, the best finale I could have asked for.

She waggles her eyebrows but says no more. Evidently she's prepared to 'behave' now she's found the answer she's looking for, saying only, 'A woman who is not afraid to speak her mind. I like her.'

'Me too,' he says.

My heart flips.

'Think we should keep her?' he asks Therese.

I mock punch him.

But Therese answers anyway. 'Oh yes. Someone's got to put some meat on those bones.'

'You sound like my yaya.'

Therese's eyes pop. 'You're Greek?'

Tom and I say it together – 'Only half' – then giggle like teenagers.

'What's the joke?' asks Therese, brows knitted together.

'Nothing,' I say. 'We just have some things in common.'

'Like Greek grannies who worry too much.'

'Granny!' says Therese in mock outrage. 'I'm only forty-five…'

Tom raises a brow. 'Oh, I see, do we count in dog years in Greece? I forget.'

She smacks him. 'Okay, fifty-four?'

He laughs. 'I'm not sure it works that way.'

She pats him on the head and says, 'So young… so stupid.'

'Hold that intriguing insult for just a sec, while I pour the coffee.'

I'm enjoying this.

He hands me a cup and I take a sip. 'Ah God, that's sublime.'

Therese's eyes widen in delight. 'An English girl who knows good coffee, yes, we have to keep her,' she says.

Tom and I share a grin.

We leave when Therese says she'd better get the shop ready, as the first customers are already starting to queue outside. I give her a hug. 'Thank you for a wonderful time,' I say.

An American woman with short brown hair, sun-kissed shoulders and a wide smile is standing in the doorway. She says to her partner, 'You see, honey, that's why everyone loves Crete – the people here are just so friendly.'

She makes her way over to Therese, places her arms on her shoulders and enfolds her in a hug, to Therese's amused bafflement. 'We know we'll have a wonderful time here as well,' she assures her. Therese pats her on the back somewhat awkwardly. 'Okay, okay.'

Tom and I leave in hysterics.

'Did you see her face?'

Tom wipes his eyes. 'God, I love Americans.'

'So do I – I can't imagine an English person doing that.'

'Would you?' he asks with a raised brow.

'Good lord, never.'

And we laugh uproariously again.

He takes my hand and my heart flutters again. I'm in that glittery state of being, somewhere past exhaustion, where the world and its colours are brighter and more beautiful because of it.

'So where to now?'

'I think I'd better go home.'

'Okay, do you need a lift?'

'Yes please, Caroline took the car last night.' At the thought of Caroline I bite my lip. I hadn't said goodbye to her last night…

and hadn't come home. Goodness knows what she must think of me... Then just as soon as I think that, I can't help but smile. She'd probably approve a lot, actually.

We head towards Tom's car, parked just ahead.

He opens the door for me and I get in.

I have to chuckle. The last time I'd seen this car I thought that Tom was trying to kill me.

'What?' he asks, with a smile.

God, he's gorgeous. With his pale blue eyes, dishevelled hair, shirtsleeves rolled up and half-loose black tie, he looks like a member of the Rat Pack.

'I just thought about the first time I saw you in this car... I thought you were going to ride me off the cliff.'

He laughs. 'That was your guilty conscience talking. That, or...' He looks at me suspiciously, his eyes darker. 'You actually did think I was an arsonist.'

'You know,' I say, my face serious, 'I don't think I ever did.'

His blue eyes study me. 'Never?'

I shake my head.

He shakes his head. 'But how could you know I was innocent when there was no proof?'

I say it before thinking. 'But there was!'

'What?'

Oh God. I hadn't told him everything... I'd started to but one bombshell was enough for any evening, let alone a date. And if I'm honest, it's more than that. Stenalis' words had echoed in my mind, even when I thought of telling him last night. Wildcard.

This isn't something I can lay on his shoulders right now. There's just no telling what he'd do, and we can't risk the investigation. Part of me, a big part, just wants to tell him everything, but I know I can't do that to him. If he finds out that the worst day of his life – the one that was blamed on him, the one that had led to the loss of everything he had ever held dear, and a few more things besides – was linked to his brother and his wife; that their connections had led to evidence being buried, that this thing went as far as the chief of Chania police himself... there was just no telling what someone who learned all that could do.

It was something that I knew only too well. It was the exact same reason that Yaya had stopped me from speaking to the drink driver who'd killed Christopher, when he had asked to see me because there was just no telling what I would have said.

I have to protect Tom. I just need a week – one week – to save him from himself.

One week to make sure that Stenalis gets what he needs and to make damn sure that this time the evidence isn't buried.

I look at him with a fixed smile. 'I just meant that according to the judge there wasn't any proof... so that was proof in its own way,' I finish rather lamely.

'Oh... right, but that's not exactly proof,' he says, tucking a stray lock of hair behind my ear.

'It should be,' I say.

'I'm surprised at you.'

'Why?'

'I just thought that a journalist would need more than that.'

I make a joke. 'Yes, but you're forgetting that I'm really a writer.' I'm hoping he won't question it further. Thankfully, he just smiles and starts the car.

'So,' he says while we head towards the hazy Lefka Ori up ahead, my eyes growing sleepy as I snuggle in the seat with his jacket over my shoulders.

'Yes?' I ask, one eye open.

'I was thinking...'

'Is this a new sensation? Usually if you ignore it, it just goes away… like a rash.'

'Ah, so you do get feistier as the hours pass. Interesting… I may have to keep you sleep-deprived a bit longer to explore this.'

My eyes open wide.

'I was thinking about us.'

'Yes?' I perk up immediately. Which makes him laugh.

'Well, it did look like you'd wanted us to have a picnic the other day. I couldn't help but notice the basket in your hands… while your feet left scorched rubber tracks behind.'

I cringe, and put my hands over my eyes. 'Er… yes, a picnic.'

He laughs, a bit too loudly I think, as I cringe a bit more.

'Well, seeing as I blew the last one, can I make it up to you? How about a picnic tonight in the vines?'

I think about teasing him, I really do, but then how many times does a handsome man offer to make you a picnic? I remember what Yaya always said about jewellery, 'Never criticise a man when he buy yew jewellery or next time he buy a washing machine instead.' Wise words.

So I just say, 'Okay,' and smile like an idiot instead.

THIRTY-ONE

Of course, after I get home I don't sleep.

No. Instead I moon around like the lovesick twenty-eight-going-on-fourteen year old that I am. Who is sometimes feisty and kickass, (the last two descriptions were, of course, what Tom and Xena Alberos had labelled me). Kickass. It was perhaps the first time in my life I'd been called that.

I quite like it, to be honest. Though I know I'm not, you know, *kickass* in the traditional sense. But these past few months I'd found that I'm not a pushover either; in fact, quite the opposite. I think I discovered that at about the same time everyone else did.

Perhaps when Yaya had passed, she'd given me some of that on her way out. Or Chris, though he'd been more charming than kickass. Though he would argue, I suppose, that anyone who made robots for a living was kickass by definition.

I figure my judgement of myself would even get a Kimberley Mondsworth-Greene nod of approval – objective and well-researched, two outside sources, one internal. Very good indeed.

I suppose I'm punch-drunk, really.

I slip off my dress of stars and have a shower, where I spend an hour letting the water fall on me while I keep my eyes closed and hum.

I get out and get dressed in a pair of shorts and a T-shirt, and close my eyes for a second. Next thing I know, I hear Caroline's voice calling me from what sounds like the end of a long tunnel. I struggle to wake.

'Is it a coma, do you think?'

A wet snout finds its way into my hand.

'Good thinking, check the pulse… we can't be too sure… she does look awfully pale.'

I groan.

'Ignore that, Yamas, sometimes when they go… they make little death noises.'

I snort.

'Yes, like that.'

'Death noises?' I ask, trying but failing to open my eyes, which feel painted shut.

'Sometimes they speak but we can't know, without offering some sort of resuscitation…'

Yamas licks my face and I gasp; his fishy breath is foul. The little dog dives onto the bed and jumps onto me.

'Good thinking, first mouth-to-mouth and now some CPR. You're an excellent doctor.'

'Okay, Dr Doolittle.' I quirk a brow. 'Enough with the animal husbandry… I'm awake.'

'Dr Doolittle, honestly…'

'Well, if the big red shoes fit?

She giggles. 'Darling, you should drink more. You're hilarious.'

'That's what Tom said.'

She gasps. 'Tom?'

I open my eyes wide – or as wide as eyes that had been up for twenty-four hours straight could go – and nod, happily, enigmatically, and probably somewhat dementedly, really.

'You were with Tom last night!' she exclaims.

I grin. 'Yes.'

She sits on my bed.

'Tell me everything.'

'First tell me why you have Nigel's dog.'

'Rather innocent, really. Nothing to tell. A night of passion... and he forgot his dog.'

My mouth falls open. 'Really?'

She laughs. 'No, darling.'

'Oh.'

'You look disappointed.'

'So how did you get the dog, then?'

'Well... Nigel came over for breakfast with Yamas, and then when he left, Yamas decided to stay.'

'Really?'

'Yup. For a visit. I'll run him up later in the week. Now tell me everything,' she says, blue eyes serious. Yamas puts his head on my chest and peers at me as if he'd also like to hear me tell everything.

So I do.

Well, not everything. But almost... about how I'd told Tom about Christopher, how great he'd been, how I'd invented a reason to go to the vineyard...

'You told him that!' she exclaims. Her blonde hair shakes out from its makeshift chignon, which was really just a pencil she'd twisted into it.

I grin at the sight. 'It's so strange, in so many ways Tom is a very soulful man. Reserved... flinty... stoic...'

Caroline shakes her head. Her lips curl upwards in amusement. 'Focus. Fewer adjectives, more verbs...'

'Sorry, got a bit lost there.'

'I'm sure,' she says with a wink.

'No. I mean, he's... I don't want to do that awful thing where you compare, but Chris was like an open book. He was so charming. You felt like you were sitting under a ray of sunshine when you were around him. Like everything would be all right. Very little bothered him. Whereas Tom... Tom's had the weight of the world on his shoulders. He grew up fast, and has been through so much. It's made him serious, but in a good way. Yet… when his guard is down, he's…'

'The one person you feel who gets you?' she asks.

'How did you know?'

'Well, darling, that's what he said about you.'

I look at her and blink.

She shrugs. 'It's true. You know, I think he was a lot like your Christopher when he was younger. Not the life of the party like you described, but easy to be around. Though he's always had a kind of magnetism, an allure, really.'

I giggle. 'Okay, Jackie Collins.'

She snorts. 'It's true though, he's very handsome, and growing up I think there were a lot of girls who lost their hearts to him.'

I sober. That's what concerns me. 'You think he was… a womaniser?'

She shakes her head. 'Tom? No, not at all. Those types of men are often shallow, vain and, well, rather glib. They're always after the chase. No. I'd say Tom was the opposite, really.'

I bite my lip. 'Soulful,' I repeat.

'Consuming is a word I'd use.'

We look at each other without saying anything because that was worse, much worse. You could fall for Don Juan and survive, but there was no recovering from Heathcliff.

'I'm screwed.'

Yamas looks at me in sympathy.

Caroline just nods her head sadly. 'I'd say so, darling.'

The picnic is set under a blanket of stars. I find my way by the light of a winding path of lanterns dotted through the vineyard towards a small hill that overlooks the mountain and the sea in the distance.

Tom stands waiting for me in the moonlight, his smile enigmatic.

'This is beautiful,' I say, touched.

He gives me that smile that does things to my heart. 'I'm glad you like it.'

I take a breath, feeling nervous.

As if reading my thoughts, Tom says, 'Wine?'

'Please,' I say with a bashful smile.

He grins, and invites me to take a seat on the soft blue blanket he's laid down.

I stare at the lanterns dotting the vineyard and casting a magical glow. Tom whispers close to my ear, 'Don't worry, they're battery operated.'

I laugh, relieved.

'Have you ever had some of the old Elysium wine?' he asks, pouring me a glass from an old bottle, the label faded with age.

'Caroline opened a bottle – the Syrah, I think – when I first started working with her. To celebrate.'

He smiles. 'Really, that's great. Well, this was our signature wine, the seven feathers of Elysium, there are only a few bottles left now, though,' he says and hands me a glass.

'Are you sure you want to use it on me?'

His face is serious. 'Yes.'

My breath catches. I take a sip and close my eyes while Tom stares at me.

I breathe in the aromas. 'It's a blend, Merlot definitely… bold, really… but afterwards it's… light, but lingering, some kind of berry?'

He nods. 'Excellent. It's a blend with the Pinot… and that's the berry you're referring to – strawberry.'

'It's heavenly,' I say.

'I thought you'd like it.'

'I do.'

We share a grin.

'So… I'm not sure it will be as nice as yours, but I got olive bread, some cheese, tapenade, houmous…'

'Sounds amazing.'

'So is this what you did when you left?' I ask.

He shakes his head. 'No, I had a lot of work to do, tying up some of the vines.'

'So you haven't slept?' I ask.

He shrugs. 'I don't need a lot of sleep. Did you?'

'Yes – sorry, I passed out.'

'I'm glad you slept. I felt bad for keeping you up all night.'

'You did?'

He eyes twinkle. 'Well, maybe not that bad.'

I laugh. There is a part of me, while sipping wine under the star-strung sky, drinking in the magical setting of the hilltop vineyard with the mountain on one side and the sea on the other, in the company of a handsome man, that can't believe how my life has changed, or that I've had two such romantic evenings in a row.

It's strange how he made me at once quite nervous, but at ease as well, so that I'm comfortable just being with him. By rights, it should be difficult to talk to Tom when looking at him, he's almost intimidatingly handsome, but it isn't. I think it's because his looks just aren't that important to him, so you almost forget in a way.

And of course, the wine helps.

There's something else that I've been wondering about and, despite the romantic setting, I need to ask, even if it changes the tone.

'Did you see Tony last night?'

Tom's face is tight. 'Yes.'

'What happened?' I ask, wondering how I'd missed it.

'The usual. We got into a fight. Iliana got involved – so I left.'

'You left because of her?'

'No, but I didn't want to cause a scene. Nigel had invited me, after all.'

'But… you came back?'

'Yes.'

'Why?'

'Why do you think?'

I blush and look away.

'I wanted to see you… to speak to you. It was the only reason I went, really.'

My eyes widen. 'But how did you know that I would be there?'

'I have my sources too.'

'Nigel?'

'Nigel,' he agrees.

'Tom,' I start, somewhat apprehensive because I'm afraid I'll risk our evening. But what he'd said about Iliana made me wonder yet again about that night ten years ago… and why he and Tony fought, and still hate each other.

'I'm sorry to ask, but I have to – were you and Iliana… lovers?'

Tom's face turns grey and he just stares at me for a while.

'It's just – it would explain—'

He looks sombre. 'Everything?' he asks.

I nod.

He takes my hand, as if for support. With his other, he rubs his mouth in frustration. 'Yes. We were lovers.'

I have to force myself not to drop his hand, though in an irrational way I want to. Even though I've always known deep down that that was the case.

'It was… complicated. I was just twenty-one.'

'I'm sure… sleeping with your brother's fiancée would be complicated,' I say, somewhat horrified that he thought age was an excuse.

He exhales sharply. 'No, you're right, of course, it was awful.'

'But you were twenty-one… sowing wild oats or something,' I suggest, trying to understand.

'No. Oh God… I just meant that I was twenty-one and stupid. I'd fallen in love with my brother's girlfriend. And I thought she felt the same way about me.'

I close my eyes for a second. I can't help feeling truly sorry for him. 'And did she?'

'I thought she did, but I was wrong… in the end.'

'How did it start?'

'Innocently enough. I mean I never set out to fall for her… not after Tony and she got together. Her parents knew my father. Her dad wanted to start producing his own wines here at Elysium so we started seeing a lot of them. Tony wasn't all that interested in the vineyard – he was more of a businessman, always has been. I was busy in the vines most of the time, so I never saw much of them. Then one night she was up late and so was I… and it just sort of grew from there.

'I was… lonely,' he admits. 'And I thought…' He fluffs his hair in annoyance. 'I thought she loved me, she spoke about ending it with Tony, finding the right time to do so. She said that he was jealous so she had to be careful, and she also didn't want to ruin the relationship with our fathers, so I believed her. I waited.

'Then on the night of the fire, Tony and I got into an argument over the direction that the vineyard was going, as usual he told me that I had no say. My dad got involved and told Tony that we had to work together, that one day we'd be partners. The same thing he'd been saying for years, I guess, and Tony said that we never would, I'd always be a bastard, that he and Iliana would run the vineyard together, modernise it. I could either work for them, follow his vision or leave, and I... snapped. I told him that he shouldn't be so sure that Iliana would marry him.

'He asked me what I meant and I told him that he should speak to Iliana, but basically she was leaving him. My father put a stop to it – he told me to go and get some air and I went to Iliana. She was staying at the cottage we had at the back of the farm, and I told her that she had to confront Tony tonight or I was ending it, I was tired of living a lie, and she agreed.

'I left her and went for a walk to cool down, and to wait for her to do it – we always met by the old well, by the west barn where we could be alone. So I waited, but she didn't come, and soon afterwards the fire broke out.'

'She never came?'

Tom shakes his head. 'I don't know, everything went so fast. We all tried to stop it, but the fire spread so fast...' He looks away. 'Afterwards... after I found my father, and the police were there, I guess I still thought we were together... but she seemed afraid to come near me after that.'

'She was afraid of you?'

'No, it wasn't that, it was just a feeling really, but I felt that she was afraid of Tony.'

My brows raise. 'Did she ever speak to you? Try to explain?'

Tom shakes his head. 'No, after the fire we were just over.'

I feel so sorry for him. On the same night, he'd lost every-thing he ever loved. Worse, after that awful night, he was blamed for causing it all.

'Didn't you tell the police what had happened – with all of you?'

Tom shakes his head. 'I told them that I thought it was Tony, but I didn't say why – just that we'd had a fight earlier and that he didn't want me there. As far as the police were concerned, that just proved even more that he'd have no motive to destroy the place, whereas I did. I'd just been told that I didn't belong, and that I had to follow Tony or else, so they thought I'd started the fire as some twisted form of revenge. Like if I couldn't have the vineyard, neither could they.'

I gasp. That was horrifying. I shake my head. 'This whole time – she could have cleared it up. Told them what really happened – that it could have just as easily been Tony who was about to lose his home.'

I hold his hand, thinking about Iliana, about her betrayal… and why she had gone to such great lengths to ensure that it didn't come out that she had identified him.

'Ria,' he says, 'I just want you to know that whatever I felt for her died that day too.'

I shake my head. 'Tom, you didn't need to tell me that.'

'I know, it's just that I wouldn't want you to think that I still had feelings for her.'

I shake my head. 'After that? Tom, we may not know each other that well yet, but after losing your dad and your home and having her abandon you on the worst day of your life, well, I would think that mostly you hated her.'

Tom's eyes are clouded. 'I did. To be honest. I was full of hate… and anger. For a very long time. It consumed me. Pushed me, brought me back here too.'

'And now?'

He exhales. 'Now I feel like I've come alive again.'

THIRTY-TWO

'Are you mad? It's *Hugh Grant*. Hugh *flipping* Grant – you cannot leave him out.'

Caroline gasps, suddenly appalled at her error. 'You're right! What the bloody hell, I mean what the bloody hell… I almost cut out Hugh Grant!' Her eyes appear a bit wild. 'We must need a break.'

'I quite agree… there's just no cause for that kind of lapse in judgement so close to the finish line here. I mean, next thing we know you'll be telling me that you're going to leave out tracking wallabies with Joanna Lumley.'

Caroline's eyes mock bulge. 'Heaven forbid, darling. Anyway, it was the duckbilled platypus, but I see your point. More wine?'

'Please.'

We are now on the final leg of the memoir, and have at last something resembling the first draft. Only it's around two hundred pages too long and we're in that awful cutting phase. Caroline had almost cut Hugh Grant from the mix. I mean, let's not get hysterical here.

One does not throw out the actor responsible for the best portrayal of Edward Ferrars that ever existed.

And if your tastes run to that type of thing – which mine definitely do – Daniel Cleaver.

I mean, I'm speechless. If speechless means that I'm actually babbling incoherently.

It turns out, though, that Caroline had not watched that production of *Sense and Sensibility*.

Of course, that makes me go out especially and rent a copy… which is dubbed in Greek. But still, he's lovely, and Caroline agrees, after three and a half hours and three rewinds to catch Hugh's fabulous smile and to replay the scene where Elinor is hysterically happy that he is not, in fact, married. Caroline declares that we're quite obviously overworked. Of course, this is when she starts plying me for more information about my date with Tom.

'So you didn't stay the night?' she asks for the hundredth time. Even though she saw me get home after 11 p.m.

'We were tired. Tom hadn't slept for two days.'

'Because of your all-nighter the day before?' she says.

I shoot her a look. 'Yes. Why don't you ask me what you really want to ask me?'

'Darling, I have absolutely no idea to what you are referring,' she says with studied nonchalance.

'All right then,' I say, pouring some more wine and humming to myself. I count to three.

'So you haven't slept together?'

I splutter my wine.

'Caroline!'

She waggles her eyebrows at me.

I raise mine at her. 'May I remind you that you are my employer, and I do not need to discuss my sex life with you?'

'May I remind you that you spent a full hour grilling said employer about the exact shade of Hugh Grant's eyes… and if the rumours were true that we'd spent a steamy night together and inspired a hit eighties song about a one night stand.'

Oh yes.

'Well, may I remind you that you neither confirmed, nor indeed denied the rumours…'

'Okay, okay but I'm not allowed to tell you... there's a difference.'

'Okay fine... no, we didn't.'

'Why not?' She narrows her eyes and shakes her head. 'Let me guess, you want it to be special... it's all boring candy hearts and rose petals with you young people nowadays. You've sucked all the fun out of it, so you have.'

I suppress a giggle. 'Most people would think that would be nice.'

Caroline shakes her head. 'Sad sods, darling, that's who. Come on... where's the action? Where's the sizzle? I mean in the sixties we were...'

'You were what?'

'Well, sizzling.'

'I thought it was swinging?'

'Er, that too.'

We both laugh like mad.

But I say, 'There's sizzle, trust me.'

She winks. 'Good for you.'

I shake my head, and later get back to work.

I had got home last night and stayed awake, sitting on my little step by the front door of my cottage, staring at the stars for hours.

After we'd kissed, I'd left.

Not straightaway. But almost.

There was a part of me that wanted to stay; staying would be the easiest thing in the world.

But I tore myself away, afraid: afraid of the future, of letting go. Being with Tom like that would make it final somehow.

It was ridiculous, but I wondered what Chris would say, if he would think it was too soon, if he'd think that I'd forgotten him.

For so long I'd been living in the past, had set up home there in a way, that thinking and living in the present without him was terrifying.

I wished I could speak to Yaya about it. Yaya always understood.

With only unanswered questions for company, I'd got into bed, and sometime before dawn I fell into a deep and dreamless sleep.

In the warm morning sun and the light of Caroline's smile, the tug of ghosts had left me.

After Caroline and I called it a day, and we shared a bottle of 'fine Australian plonk', as she termed it, I make my way back to my cottage and do the unthinkable.

I phone Trish. Christopher's mother.

Now, you would think that phoning your dead fiancé's mother to tell her about the new man in your life would be the stupidest idea I'd had yet. And you'd be right.

Except it was Trish, and she, I realised, out of everyone, would really be the person who understood best.

It's been almost a year since we've spoken.

The last time had been so hard. She was in that phase, the one where you're 'keeping busy' and had taken up painting furniture with somewhat manic enthusiasm. It had been exhausting to watch.

I had been in that other phase, you see. Denial. I'd lived there for years.

The phone rings for three beats, then a posh woman's voice says, 'He-llo?'

'It's me.'

'Oh!' says Trish.

I take a deep breath, and say with a heavy heart, 'I'm sorry.'

I hear a sharp intake of breath before she says, 'Oh sweetie, I'm so glad you called. Are you okay?'

I nod, but of course she can't see me, so I say, 'I'm in Crete.'

'I heard!' she says, her voice full of excitement.

'You did?'

'Your mother,' she explains.

'Of course.' Mum and Trish got on very well, especially after it happened.

'She's very proud of you – so am I,' she says.

'You are?'

'Yes.' Then firmly. 'Very.'

I feel ridiculously relieved.

'Sweetheart, it wasn't my place to say… Though, you know, I did anyway. But it was hard to see you like that, so—'

'Stuck?' I answer boldly. The word is an apt description for my life since it happened. 'I'm not stuck any more,' I say.

'I'm glad,' she says, and I can hear that she means it.

'It's just, well, things… were horrid, but they made sense and now…'

'Now they don't?' she asks, trying to understand.

I sit on my bed and look out at the olive grove, which is painted in a swirl of mauve and amber sunset.

'Not really. It's like everything is moving fast.'

'It will, though. That's life, it's always hard to accept when you re-enter it.'

'Is that what I've done?' I ask. Though, of course, I know that it is.

'Yes,' she answers.

'Trish—' I say, wanting to tell her about Tom, but not sure how to start.

'Sweetheart, living in the past won't honour him. It's taken me a long time to think that, but I know it's true. Chris was so full of life. So vibrant, he wouldn't want this for you. He hated to see you sad, for anyone to be sad, really.'

I exhale sharply. I hadn't thought of it that way, but of course she was right.

'Sweetheart, if you've managed to find yourself some happiness there, then I say this from the absolute bottom of my heart. The heart that has been worrying about you for so long. Grab it, take it with both hands and don't let go. You've been through so much, so much pain and heartache, and I know that it won't ever truly go, that it will be something you manage. But if you can… if you can find happiness in this world, then I know he would be happier for it, and honoured by that.'

The tears leak down my face, and the knot that had lodged itself in my chest for so long finally seems to loosen.

I tell her about Crete. About Caroline, the countryside and the Lefka Ori, the scent of the wild mountain herbs, and how waking up here with the wind blowing is the most beautiful scent in the world. I tell her about the vineyards, about Elysium and what happened. I don't get into too much detail about us, but I suppose she guesses anyway.

'And the young man, Tom, is he a new friend?' she asks.

'Yes, he is.'

'He sounds…'

My heart starts to beat a little fast, but she giggles. 'Well, rather fabulous, actually.'

'He is.'

'Quite admirable, to face all that and start again. I like that in a man.'

'Me too.

Before we hang up, Trish says again, 'I'm so happy about this, sweetheart, more than I can say.'

When I set down the phone, I have to agree.

THIRTY-THREE

The next morning, I take my bicycle down to the local bakery, thinking that I'll pick up some patisseries for breakfast. Caroline, like me, was very partial to a *kataifi* to start the day. The traditional Greek dessert is bathed in lemon-scented syrup, made with roughly chopped walnuts and cinnamon, and wrapped into buttered crispy *kataifi* dough. Heaven. The morning sun is warm on my shoulders, and I am feeling light and free.

I love the ride into town, even though there are steep hills and the mountain pass is always heady to traverse. I never would have pictured myself as much of a cyclist but living here these past few months has made me something of a convert.

Plus there is something magical about gliding past wild mountain herbs, the Lefka Ori and the sparkle of the ocean from the seat of my bicycle, something that makes me feel alive.

I head into the small honey-cobbled town, and feel a lift when I see it.

Called simply Yum, it's the most idyllic little patisserie in the heart of the pretty postcard village. I park my bicycle against the sun-coloured stone of the bakery and head inside.

Maria is at the counter today; her smile turns bright when she sees me.

I'd met her a month ago, and had been coming in almost every week since. She's dressed in a red and white polka dot dress, which sets off her beautiful long, black curls.

'Yew must have gotten my message,' she says, with a twinkle in her large coffee-coloured eyes. Her wide red-lipsticked mouth curves in a grin.

'Your message?' I ask, eyes alight.

She taps her nose conspiratorially. 'W-e-l-l. I decided today, being a fine summer morning, that I'm in the mood to bake the honey *kataifi*, which my young friend seemed to like so much the last time she was in the area, which was what – yesterday or the day before?'

I smile widely. 'Both. I'm here at least twice a week now. See, I must have got the message loud and clear, because something said to me this fine morning… I wonder if Maria will be making those *kataifi* of hers? And here I am.'

She gives me a wink. 'Very strange.'

'Very.'

'We have some chocolate hazelnut croissants too if you like?' Looking every bit the temptress.

My eyes light up. 'Oh, I like,' I breathe.

She shakes her head. 'Where you put it all?' she says, eyeing my thin frame.

I shrug. To be honest, I hadn't eaten much over the last few years, everything had sort of tasted a bit like ash. But now I was making up for lost time.

And I really didn't care that much if I put on weight. Well, not really.

I leave Maria with a promise to come by on the weekend to get some *kalitsounia* – sweet cheese pastries. I place the two boxes carefully in the basket of my bicycle.

'I thought I'd find you here.'

I whirl around to find Tom standing casually outside the bakery, dressed in dark blue jeans, a white T-shirt and his Converse trainers, as usual effortlessly handsome.

The breath catches in my throat.

'Hi,' I say, feeling a little bashful.

'Hi,' he says, the lines by his eyes crinkling.

We haven't spoken since the picnic, since I'd left in a rush, and I knew that was because of me.

I stare at him; God, he is beautiful. I mean, it's not like I could forget, but he has the kind of magnetic presence that when you confront it after an absence, it takes your breath away.

'I like your hair like that,' he says.

It is just loose. 'Thanks,' I say.

'You hungry?' I ask.

'Sure.'

'Well, I bought half the bakery…'

'I can see that,' he says, blue eyes dancing.

'Well, Tom… see, I have a problem.'

He cocks his head to the side. 'Really?'

'Uh-huh. An addiction, really.'

'Does it have anything to do with Maria?'

I sigh in mock despair. 'It does.'

'I'll have to tell my aunt on you, you know.'

I open my eyes wide. 'You wouldn't. She'd never understand… and anyway it's only been this one time.'

Tom looks amused. 'Today?'

I press my lips together to cover a smile. 'Well, yes.'

'So what did you get? I can't believe you're going to eat all of that by yourself,' he teases.

I narrow my eyes. 'Well, for your information, I got Maria's *kataifi* and—'

'The lemon drizzled one with walnuts?'

I nod.

'And you only bought two boxes! Rookie mistake, Laburinthos,' he says, turning on his heel and entering the bakery.

A minute later he comes out empty handed, shaking his head. 'Like I said, Laburinthos, rookie mistake.'

I laugh, 'Actually… I took the entire last batch… and since I've cleared them out, why don't you come over for breakfast? I was going to share them with Caroline.'

He gives me a wide grin. 'All right.'

Tom doesn't have his car with him, so we walk back, Tom pushing the bicycle along while we head up the mountain road.

'How are things going with Elysium?' I ask.

He smiles. 'Good, we'll be starting in the next six months or so, as the Syrah will be ready for picking by then.'

'You know by the date?' I ask, astonished. I thought that there was much less of a science to it.

'Well, Kokes thinks so, we'll do the harvest then. The Pinotage should be ready by then.'

'Really!' I say in delight. 'So that's what – three hundred bottles I need to pay for, if I remember correctly?'

He laughs. 'Sure, we'll even throw in free delivery.'

I grin. 'Well, the timing is good, the article should be out about a week before the harvest, so it should offer some great publicity.'

His face grows serious. 'Thank you.'

I wonder if he's thinking of Tony and his threat to burn the place down. I wish, not for the first time that week, that I'd heard something, anything, from Stenalis. But he hasn't been in touch and I'm reluctant to push him. As it is, what we'd done – getting the fingerprints through Stenalis' connections, which would ensure that we'd get the results so soon – was all a bit nefarious. I can't push for more. Even if I want to.

I wish I could tell Tom about it. So that I can take away that frown that has settled between his brows.

I touch his hand. 'Are you worried about Tony, about him coming there and trying something?'

Tom's face hardens. 'No, if he tries anything this time, it will be the last thing he ever does, I promise you.'

That's what I'm afraid of.

I just hope that it won't get to that. I couldn't face it if Tony destroyed everything Tom had built again, before we had a chance to clear Tom's name. I don't know how it will work, how Stenalis will be able to do it, how he'll be able to prove it once Tony's fingerprints are identified, considering that the way we'd obtained the evidence wasn't legal. But Stenalis has a plan, and despite everything that has happened, despite all the cover-ups, and the lies, somehow, against all the odds, I trust him. I know that he's going to help Tom, I just hope he can do it soon, before it's too late.

After the heavenly feast of *kataifi* and croissants, enjoyed al fresco in Caroline's olive grove, Tom and I each have a cup of Greek coffee. Caroline just shakes her head over her cappuccino and laments our lack of taste. Tom leaves shortly after, as he has to see the PDO representative.

'The PDO?' I ask.

'Stands for Protected Designation of Origin. The wine is inspected and declared good enough to drink, bottle and sell commercially. While I won't qualify for a wine of origin with the Pinotage, they still can declare whether it is good enough to bottle or not,' he explains.

'Oh wow, I thought there wasn't such a stringent rule with Greek wine?' I say, thinking of the thousand-year-old ritual of home-brewed Cretan wine, and how so many Cretans seem to have their own family recipe with varying degrees of quality. It seems odd to think that there's someone who declares whether the wine is fit for consumption in light of these traditions.

'You're thinking of the home-brewed wine.'

I nod.

'Well, in commercial practices, it's a bit different. We follow the French method, in that if you are going to sell it as a certain quality, it needs to meet the international standard for quality. It's to protect the consumer, really.'

I suppose that makes sense, particularly if it's to be sold internationally. 'And if they don't find it good enough?'

He sighs. 'We start over… and go through it all again the following year.'

'Oh no!' My hand flies to my mouth. That's a lot of power for one representative.

'Here, give him the croissant… your need is greater than ours,' says Caroline.

He winks, and gives me a kiss goodbye. 'Depending on how it goes, I may need someone to celebrate with me later, or to commiserate. Will you come?'

I nod. 'Seven okay? I'll bring both champagne and tequila, just in case.'

'Sounds good,' he says, kissing me so that shivers run down my spine.

There is a universally acknowledged truth that a watched phone will not ring.

For three days I resisted checking my phone for Stenalis' call. And even though he'd said that we couldn't expect an answer for a week, I couldn't help but check that day.

And keep checking.

When I did a round of laundry, making liberal use of Caroline's washing machine, I ran back inside the cottage and checked.

And after I hung the clothes up on the line outside by her kitchen garden, where I picked fresh rocket leaves and vine-ripened tomatoes for dinner, I checked again.

Caroline had gone to visit her old producer from her show *Off the Beaten Trek*, who was yachting in Agios Nikolaos for the summer… as you do. She'd be gone for two days, and I was glad that she was taking a little break from The Book.

Later when I put the pastitsio in the oven – I thought I'd surprise Tom with a home-cooked dinner – I check my phone again.

Of course it rings as soon as I pour myself a glass of rosé and take a seat at Caroline's scrubbed farm-style table with my feet up and her manuscript for company.

My heart stops completely. And I jump out of my chair to answer it.

It's a number I don't recognise, but I click 'accept' nonetheless.

A rich, throaty voice barks at me. 'Have you heard?'

I sigh, and sit back down.

Xena Alberos. The Cretan journalist.

'No, sorry.'

'Okay, phone as soon as you do.'

'Okay, I will, promise.'

The phone goes dead, and I have to laugh. Alberos had turned out to be my unlikely conspirator. And despite her abrupt tone and style, I like her spunk. In another life, she's exactly the kind of woman I would like to be.

Playing with my phone, I think about the evidence again, wondering what the outcome will show. I have to remind myself that even if it doesn't prove that it was Tony, that it's not a dead end, it will prove that it wasn't Tom.

And if it did nothing else, at least, once and for all he could clear his name. I wish yet again that I could share that with him, and explain why I know he didn't do it, beyond just knowing in my heart that he is innocent.

But doing so would mean risking his reaction. There was a chance that could endanger what Tom had spent two years trying to rebuild, and I would never allow myself to expose him to that risk.

I take a sip of rosé, thinking of Tom. I'm not a wine expert, but if the wine I'd sampled months before was anything to go by, there was no way that the wine representative wouldn't give it the seal of approval.

But for all that, I know that sometimes these things are political, and Tom, with his past and the cloud of suspicion that followed him, hadn't always had the gods in his favour. Not only that but with the deep connections and associations that Iliana Kirosa and Tony could lay claim to, I had to wonder, would he really be able to get it certified? That family had already gone to such great lengths to destroy Tom by infiltrating the police, changing reports and getting someone moved to another police department. And I knew now with certainty that they'd got rid of Stenalis to make sure that they could put their own man in charge – Chief Mino, who wasn't afraid to cross a few moral boundaries in favour of an elevated position. Considering the extremes they had gone to, and Tony's threat to destroy Tom, would they find another way to prevent Tom's wine from being certified?

I set down my glass, my face grim. The truth is, it should have occurred to me earlier. The chances are high that Tom's beautiful wine won't be approved today. Not if Tony or Iliana can help it. Perhaps, somehow in the years since losing Christopher and then Yaya, working for someone like Janice, I'd finally become what no one, least of all me, ever thought I would: a realist.

I find Tom sitting alone in his dark kitchen, his face tight, blue eyes cold.

For some reason, despite the evidence – the tumbler of whisky in his hand, and the grim line of his jaw – I still have to ask. 'He didn't approve it?'

He cocks his head in assent, and takes a sip of the whisky.

I sit down next to him and take out the tequila.

He gives me a grim smile. 'That will help.'

I get up and find us two glasses, and place the food by the fridge. He doesn't even ask what it is.

I know that we won't be eating any of it, not tonight at any rate.

I pour us both a double shot and sit down opposite him.

'What did he say?'

Tom stares at the tequila, then downs it in one. 'It isn't ready.'

'But that's not so bad then, surely? I mean, maybe it just needs a little more time?'

He shakes his head. 'That's what I thought. Except when he left, he said he didn't think it would ever be ready.'

'Tom,' I say, not knowing what else I can say. I put my hand over his. 'Is that it – can't you speak to someone else?'

He picks up a card that's lying close to his glass of whisky, and starts turning it over and over. His voice is taut when he speaks. 'Yes, there is someone I can speak to.' He puts the card down and takes another sip of whisky. 'And when I'm through with him... well, let's just say it will be over one way or another.'

I frown. That sounds ominous. I pick up the card Tom had been twisting in his fingers and then understand.

There in black and white was printed the name of the PDO representative: Michael Kirosa.

I slam it down hard and stand up.

'That BITCH!' I explode.

Tom looks at me, taken aback. It's the first time he really has since I got here tonight. I don't care, I am furious.

'That UTTER, UTTER bitch… with her little swishy walk, and that voice, like Moaning Myrtle's but worse, Moaning Myrtle… in Greek!' Then as I work up some more anger, I continue, 'And him… that slime ball wearing his little man suits… those assholes. How dare they?' I hiss. 'And with this… it's not even like they're trying to pretend. Bloody bastards,' I fume.

To my surprise, Tom starts to laugh.

He stands up and gives me a hug, his shoulders shaking. 'You're wonderful,' he says. Then wiping tears of mirth from his eyes, he repeats, 'Little man suits… Oh my God.'

Despite myself, I grin. 'Well… I mean, where does he find them?'

Tom starts howling again.

Then between breaths he manages, 'Moaning Myrtle… in Greek!'

I laugh. Pouring him another tequila. I joke, 'I'll be here all week.'

He smiles. 'You will?'

I smile back, down my tequila shot in one and, despite the sudden hit of alcohol, I sober up. 'Tom, you can't go to Tony.'

His face grows tight. 'I don't have a choice, I can't let him just get away with this. I knew it wasn't going to be easy coming back here, that he'd make it hard. It's his way, but he just won't see reason. And to be honest, I'm sick of it. It's time that people know what really happened.'

'I agree.'

He looks at me, surprised.

'I agree,' I repeat. 'And he won't get away with it, trust me on that.' I take a steadying breath. 'Tom, there's something you should know. I was waiting to tell you about it because, well, I was afraid that it would lead to this – you rushing there to kill him before we could get it all sorted out. But since it's likely to happen anyway, I'm going to tell you. But—' I take his hand in mine, 'Tom, I need you to promise me something.'

He frowns. 'What's going on, Ria? What's this about?'

'I'll explain, but please, Tom, I need your word.'

His brow furrows further. 'My word on what?'

'That after I tell you what I know, you won't go to Tony, that you'll leave it to the police.'

Tom's eyes widen. 'The police! Ria, what's going on?'

'Tom, your word, please.' I beg.

He exhales. 'Very well, you have my word.'

And I tell him about how the evidence was covered up, how the report was changed, how Stenalis was taken off the case, how they said that the witness was actually Mr Portcullis.

'Our old vintner – but he died the day before,' he exclaims.

'I know.'

Tom looks at me oddly. 'You found out all this – when?' he asks.

My heart is pounding in sudden fear. 'I've been researching it for months. After I met you, I started going to the library – translating articles that I found. Despite what Chief Mino said, the report wasn't made public, but I managed to get hold of it, and when I read it alongside old articles in the *Chaniá Ilio*, it seemed to be giving a different story. Such as the fact that the source was female, and I had a hunch that it was Iliana, so I met with the chief of police and later the journalist from the *Chaniá Ilio*.'

He tilted his head, his face hard. 'A hunch?'

'Yes, it just didn't add up. Nigel agreed with me.'

Tom's mouth forms a thin line. 'Nigel? Oh Nigel, your editor. I see, so you were going to write a story,' he waves a hand expansively, 'about all this. I see.'

I nod. There's no use denying it now.

He stands up, livid. 'So the other night, when you told me that you'd been interested in the vineyard and that you felt drawn to it, to me. It was because you were really just drawn to the story, to the right story – the one that would make your career. Well… well done, seems you found it.'

I stand up quickly. 'No, Tom, it wasn't like that, I promise! It was you, your story. I wasn't thinking of me at all.'

He snorts. 'This whole time, Ria, I thought… I thought this was something else. You even said the other day that you're more of a writer than a journalist, which was a joke. I mean, even to-day when I told you about the PDO rep, you knew… you knew then that he'd never okay it. It was all just a story to you.'

'Tom!' I exclaim, devastated. 'I didn't know that! I mean later I suspected it could happen but—'

'Oh yes, of course your suspicions are always right.'

'Tom, please. You're turning this into something it's not. I'm not some god-awful journalist who puts the story first. You have to believe me.'

'You're not?' he spits, his eyes cold and harsh. 'Ria, you could have told me about this from the start, but you were worried that I'd blow the lid off before you got the story out. I'd say the bloody shoe fits, wouldn't you?' he scoffs, then turns on his heel to leave.

'Tom – please don't go!'

He turns back and looks at me so venomously that I flinch. 'I won't go there if that's what you're worried about, but I am leaving. See yourself out.'

I run after him, but he just ignores me. Even when I try to pull him towards me, he flings my arm off him, jumps into his car and speeds off into the night.

I stand in the moonlight, tears choking me, wishing that I'd never told him, wishing that I'd told him from the start.

I walk home, trailing my bicycle beside me, the tequila bottle standing sentry in the basket. Every now and then I take a helpful numbing sip. It takes over an hour to get home, and as soon as I make it to my door the world starts to spin. Somehow I manage to get myself to the bathroom in time to throw up. Sometime after that I fall asleep on the cold tiled floor.

THIRTY-FOUR

I wake up to the sound of my brain attempting to burst my skull; the pain is one thing, the noise is insufferable.

'Die quietly,' I admonish my brain and groan, as speaking aloud makes it worse.

When it won't obey, I realise that the ringing noise is coming from somewhere else.

My mobile phone. I dive for it, thinking only: Tom.

I fish the phone out of my bag and answer breathlessly, 'Tom?'

'Stenalis,' a voice barks out.

'Inspector!' I exclaim.

'We've found a match.'

My heart starts to pound.

'Who – who is it?' I cry.

'Not over the phone – can you come in?'

'Come in?' I ask in disbelief, cradling my pounding head on my arm. 'Where?'

'To the Chania station – we're pulling them both in for questioning. You should come.'

I sit up, my head throbbing. 'But I thought you were going to wait?' I say, shocked.

'I'll explain when you get here – get here soon,' he says and hangs up.

I feel sick. I stand up, brush my teeth, take two paracetamol and jump into the shower for a thirty second rinse, then get dressed in record time.

My head is still hammering when I pull into the Chania Police Station car park and make my way to the doors. Stenalis is waiting outside, smoking a cigarette, which he throws on the ground as soon as I arrive.

'Laburinthos.' He raises a bushy black brow. 'You look like hell.'

'Inspector,' I say, not bothering to correct him.

He steers me by the arm, past reception. 'We got the match this morning, they're bringing them in now – had to fetch them from Elounda, but they'll be here any minute.'

'It was Tony?' I ask, feeling ill and not just because the tequila is still playing havoc with my system.

He shakes his head. 'You won't believe it.'

I gasp. 'Iliana?'

He nods.

I shake my head in amazement. 'But – but why?'

He shrugs. 'Goodness knows. Rich little girl. Explains why there was such a cover-up, though.'

That does make sense, but still it's dreadful to contemplate. That awful woman.

'Do you think Tony knew it was her?'

Stenalis shakes his head. 'I don't know, but for us it was a lucky break.'

I look at him in surprise. 'Why?'

He smiles. 'It turns out that her prints were in the system already.'

'What?!'

'A few years back there was a robbery at one of her resorts. Two Monets went missing – it made international headlines.'

'The Monet Escape, yes! I heard of that,' I exclaim.

'Yes, well, one of the paintings was in Iliana Kirosa's private suite, so the Elounda police fingerprinted everyone – including Iliana.'

'No!' I exclaim.

'We couldn't believe it either. Harvesos ran the prints against the database, and we compared it with the recent evidence – and there it was, a match. We've had to work quickly to get everyone here now before anyone has a chance to try something.'

'You mean before she tries to cover it up again.'

'Exactly.'

Loud angry voices in rapid-fire Greek erupt just then. Stenalis and I both turn to see Chief of Police Mino being led in by two police officers.

'This is outrageous!' he shouts. 'Take your hands off me! Do you know who I am, you idiots?'

They ignore him, but Stenalis calls out, 'Oh yes, Chief, we know who you are, all right.'

The chief turns to glare at him. When he sees me, his face goes from red to white and back again. 'You!' he exclaims.

'Yes, me. Hi.' I wave.

His face turns puce.

'Turns out I did read the report… the real one,' I call.

He shouts several expletives that carry the length and breadth of my mongrel pedigree, but I'm spared the rest as he's led into a room just off the hall, where a door clicks firmly shut.

Stenalis looks at me, a wide grin on his face. He pokes me in the ribs with his elbow. 'Hi,' he mimics in a high-pitched voice.

I smile in return, but it dies as Tony and Iliana are escorted in. They both look worse for wear.

'What is this about?' exclaims Tony, seething with suppressed rage. 'I demand to know! This is inhumane. You have no right to do this. None! How dare you drag us out here? Somebody had better explain it!'

Stenalis springs forward. 'Gladly,' he answers in English, for my benefit. Though he needn't bother – my Greek is better than it's ever been.

Tony's eyes bulge when Stenalis moves toward Iliana instead. He unhooks a pair of handcuffs, and switches back to Greek, saying, 'Iliana Kirosa, you are under arrest for arson to the vineyard Elysium, and manslaughter resulting in the death of Gyes Bacchus. Furthermore you are charged with fraud, bribery and corruption. Please come with us.'

Iliana's face pales. 'What?! I never!'

Tony looks dumbstruck. He looks at Stenalis. 'This is impossible. What are you talking about? Iliana had nothing to do with that… she never…' His eyes are wild, then he spots me, and like Mino he explodes. 'It's her!' he shouts, pointing at me. 'She's at the bottom of all this. She's… she's involved, she's fed you some stupid lie and you've dragged us all here… When I'm done I'll have all your badges for this!' Tony shouts.

Stenalis snorts. 'Our badges… what is this, America? It doesn't work that way, and if you are referring to my colleague here, Miss Ria Laburinthos, who discovered that your wife provided false testimony against your brother, and ensured that the evidence from the night of the fire was buried, then you are quite correct – she was involved. But the only one, if I may be so bold, who seems to have fed us all a lie, is standing right here,' he says, snapping the handcuffs onto Iliana Kirosa's wrists.

Iliana doesn't say anything, her chin only wobbles, and she looks at Tony pleadingly. 'It's not true.'

Tony just stares, his mouth opening and closing wordlessly. A part of me can't help feeling sorry for him.

Stenalis leads her towards another room down the hall, and Tony and I both follow, though I'm not sure if I'm allowed. No one makes any objection, though.

Iliana is escorted to a chair opposite a steel table. Stenalis sits down across from her, and a police officer hands him a file and a small recorder.

He looks up at the people in the room: there are two police officers, as well as Tony and me. One of the men asks Stenalis if Tony and I should be there.

'I'd like them to stay for now,' he says.

Tony looks nonplussed. 'This is ridiculous – you don't have any evidence. You all know who started that fire.'

Stenalis holds up a finger for silence. 'You're wrong on one count, and quite correct on the other.'

Tony frowns.

Stenalis, however, starts the recorder and dives straight in. 'Iliana Kirosa, we have evidence that your fingerprints were on the petrol bottle that was used to start the fire at Elysium ten years ago. We have also discovered that the original report written by me was altered. The original, as you may recall, testified that you saw Tom Bacchus leave the west side barn minutes before the fire broke out. It also mentioned that the petrol bottle was booked for fingerprinting and that all the staff at Elysium had gone in for questioning. This evidence was buried. Three months after the case broke out, before Tom Bacchus was sent to trial, I was transferred to Iraklion and Mr Carlos Mino took over – your cousin, I believe?'

Iliana says nothing. But I see her shift uncomfortably in her chair.

'Well, I must say we were all surprised that within only a year of being a junior officer, and a desk officer at that, Carlos was made chief of police, but now we understand why. Mino rewrote the report, claiming that it was in fact a dead man who saw Tom Bacchus that night – the old vintner, Mr Portcullis,' says Stenalis. He picks up the false report. 'This was put into the system after I was transferred and the original was destroyed. Luckily I keep a copy of everything I do. As does the *Chaniá Ilio*. Still, it's likely that no one would have discovered this had it not been for Miss Laburinthos who, while researching her article on the vineyard, read the articles by the *Chaniá Ilio* – the ones that of course referred to the original report. She found an anomaly that wasn't in this fabrication that your family had supplied. Namely, that my source had been female. It was this that led her to become suspicious enough to contact both the *Chaniá Ilio* and myself, only for us to discover that you have been keeping a lie, with your cousin's help, perhaps even the former mayor's himself, for over ten years.'

Iliana looks distraught. Tears begin to fall from her eyes. 'No.'

Tony looks wretched.

'Iliana?' he says, 'This can't be true… can it?'

She shakes her head. 'Tony…'

Stenalis barks, 'Stop lying! Your actions led to the death of your husband's father! You destroyed his home. You tried to frame your brother-in-law and let him take the blame for what you did. We know you did!'

Iliana's shoulders shake and she sobs, 'It wasn't like that! I never meant to hurt anyone!'

Tony's voice breaks. 'Iliana?' His wide eyes are full of bewilderment.

She starts to sob painfully. 'It was an accident. Tony, I promise, I never meant to hurt anyone.'

Stenalis scoffs. 'An accident? It was no accident! You deliberately set fire to his home – we have the evidence to prove it. Or are you going to suggest that you were carrying around the petrol bottle, and a box of matches, and tripped?'

Iliana sobs louder. 'No! No, it was an accident, I promise you.'

Tony looks dumbfounded. 'Just tell me.'

Iliana lifts her handcuffed wrists and wipes her nose on her sleeve, covering her mouth in agony. 'It was after... you saw us.'

Stenalis looks from Tony to Iliana. 'Saw what?' he says.

'Tom and Iliana... they were having an affair,' I answer.

They all look at me in surprise.

I shrug.

Tony closes his eyes, a small angry laugh escaping his lips. 'She said...' He shakes his head, then opens his eyes, which are raw with pain. 'You said that he kissed you... that he was in love with you, wouldn't leave you alone.'

Iliana starts to shake even more. She looks away.

Oddly I don't feel sorry for her. Not at all. I realise watching her that her cowardice hadn't ruined just Tom's life but perhaps Tony's as well.

'That,' I say, 'would be another lie – they were in love.'

Tony looks at Iliana for confirmation.

Iliana starts to cry. 'I'm so sorry, Tony...' Tears turn to sobs.

'Is that why you started the fire?' I ask.

Iliana's eyes look wild. 'No... yes. I started it because Tony said that he was going to kill Tom... and he meant it... he always hated him, so I had to do something... anything to get him to stop. I remembered that there was a can of petrol in the barn for the tractor... I'd seen it there after...'

'After?' asks Stenalis.

Iliana looks down, ashamed. 'Tom and I had made love in the barn and we'd knocked the bottle over... the night before.'

Tony looks like he's been shot. He slides down the wall and comes to a stop on his haunches, his head in his hands.

Iliana hastens to explain. 'I just... I just wanted to distract you, I didn't mean for it to get so out of hand... I'm so sorry, I never meant any of it,' she says again.

Stenalis looks at her with disdain. 'You didn't mean it when you blamed your lover for what you did? Or when your actions caused two brothers to hate each other for the rest of their lives and lose their father… or what about when you decided to cover all of it up with the help of your cousin?'

Iliana just shakes her head. 'No… I never meant any of it, it was my father, he got involved… and it just got out of control, one lie on top of another. It's been killing me.'

Tony stands up slowly, looking like the fight has gone out of him. 'It's been killing you? So afterwards when you married me, what was that? Guilt?'

Iliana's eyes widen. 'No, Tony, I love you.'

Tony's eyes look dead. 'Did you? What about Tom?'

Iliana blinks, the tears falling rapidly from her eyes. 'No, it was a… crush, that's all… I promise you.'

Tony just shakes his head. 'You promise… your promises mean nothing to me,' he spits. He looks stricken. He stands in silent agony for a second, then turns and leaves. No one tries to stop him.

Stenalis stops the recorder. 'Ms Kirosa, you will be taken to a cell for the night. Based on this testimony, you will be charged in due course for arson and fraud. I suggest that you use your phone call to contact your lawyer… and not your father. As you can well imagine, he will be brought in for questioning with regards to his involvement in this case later today. Good day.'

As Iliana is escorted out of the room, her eyes fall on me and she sneers. 'You loved this, didn't you – ripping apart someone's home for your little story?'

I shake my head in disgust. 'The only one who ripped apart anyone's family was you.' I frown as something occurs to me, something that should have from the start. 'You loved him, didn't you?'

'What are you talking about?'

'Tom. You loved him. That's why you started the fire, and it's why you dropped the testimony later. It was your father who wanted you to set him up, wasn't it? Perhaps that's why his mother lied and said Tony was with him – you asked her to, didn't you?'

She glares at me.

'I'm right, though, aren't I? He said he wouldn't help you unless you blamed Tom... so later when they changed the report, you made sure that his case was thrown out.'

Iliana's mouth fixes itself into a grim line. 'You can't prove it.'

I scoff. 'That you have a heart? No, I suppose I can't, but I'll never understand women like you. For the sake of your money and privilege, you let go of the man you really loved, destroying him and his brother in the process. I have to wonder – was it worth it?'

'Fuck you,' she spits venomously.

I guess that is a no.

Stenalis just shakes his head and leads her out of the room.

I walk out too, feeling suddenly adrift, and I walk straight into Alberos, her dark hair long and loose, looking even more Amazonian than usual in a pair of olive green leggings and a black vest. Her dark eyes are serious. 'Laburinthos, is it true?' she asks, black eyes sharply focused on me.

I nod.

She looks at me for a second. 'How are your Greek writing skills?'

I frown. 'What?'

She explains. I take a deep breath in and close my eyes.

'No... I couldn't.'

'What?' she exclaims. 'You have to, come on.'

'Xena – I can't. You don't understand, Tom and I... we're... well, we were together, but it all blew up when he found out that I was investigating it. If I do this, there might not be a chance for us again.'

She shakes her head angrily, black curls bouncing wildly. 'Typical.'

I frown. 'What do you mean?'

'You clear his name – and he gets to be angry. It's just typical.'

'No, it's not like that. I didn't tell him that I was doing a story.'

She looks at me. 'Look, Laburinthos – you have no choice. It has to be you, and you won't do him any favours by not writing it.'

I stare at her: she just doesn't seem to get it. 'But if I did it, I'd be doing exactly what he accused me of,' I say.

'What?' she asks with a frown.

'Chasing the story, being a journalist!'

'And?' she looks genuinely perplexed.

I attempt to explain. 'It wasn't about that. I mean it was, but it was also about him, helping him.'

She snorts in derision. 'Obviously. Come,' she says, pulling my arm.

'What?' I ask, confused. 'Where?'

'Across the street – we'll have a coffee. Hear me out.'

I follow her outside, blinking in the harsh sunlight. My head still feels like it's going to explode, and despite everything that has gone on all I really want to do is go home and sleep.

Alberos, however, is unmoved. 'Christ, you look like hell. Here,' she says, handing me a pair of sunglasses, which I slip on gratefully as she marches me across the street. We sit down at a local coffee shop with little tables and chairs that spill over onto the pavement.

We take a seat, and I order an espresso as soon as the waitress comes over. 'The same,' says Alberos.

'Now, look,' she says after the waitress leaves, 'this is just nonsense. I mean, for God's sake, it's not like you're a news reporter, you work for *Eudaimonia*.'

I frown. 'Hey, what's wrong with *Eudaimonia*?'

She waves her hands. 'That's not what I meant and you know it, Ria.'

It's the first time she'd ever used my name.

'You're a features writer... Nigel Crane says you're a good one, too. Now, you're not someone who "chases the story", you care about the people you write about. And another thing, sure, there are journalists who only care about getting a story, just like there are crooked cops, but you and Stenalis are the good guys here, you've cleared up a ten-year conspiracy, and I think you deserve to get the credit for it.'

'I hear you. I'm just not sure that he'd see it that way.'

'Well, we'll make him. I've spoken to Nigel already. We're going to run the story at the same time – we've got to get it in within the next two hours in time for tomorrow's print. *Eudaimonia* is going to do an early print edition to time it especially. So it has to be you.'

'But...' I was a bit speechless. 'But – don't you want to do it?' I ask.

She shakes her head. 'Look, it's a great story, I'd love to break with it, but Ria – it's your story, you deserve to tell it. But like any good editor, and considering it was my article that led you on the right path, I feel that my paper deserves it too – that's why I phoned Nigel yesterday. I thought we could share it.'

I shake my head in amazement. 'Wow.'

'Tell that to your Tom, who thinks we're all lying snakes.'

I laugh. 'But that's my point,' I say. At her frown, I explain. 'No, I mean I'm not sure that he'll see it that way. He'll just see that, after everything, now my name is in not just one but two papers – he'll think that's what it was all about. That I didn't care about him, just the story.'

She shakes her head. 'Then tell it like that… tell the real story.'

'What do you mean?' I ask.

'Ria, this is Crete, you don't need to tell some bald news story – tell your story, the real one, and I'll print that. Our readers would prefer it anyway.'

Maybe they would.

THIRTY-FIVE

It isn't the Sunday night blues.

And my fingers haven't yet gone numb.

But the fear is there nonetheless.

The same fear I'd had every Sunday night for the past three years straight, knowing that *The Mail & Ledger* would be out and I'd have to deal with whatever came my way.

Knowing that in just a few hours, two national newspapers would cover my story.

But unlike *The Mail & Ledger*, I knew that this time it wouldn't be a little old lady crying outside my cubicle. There may be no one there at all, and that was so much worse.

I'd done as Alberos had suggested and told my story, my way. I'd written about my arrival in Crete, and how the vineyard had come to mean so much to me, about Tom's dedication and how I came to believe in his innocence and had put the clues together till finally I'd met Alberos and Stenalis and we'd all helped to uncover the truth. I didn't speak about the fingerprints we'd stolen from Tony and Iliana, or Tom and Iliana's affair; that was their story, it wasn't mine to tell.

I don't know if Tom will forgive me when he reads it.

But I know why I had done it and I couldn't ever regret that. I know that in some way that I couldn't explain I had honoured not just him but myself too. And while I have more to lose than with any other story, a small part of me knows it's going to be okay. Perhaps it had something to do with Alberos' red-rimmed eyes and the moment of silence while she read it, or the lump Nigel had in his throat after he called to ask me if I'd be okay, or their combined assurances that together they wouldn't stop trying to help make him understand that made me think that perhaps one day he would.

After I wrote the feature and left Xena's office, I didn't go home; I was too wound up. I walked along the beach with my thoughts for company. It was after midnight when I got home. To my amazement, I found Tom sitting on the little step outside my cottage.

I stopped stock still, staring at him in shock. 'You're here?'

He stood when I neared, jammed his hands into the pockets of his jeans, his face serious. 'I didn't know when you were coming home, so I waited.'

I swallowed. 'Have you been here long?'

He gave a half smile, his blue eyes soft. 'About three hours.'

I blinked. 'Oh God. I'm sorry.'

He shook his head. 'No, Ria. Christ – I'm sorry.' He thrust his hands into his hair. 'Truly. I was an idiot.'

My eyes widen. 'You – what?' I asked, confused.

'I think I knew even as I was driving away that I was being an idiot – it took me a few hours to realise it, though. But you don't run away from someone like you. Someone who does something like that – does everything they can to help you. You run like hell towards them.'

Tears started to course down my face. He brushed them away, and pulled me into his embrace, whispered against my hair. 'I came here in the morning but you were gone. I tried to phone but I couldn't get through to you, so I tried Caroline, and when she had no idea I tried Nigel.'

'Nigel?' I asked, stunned.

Tom laughed. 'Yes, he told me everything. That it was actually Iliana who started the fire?'

I nodded.

He shook his head and looked into my eyes, his gaze serious. 'Nigel thinks that you're my knight in shining armour. He was rather unimpressed with me, I can tell you. He seemed to imply that I let you fall on your sword. I rather agree.'

I grinned, a watery grin, wiping my eyes. 'That sounds like him, he's big on honour.'

Tom smiled and touched my cheek. 'Evidently. He wouldn't let me come find you until he read me your story. So that I could see just what kind of woman you really were... and how I didn't deserve you, even though it was quite clear to everyone, as far as he was concerned, how much I loved you.'

I closed my eyes.

Tom loves me?

Bloody, blustery, wonderful Nigel.

I cried harder. He kissed my face, my hands, my lips. 'I didn't realise it,' he said tenderly, 'but of course he was right. I've been falling for you every day since we met.'

I took a deep breath and looked into his eyes, finally admitting it to myself. 'I think I fell for you the day I read about your story. I didn't know how or why, but all I knew was that I wanted to help you.'

Tom closed his eyes. 'I think you saved me, really.' He pulled me close and kissed me.

I shook my head and held him tight. 'We saved each other.'

EPILOGUE

Six months later

'So that's three hundred bottles – shall I have them delivered, madam?' asks Tom, pointing at the rows of bottles. Displayed on a trestle table in the recently refurbished cellar, they bear their new shiny labels, each with the new fallen feather motif, the secret tribute to Gyes Bacchus.

'Mmm – I suppose I may have to share, considering that you have all these people here. I wouldn't want them not to have anything to drink now, would I?'

Tom grins and plants a kiss behind my ear. 'Good plan. Anyway, we can't have you too drunk for the grape press just now, Mrs Bacchus.'

'Tom!' I exclaim.

He chuckles and dances away. 'I'm just going to keep asking… and keep calling you that until you say yes.'

I can't help but laugh, watching his twinkly eyes depart, as he goes to help the first load of customers that have arrived for the harvest.

There are so many people here. Tom and I are both amazed at the turnout. After the article went out, it seemed like all of Crete wanted to do their part in letting Tom know that he'd had their support over the past few months.

Of course, Caroline had blubbered like a baby when she read it. Then straight afterwards she declared that she still wasn't going to let Nigel get his hands on me and that, despite what he thought, she very much needed me around for the second phase of The Book. Now that the manuscript was with the publishers, there was the website to think of and the email to set up. That's what she called it – 'the email'. She said she wasn't about to lose her very best assistant, not to mention her best friend, which I suspected was the real concern – a groundless one, to be sure. She was one of my best friends too, though Tamsin would probably fight her over the title, even if it turned out that Nigel was going to be the best man at our wedding. Which was faintly ridiculous because there was not going to be a wedding.

I have no idea where Nigel had got the idea. Okay, Tom had probably mentioned it to him, but it was a little premature, as I haven't said yes yet. You have to hand it to Nigel, though; it turns out he really is quite the romantic.

The trouble is, of course, that considering what I've been through, I don't quite believe in weddings, even though I do believe in Tom.

'Laburinthos?'

I turn and am surprised to find Alberos and Inspector Stenalis walking towards me, each holding a glass of wine. 'This is so good,' says Alberos with a rare smile, her ebony eyes alight.

Stenalis nods, his smile wry. He's wearing his off-duty uniform – a golf shirt and chinos. It was nice to see him looking relaxed. 'This was definitely worth fighting for,' he says with a wink.

I look at them both happily. It's so good to see them again. My two comrades at arms.

'Definitely,' agrees an American accent from behind them. I look around her to see a lanky man with vivid red hair and green eyes standing with Nigel, a look of pure contentment on his face as he beams at me. I smile at him and he introduces himself, holding out a thin freckled hand. 'Hi there… Mathew Sprint.'

'Pleased to meet you,' I say, shaking his hand.

'I was invited here by my good friend, Nigel, who knows that I'm rather a connoisseur of the Pinotage.'

I frown. Something is tugging at the corner of my mind. Something from the *Eudaimonia* article… then suddenly it dawns on me. 'You're – the wine critic from *The New Yorker*!' I exclaim.

He grins. 'Indeed I am.' He looks rather pleased that I know who he is. 'Can you point me in the direction of your husband?'

'My hus—' I say, narrowing my eyes at Nigel. Honestly. 'He's not … never mind,' I say, shaking my head as both Nigel and Alberos crack up. Were they all in on this?

'Follow me,' I say, leading him over to Tom, whose megawatt smile meets me with full force, causing that now familiar flip in my belly. God, would I ever get used to that?

I head over to Caroline, her dark blonde hair piled on top of her head in her effortlessly elegant way. She's standing amongst the vines, a glass of wine in one hand while the other clutches at Tom's Aunt Therese, as they howl with laughter. I grin at them, but startle suddenly as I feel a pair of soft hands slip around my eyes. Familiar hands.

'Surprise!'

I turn around and see Mum, her brown eyes soft as she cups my face and stares at me. I give her a hug that could crack bones, breathing in the familiar smell of lily of the valley from her silky brown hair. 'Dad sends his love, unfortunately he wasn't able to get off work, so it's just us girls.'

'Girls?' I say, then let out a giant squeal of delight as I spot Tamsin. 'You're here?'

'I'm here!' she agrees. 'Had to meet your husband,'

I roll my eyes and growl, 'Not you too!'

She laughs. Just then I spot someone else standing just behind Mum and Tamsin – it's Dorrit, my old roommate from university. She gives me her familiar awkward smile, her black hair jammed behind her ears, her clinical style somewhat at odds with the rugged landscape of tumbling vineyards and golden sunshine. I give her a hug hello while she pats my back clumsily. 'It's so nice to see you. I'm so glad you came.'

She touches my arm. 'Me too.'

My mum, very out of character, bursts into tears. 'You look so beautiful,' she says, touching my red and white sundress.

I smile. 'It was a present from Caroline,' I explain, who upon hearing her name turns round, her blue eyes widening.

She clutches her chest, her face beaming. 'Darling!' she exclaims. 'She looks just like you!' And she rushes over to give Mum a giant hug; I'm bemused to see Mum hug her tightly back.

Mum smiles. 'It's so nice to finally meet you,' she says. 'Thank you for everything, for looking after Ria.'

'Oh no darling, she's the one who's been looking after all of us. It's we who should be thanking you.'

I shake my head.

'Now darling, it's all going to be okay,' says Caroline. 'Trust me.'

I frown at her. 'What do you mean?'

'Just go with it, Laburinthos,' says Tams with a wink.

'What?'

'If I could just get everyone's attention please?' comes Tom's voice up ahead.

We all turn to see Tom standing in the middle of the vines, looking relaxed and happy, wearing his customary blue jeans, Converse and a white T-shirt. 'The ceremony is about to begin, so if you could all make your way to the front, that would be great,' he says, his blue eyes dancing.

Ceremony?

I follow as everyone makes their way towards the vines.

Caroline whispers against my ear as I walk. 'So what's this about you not giving Tom an answer?'

From my right, my mother grumbles as well. 'Yes, that's also what I would like to know.'

I turn to look at her. 'Et tu, Brute?'

She giggles mischievously, in a decidedly non-barrister-like way. 'Mum?' I ask. She winks, brown eyes dancing. 'You know, we could do it today.'

Caroline's smile widens. 'Darling, now that's an idea!'

'Absolutely, babe,' agrees Tams.

I look at them all, flabbergasted. 'What?'

Mum touches my arm. 'Honey, I know you don't want the whole white wedding thing,' she says. 'And frankly I understand, of course I do, but you can't let that stop you from being with the person you love.'

I bite my lip. They're right.

'Is it that it's just too soon?' she asks. Beside her, Caroline's eyes view me with sympathy.

The truth is, it isn't that. The truth is that all I really want to do is to be with Tom forever. I'm just… afraid. I shake my head, tears threatening. They both share a look. A rather triumphant look. I glance from one to the other a little suspiciously.

'Well, in that case it just so happens…' says Tams.

'Darling, we fetched the priest!' says Caroline, pointing at a man standing right at the top of the long dirt path, beneath a little archway strewn with yellow roses.

'Caroline?'

'Surprise,' whispers my mother with tears in her eyes. 'Come, honey, I know you… It's what you want in your heart, isn't it?'

I blink back my own tears. Yes.

'Well, go on then, darling,' says Caroline, giving me a kiss on the cheek. Mum gives me a hug.

'You're in big trouble, all of you,' I say with a watery smile while I take a wobbly step forward, fighting the mad hysterical urge to laugh as I make my way on shaking legs up what I now realise is an aisle, while everyone cheers. Tom stands beaming at me. He hands me a single yellow rose for my bouquet and takes my hand in his. I stare into his blue eyes and I know just then that this has turned out to be the single best day of my life. And just like that, while the priest says the words, and we repeat them in the company of friends, and the vineyard we'd both helped to save, we are wed.

Tom kisses me deeply, and before my head clears he carries me over to the nearest barrel full of plum-coloured grapes and takes off my sandals, giving each foot a kiss before he lifts me in. And then he jumps in after me so that together we tread the grapes, laughing and kissing. In my bliss I send up a kiss and a prayer, thanking Yaya for helping me to see that sometimes running away is how you find yourself again.

LETTER FROM LILY

If you're wondering what's next – there's lots! I can't wait to tell you about my next novel set in Cornwall. There's sea, a mystery, some magic, and a romance… You'll find out this and much more besides by join my mailing list here:

www.bookouture.com/lily-graham

Otherwise I'm regularly on Twitter and Facebook, chatting about romantic escapes, abandoned beach cottages and much more, which I also share on my blog, which you can find in the links below. Do come say hello!

If you enjoyed the book, it would be so wonderful if you could leave a review. Your help in spreading the word is so appreciated.

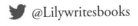 @Lilywritesbooks

LilyRoseGrahamAuthor

www.lilygraham.net

ACKNOWLEDGEMENTS

To my best friend, Catherine, who insisted I write it in the first place, set me a deadline and laughed at all the funny bits, there wouldn't have been a book without you. Sorry, Pete, for the marathon editing and WhatsApp sessions!

To my husband Rui, who was always there with a word of encouragement or a shoulder for support.

For Mom and Dad, my brothers, sisters-in-law, and the Valentes, for all their love, support and encouragement.

To Cindy and Pearl, Tami, Wayne and Esmi – thanks for everything. To Nadine Matheson, whose insight as a fellow writer, and background as a defence attorney, was invaluable. Christie Stratos, who first edited it, and Katherine Middleton who cast her expert proofer's eye over it.

Thank you to the wonderful Lydia-Vassar Smith, and Natasha Hodgson and the entire incredible team at Bookouture, who have helped bring the story to life, from the first-class editing to the incredible cover. And of course, the incredible author team who have offered their support, advice and many a well-timed laugh: you guys have made the whole experience so special.

A huge thank you to all the amazing book bloggers and readers whose support means the world, from the wonderful Isabell Homfeld to Gurdeep Asssi, Bethany Lynne, Rebecca Pugh and Barbara Little just to name a few. You guys are amazing.

To anyone who has read my books and taken the time to leave a review or let me know that you've enjoyed it, thank you so much.

AUTHOR'S NOTE

The beautiful town of Ouranó is fictional, alas. The Lefka Ori mountain range is not. Ouranó was very loosely based on the village of Vatolakkos – just with a sea view. The vineyard 'Elysium' is inspired in many ways by the remarkable Manousakis Winery in that village. The Manousakis Winery's Alexandra Manousakis very kindly helped with some of the wine references in the book, particularly the PDO information. However, all mistakes are entirely the author's, often deliberate. For instance, the PDO wouldn't in all likelihood have approved or disapproved Tom's production of Pinotage – this was done more for dramatic effect. Any other wine-related mistakes regarding the proper ageing, etc. were done to keep the story moving along. Apologies to any wine aficionados.

Similarly, a vast degree of poetic licence was applied to the structure and management of the Chania Police Department, this was a purely fictional account of the department, created solely for the purposes of the story.